"You shouldn't be up there, soldier."

Kelsey climbed aboard the base of the bucket lift and continued talking. "Who authorized you to be here? I'm going to bring you down now." She applied pressure to one of the levers on the main control panel.

To her horror, he lunged for his own controls, and Kelsey found herself in a fight over the machine.

"Stop that! That's an order!" The young man did not comply.

Kelsey eyed the key that would turn off the electricity. But she couldn't let go of the levers. She couldn't risk the equipment coming to an abrupt stop. "Ease up on your end, so I can let go of mine!" she called out, but panic seemed to have taken hold of him, and he let go.

The bucket shot downward. With a cry, the man teetered for a moment, his arms flailing wildly. Then he pitched over the side.

"No!" Kelsey watched him plummet headfirst, taking forever to reach the cement, and yet hitting it so suddenly that she hadn't finished the syllable before she saw him sprawled in a widening pool of blood.

She started forward as too many immediate needs crowded her thinking—*call the medics, stop the bleeding, don't move him, check for a pulse, get an ambulance, resuscitate him, save him….*

Midstep, she ███████████████████████ d her. On instinct she █████████████████████ ut before she could co █████████████████████ plintered through her ██████████████████

Followed by blackness.

Dear Reader,

Captain Kelsey O'Roark is certain she witnessed a young man's death. But the body has vanished, and there isn't a shred of evidence to confirm what she knows happened that night in her warehouse. As the logistics officer at Fort Belvoir, she realizes she'll need help if she's going to unravel the mystery of what happened and why. She turns to the one person she knows will have the ability to make sense of her memories, Major Julian Fordham of the Criminal Investigations Division. Unfortunately, she and Julian have a history together, which ended the previous year when he couldn't handle what they'd begun to feel for each other and she had to let him go, despite her broken heart.

I hope you enjoy reading Kelsey and Julian's story as he finds his way past the emotional wounds of his childhood while Kelsey copes with a sister whose needs threaten to distract her from her duty to pursue the truth. And if you're an animal lover like me, you'll fall in love with the two dogs and one cat that enliven the lives of these determined and loving people.

Visit my Web pages at www.elizabethashtree.com to see photographs of the real Bella and Buddy. You'll see why I had to feature them in this newest tale of love in the military.

Elizabeth Ashtree

Into Thin Air
Elizabeth Ashtree

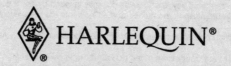

HARLEQUIN®

TORONTO • NEW YORK • LONDON
AMSTERDAM • PARIS • SYDNEY • HAMBURG
STOCKHOLM • ATHENS • TOKYO • MILAN • MADRID
PRAGUE • WARSAW • BUDAPEST • AUCKLAND

ISBN 0-373-71264-2

INTO THIN AIR

Copyright © 2005 by Randi Elizabeth DuFresne.

To the real Bella, who is also a small, white, furry froo-froo
dog and my devoted writing companion. And to Bella's
protector, the real Buddy, who is not a German shepherd
but thinks he's as big as one, despite his diminutive
size. And to the real Jasper, who is big enough to take
on either one of my dogs, or both at the same time—
thank goodness he doesn't live in the same house.

Books by Elizabeth Ashtree

HARLEQUIN SUPERROMANCE
828—AN OFFICER AND A HERO
1036—THE COLONEL AND THE KID
1089—A CAPTAIN'S HONOR
1216—A MARRIAGE OF MAJORS

Don't miss any of our special offers. Write to us at the
following address for information on our newest releases.

Harlequin Reader Service
U.S.: 3010 Walden Ave., P.O. Box 1325, Buffalo, NY 14269
Canadian: P.O. Box 609, Fort Erie, Ont. L2A 5X3

PROLOGUE

THERE IT WAS AGAIN, the whine of machinery.

Captain Kelsey O'Roark slowly unlocked the desk drawer and gently lifted the army-issue semiautomatic handgun. Holding it at eye level with a steady hand despite the quickening of her heart, she confirmed that the weapon wasn't loaded. As she reached for the ammunition cartridge, she strained to hear again the sounds of activity that had shattered the silence a moment before. Someone in the outer area was operating one of the hydraulic lifts used to move supplies.

As the post G3 logistics officer at Fort Belvoir, Kelsey knew every ping and whirr that should emanate from this warehouse. *Her* warehouse. If someone had been told to check inventory at this ungodly hour, she ought to know about it. The duty roster sat on the corner of the desk where she'd been reviewing reports. Her deputy, Lieutenant Sorrell, hadn't left any notation about work taking place here tonight. Kelsey had expected to be completely alone in the small office tucked away at one end of the enormous building.

A hollow thud from beyond the thin walls made it clear that she wasn't alone.

Eyeing the weapon in her hand, she wondered if she should call the MPs. If the person on the lift was an intruder, perhaps she shouldn't confront him alone. On the other hand, she needed to confirm that it wasn't one of her own soldiers before she could contact the MPs. It wouldn't be career-enhancing to call in the cavalry prematurely. She could just imagine the stories that would circulate all over post about her, and about army women in general, if she called in a false alarm.

Security was at an all-time high throughout the military and intruders were unlikely. But the warehouse sat close to the edge of post, surrounded by forest, and thieves were not out of the question. Caution seemed called for as she assessed the situation. Carefully, she eased the clip into the gun. The slide and click seemed to echo in the confines of the office.

She chambered a round and made certain the safety remained on. Cocked and locked, the gun was ready for action. Kelsey's nerves hummed like violin strings. Her heart drummed a quick accompanying rhythm. Hoping that her caution would prove unnecessary, she moved stealthily to investigate the activities amid the inventory.

The first thing she noticed was the missing bucket lift. It had been this ungainly electrical vehicle she'd heard, though it should have been parked at the end of the central row of huge metal shelves. Holding the gun at the ready near her right shoulder, she soothed her nerves by telling herself she would likely discover someone from her staff. Surely Lieutenant Sorrell had simply failed to inform her that he'd ordered an overnight inventory. Why else would anyone be here at this hour?

Still, her palm began to sweat against the grip of her weapon as she flicked off the safety and approached the first set of shelves. She peered around the corner into the darkened depths created by the laden tiers. Nothing. But the unmistakable groan of the bucket lifting into the heights of the cavernous building drifted her way from somewhere among the rows ahead.

She maneuvered forward to another wide aisle and carefully darted a look around the corner, then immediately pulled back and flattened herself again, hidden. Processing what she'd seen in that brief glance, she realized the man up in the lift wore the ubiquitous army woodland camouflage uniform. That was a good sign. Her heart rate began to return to normal.

Feeling foolish for her skittishness, she reengaged the safety and lowered the handgun to her side. She held it behind her leg where her loose-fitting camouflage utility pants would conceal it from view. No sense in alarming one of her own people if she could help it.

"Hello!" she called out to warn of her approach. "Hey, how come you're working so late?"

A wide-eyed man turned all at once, causing the ungainly bucket to lurch awkwardly as his hand jerked the sensitive lever. He let go of the control as if it burned him, proving to Kelsey that he had no training in how to operate the machine. He frowned down at her. "Um," said the soldier as he backed up into the shadows as far as the small bucket would allow. "No one else is supposed to be here."

From the base of the lift, Kelsey looked up into what appeared to be a youthful and confused face. Even though she couldn't see him clearly, she knew he wasn't familiar to her. He'd hoisted himself too high for her to read the name tag sewn onto his fatigues. "Do I know you?" she asked.

"Uh…no, ma'am, I don't believe you do." And he leaned back into the gloom still more so that she could no longer see his features at all.

"Well then, you shouldn't be up there, soldier. Who authorized you to be in the warehouse?" she asked as she climbed aboard the base of the machine. He made no response. "This equipment is very temperamental, so I'm going to bring you down now. We'll get this all straightened out from ground level." She applied pressure to one of the levers on the main control panel.

To her horror, he lunged for his own controls, and Kelsey found herself fighting over the machine. The bucket nodded and groaned, but it didn't come down more than an inch.

"Stop that!" she shouted over the screech of the straining mechanisms. "Let go of the levers, soldier. That's an order! Let me lower you safely to the ground." The young man did not comply, forcing the bucket higher.

Kelsey eyed the key that would turn off the electricity. But she couldn't let go of the gun. Even if she could manage to turn the key, she couldn't risk an abrupt stop. "Ease up on your end so I can let go of mine!" she called out, but panic seemed to have taken hold of him and he let go all at once.

The bucket shot downward. With a cry, the soldier reached for a shelf as if he could stop the sudden descent. Kelsey released her own lever a second too late and the soldier's grip on the ledge tore free violently before the bucket came to an abrupt stop thirty feet from the floor. The man teetered for a moment with his arms flailing wildly, then…

He pitched over the side.

"No!" Kelsey watched him plummet headfirst, taking forever to reach the cement, and yet hitting it so suddenly that she hadn't finished the syllable before she saw him sprawled there in a widening pool of blood.

She started forward as too many immediate needs crowded her thinking—call the medics, stop the bleeding, don't move him, check for pulse, get an ambulance, resuscitate him, save him, save him, save him….

Midstep, she suddenly sensed that someone was behind her. On instinct, she began to lift her weapon and turn. But before she could confront the second intruder, pain splintered through her skull.

Followed by blackness.

CHAPTER ONE

"I...I DON'T KNOW what happened to the body."

From behind his desk, Major Julian Fordham looked up at the woman who had just walked unannounced into his office. He couldn't help feeling as if he were in a film noir that began with a narrator intoning "Of all the beautiful dames in all the world to walk through my door, why did it have to be her?" But then he got past the fact that Captain Kelsey O'Roark had suddenly reentered his life and focused not only on her bizarre words, but on her appearance as well.

"My God, what happened to you?" he asked as he rose from his chair and circled his desk. He reached a hand out to her, but dropped it again when he remembered he probably ought to maintain a professional distance. At least until he understood what had occurred.

"I...I...was working, trying to catch up on some reports after being away for a few days. I have a meeting tomorrow." Her gaze shifted to the window where the sun had just begun to brighten the horizon. "I mean today. And... and I lost the body, Julian. Sir."

"What are you talking about, Kelsey?" he asked, taking note of the smudges of dirt on her face and hands. One sleeve of her uniform was crumpled up past her elbow while the other hung loosely at her wrist without its button, a small tear in the material.

"It's a long story, sir." She stood at rigid attention, but she looked as if she might keel over any minute. He admired her determination, but he couldn't let her pass out because of it. And her appearance and tone were downright alarming.

"Sit down, before you fall down." He pulled the guest chair around behind her so she could more quickly ease into it. "Can I get you anything? Here, have some water." He reached for the plastic bottle that sat on his desk half finished and put it into her hand, then wrapped her cold fingers around it. He hunkered down in front of her with his bigger hands enveloping hers for a moment until she felt warmer to his touch. Before his thoughts could wander inappropriately, he released her and eased back.

She looked at the bottle as if she couldn't tell how it had gotten there, then she drank greedily, not caring that he'd sipped from it before her. His focus dropped momentarily to her mouth and memories threatened to swamp him. He pried the empty bottle from her clutching grasp.

Possibilities about what might have happened to her began to swim through his mind. All of them made him want to strangle someone. "Let me bring you to the hospital," he urged softly.

"No!" she nearly shouted. "I have to tell you what happened. You have to help him. At the warehouse…there was this man and…I heard a noise…" Her voice quavered and she stopped in midsentence.

He wanted to take her into his arms to comfort her. But he had no right to do that. And he felt certain she wouldn't appreciate the gesture. She'd come to him as a professional, not as a friend. She would have no other use for a man who, only a year ago, had run the instant their friendship had blossomed into something more.

"Start at the beginning, Captain." He stood and gently lifted her black beret from her head. This woman was an officer and would want to be treated like one no matter what had happened to her, he thought, handing it back to her. Stiffly, he returned to his seat behind his desk and took out a small, green, military-issue notebook and scribbled a heading that read *Captain K. O'Roark* under the date and time.

Sitting forward, her wrists on her knees, an earnest expression on her face, she took a breath and composed her features. But she betrayed her tension by continuing to turn her beret around and around in her two hands. "I saw your car in the parking lot," she said. "I'm not sure I would have been able to make myself come in here otherwise."

"Yes, you would have. You always do the right thing." He saw that this comment seemed to nearly break the calm she'd barely achieved, so he tried a new direction. "But it's lucky I volunteered to work the night shift for one of the lieutenants with a sick baby," he said, trying to put her at ease until she could make herself speak of the events that had brought her into his Criminal Investigation Division office.

To his relief, the corners of her mouth turned up into a tremulous smile. "That would be just like you—to volunteer to help someone out."

His concern for her subdued any happiness he might have felt that she remembered something good about him.

"I came to you because I hoped you wouldn't think I'm crazy, despite what I'm going to tell you." She eyed him as if to gauge his reaction, but he kept his face as expressionless as he had on countless investigations during his years in CID. When he said nothing, she stumbled on. "I thought, since we know each other, you'd be more willing to resist the urge to cart me off to the psych ward."

"Did someone hurt you, Kelsey?" he asked quietly, praying that she would deny it and yet knowing that her appearance indicated she wouldn't. His anger at the as-yet-unnamed attacker appalled him. He knew he had to retain control now, if ever he needed to. He must remain objective, professionally detached, neutral. But his gaze kept drifting to her missing button and the torn sleeve—indications she'd been in a scuffle. And rage suffused him, despite his legendary sangfroid.

She noticed the direction of his focus and looked at her wrist herself. "Oh!" she said. "I guess that must have happened when I was dragged into my office."

Horror lanced through him at her words, but she only rested her beret on one knee and proceeded to roll up her two sleeves neatly so that none of the muted interior colors of the cloth could be seen, as regulations demanded. Kelsey was nothing if not by the book.

"You were dragged into your—" With a muttered curse, he cut himself off. Had she been attacked, raped? He'd kill anyone who'd laid a violent hand on Kelsey. But he managed to keep from uttering those words. "Please, start at the beginning," he said without betraying his inner turmoil.

So she started with the moment when she'd heard the noise in the warehouse and had armed herself. When she finished, he remained nearly as angry and confused as when she'd begun.

"So you were knocked out cold?" Julian asked as he concentrated on scribbling another note. "Nothing else?"

When she didn't respond, he forced himself to look up at her—and found himself caught by her familiar eyes, usually so full of laughter and intelligence. Now they were frightened, despite her efforts to appear calm and unaffected. But they were still beautiful. Memories flashed through his mind in the space between one heartbeat and the next.

A year ago. A casual date filled with laughter. Then others filled with deeper feelings. Finally, a kiss. He'd meant it to be brief and respectful. But he'd made the mistake of meeting her gaze before he'd lowered his mouth to hers. Something he'd seen there had ignited him. He'd kissed her long and hard until he'd been gasping for air, terrified by all that he'd felt.

"I blacked out," she said after a moment. "So I can't be sure, but I think that's all that happened to me. But..."

"You should go to the hospital," he said. "You could have a concussion."

"I'm fine. I'll go later. Right now, I need you to help me figure out what happened." She shook her head back and forth mournfully. "That young man..."

"It was an accident, Kelsey," he said with as much reassurance as he could put into those few words. Watching her eyes turn shiny with emotion made his heart go tight. "There must be something going on in your warehouse. Theft, maybe. We've had some anonymous tips about something like that going on at the fort, but we could never find anything specific. We'll need to send a team over to investigate. And to retrieve the body." Beneath a note that read *victim knocked out: find heavy object/weapon,* he added to his list *retrieve/identify body: HAZMAT team: blood/cleanup.*

"But that's just it," she said, "there is no body."

That made him lift his gaze to hers again. "How can that be?" he queried as he studied her worried face. "I thought you just told me..." And he automatically glanced briefly at his notes to make sure she'd said that the young soldier in the lift had fallen thirty feet onto cement.

"Yes, I saw him fall. Headfirst. There was so much blood. His neck was all crooked. He couldn't have survived. Could he?" A hopeful edge lifted her tone and made Julian wish he could offer her another possibility.

Taking a breath and reminding himself to remain dispassionate and open-minded, he ignored her question and asked the obvious. "Then where's the body?"

"I don't know," she said, evading his mystified stare. "I told you before, I can't find it."

"When you regained consciousness, you'd been dragged into your office?"

"And when I went out into the warehouse again, there was no body. No blood even. My gun was back in my desk drawer with the clip sitting beside it as if I'd never taken it out or loaded it. The bucket lift was back where it was supposed to be, too." The beret turned and turned in her nervous fingers. At last, she looked directly at him again. She lifted her chin slightly and spoke almost defiantly. "And there was no body anywhere."

"I see." He knew she needed more from him than that, but for the life of him, he couldn't think of another thing to say.

"So, will you come to the warehouse with me? Maybe you can find something I'm not trained to notice."

"I'll send a team…."

"No, just you and me. Because if the story gets out like this, people will think… Unless you can find something to support what I'm telling you, my sanity could come into question. I can't have my staff whispering about this or risk my standing among my fellow officers. Please. Sir."

He knew how fragile any female officer's career could be in this man's army, no matter what the advertisements said about equal opportunity. "Don't keep calling me 'sir,'

Kelsey, as if we were never…" He stopped, unsure of the word he should choose to describe what they'd been to each other. *Almost-lovers* came to mind, but he wouldn't say that out loud. It would sound mournful and presumptuous at the same time.

She nodded her understanding, but her eyes were pleading. "For the sake of our friendship, will you come with me? If you don't find anything, my story will seem even more insane. But at least it'll just be between the two of us for a while longer and maybe I can come up with some sort of explanation for the events I witnessed."

"It's probably a conflict of interest for me to be involved in this and…"

"Please," she said softly, reminding him of the smooth-as-wine tone she'd used when she'd whispered his name a year ago.

There was no way he could turn his back on her despite the certainty that he could be in too deep with this woman in no time at all. He had to help her and he also had to find a way to remain aloof. Despite his reputation for cool composure in all circumstances, he wasn't sure he could do it. But he'd have to try.

She must have read his hesitation as an unwillingness to accept her story because she stood and said, "You should feel the knot on the back of my head, if you don't believe what I've told you." Before he could reassure her, she'd made it halfway around his desk toward him.

Resisting a surge of tenderness, he stood—a better position from which to keep her at arm's length. But when she drew near, she faced away from him and indicated the spot where he should touch her head. With her back toward him, he thought he would be safe from her allure. So he did as she asked.

His touch hesitant, he sifted through her short, golden-brown hair and remembered its silky texture from the last time they'd been together all those months ago. With memories crowding his mind, he managed to find the egg-size bump on her head which he touched very gently. But then his fingers seemed to drift on their own through her thick waves. She didn't pull away and in another second, he felt her relax against his touch and heard her sigh.

"You've been through hell," he whispered next to her ear.

It was an excuse to keep on touching her. She seemed willing to let him. So he gently massaged the base of her scalp, her neck, her shoulders—avoiding the place where she'd been hurt. But after a moment, she shook herself slightly and slipped out of his grasp. He came to his senses the instant she stepped beyond his reach. What had happened to his determination to remain aloof? Gone, with one touch!

"Will you come with me?" she asked again.

"Yes," he said, dooming himself to an involvement with her that was bound to be an emotional roller coaster. He led the way to the exit, taking long strides to keep enough distance between them so he couldn't detect the current that seemed to dance along the nerves of his skin when she drew close. "We'll get to the bottom of this, one way or another, Kelsey."

"That's why I came to you, Julian. I trust you."

He closed his eyes briefly, shocked that she would trust him after the way he'd dropped out of her life so abruptly. It meant so much to him and yet he shouldn't let it matter. He *couldn't* let it matter.

Because Captain Kelsey O'Roark was the marrying kind of woman. And after his own brief and disastrous marriage, he would never risk making that kind of commitment again. He had made an orderly life for himself in the army, he wouldn't bind himself to inevitable disaster.

Not even for Kelsey.

Julian had vowed to avoid her. He'd succeeded for an entire year. But now even if he wanted to escape, he couldn't.

Kelsey needed him and he couldn't deny her.

THE YOUNG SOLDIER OPENED his cell phone and dialed with shaking fingers. When he heard the voice on the other end of the line, he spoke frantically. "She's gone to CID! She's in there right now! What should we do?"

"Nothing at all," came the reply. "I told you to watch her and that's what I want you to do. Don't let her see you. Just follow her and tell me what she's up to."

"But she's got CID involved. They'll be all over us!" His free hand gripped the steering wheel of his beloved black truck. He'd trailed her from the warehouse to this office building at a safe distance, fearful that his truck would be easy to identify if she noticed it.

"Now why would you assume that? We've cleaned everything up. There's nothing left for them to find. It's this kind of defeatist thinking that will keep you from ever making NCO," said the other man, referring to noncommissioned officer status that all enlisted soldiers wanted to achieve. "Just keep a cool head. Those bumbling idiots in CID will keep spinning around in circles, now that they have this distraction. Everything that's happened could end up working in our favor."

The private gulped air. "She's coming out of CID now. I can see her. Someone is with her. A man. He's an officer."

"Get a grip and follow them, Private. But be careful. If they get suspicious of you, I'm throwing you off the raft, you understand? You'll be on your own and I won't be able to save you."

Private Earlman swallowed hard and nodded. "They're getting into separate cars. Which one do I follow?"

He heard a deep sigh over the phone. "I told you to follow *her*. Always follow her. And call in every few hours to tell me what she's doing."

Earlman thought back to the events of the night and felt as if he couldn't breathe. But he knew he was in too deep now to back out. "O-okay," he said into the phone. But then he thought about the other guy—the one who'd fallen— and had to ask. "And what about—"

His mentor in crime cut him off. "I'm taking care of everything else. You just leave it to me."

CHAPTER TWO

KELSEY LED THE WAY through the entrance along the side of the huge warehouse and found herself walking almost on tiptoe. The cavernous interior seemed to amplify everything, even the sound of her own breathing.

"Show me the office and then retrace your steps for me so I can understand how everything happened," Julian said. She could see his eyes glancing at every surface, penetrating every corner, his face a study in concentration.

"This way." She led him to the office where she'd been working. "Do you want to see the semiautomatic?" He nodded so she turned the key in the lock and pulled on the drawer handle, noticing for the first time the low screech of metal on metal as the thing opened. Had it always made that noise or were her senses on overdrive?

There sat the weapon, for all the world to see and as if she'd never touched it. The ammunition clip rested next to the gun as if it had never been snapped into the grip. Fingerprints might have proven that someone else's hands had held the thing, but whoever had gone to all the trouble of replacing it in exactly the same position as before would not have forgotten to wipe it down, too.

"I'll have someone dust it, but I don't expect to find prints," Julian said. "Leave it there and show me where you found the young soldier. Try to reenact your steps."

Blushing with embarrassment, she tried to do as he asked. Sneaking through the warehouse on the trail of an intruder hadn't seemed silly at the time, but doing it again under an investigator's scrutiny made her self-conscious. If only she could stop remembering the way this particular investigator could kiss, she might be able to better maintain her composure. Unfortunately, every time she glanced his way, her eyes seemed to hone in on his mouth. Her own lips tingled.

"Is this what you did? You just walked toward the sound?" he asked.

"Well, no," she admitted. "I hunkered down a little and moved from one end of the shelving to the next." She put words into action and Julian gave her a nod of satisfaction. "Then I popped my head out for a second to see if the noise had come from this aisle." She showed him, using her hand and pointed finger to imitate the gun she'd held. "Then I noticed that the bucket lift wasn't in its parking space." Kelsey pointed to the big machine.

"It's parked there now," he observed.

She squinted at him in exasperation. "I told you. Everything was put back where it had been by the time I regained consciousness. There's nothing here to corroborate my story."

"Let's have a look at where you think the man fell," he said and Kelsey bristled at the implication that a man hadn't *really* fallen. But almost as soon as the irritation surfaced, she realized he might not have meant to question her story, only the location of the accident. She shook her head slightly, hoping to settle her rioting emotions, but regretted the action when pain streaked through her battered skull. She lifted her hand to the bump near her crown, remembered the sensation of Julian's fingers gently sifting through her hair and knew that her emotions would be out of her control as long as she remained in this man's company.

She gestured toward the place where she'd seen the bucket lift idling and Julian moved down the wide corridor created by the ceiling-to-floor metal shelves. Kelsey watched as he stooped to look at the polished cement beneath his feet and gave the surrounding area a thorough inspection. She couldn't imagine what sorts of things he might be looking for, but his gaze scanned the gleaming floor inch by inch. She'd already scouted the area and had found nothing.

She'd found so much nothing that she would've doubted her own memories if not for the lump on the back of her head. Unfortunately, she knew that it would take more than her swollen head to convince Julian—or anyone else.

"Is the floor always this clean?" he asked.

She nodded, but frustration made her add, "Except when there's blood all over it."

He gave her a small smile and Kelsey remembered how wonderful his rare laughter could be. Why hadn't she called him for another date after those last electrifying few hours they'd spent together? The reason completely eluded her as she gazed at him now.

"Someone must have cleaned up quickly and completely. I don't see anything that looks like blood. There isn't even any dust on the floor."

She shrugged. "It's an army warehouse. We mop up every night. Lieutenant Sorrell would have followed that protocol before locking up at eighteen hundred yesterday."

Julian's brow furrowed. "Lieutenant Sorrell?"

"Mark Sorrell. He's my deputy. He was in charge yesterday because I was on temporary duty at a class in

Charlottesville. I only came in to get ready for a meeting in—" she checked her watch "—three hours."

"So, you weren't supposed to be here at all," he said as he tipped his head to gaze along the length of metal shelving, apparently trying to find smudges by catching the proper lighting.

"That's right." She'd already explained this to him. Did he think her story wouldn't bear up under the strain of repetition? "I told you that before."

He shot her another half grin. "So you did. Sorry. Getting a witness to repeat things is just a habit. The variations that creep into different renditions can be very revealing."

Well, at least he was up front about his tactics. And if she were in his shoes, she'd test her story, too. "Have I provided you with any variations?"

"Not yet," he said as he shot a devilish look her way. "I don't see anything here. Let's take the lift up to the level where you saw the intruder messing around."

"The bucket lift?" The idea of touching that thing again, after what she'd seen happen the last time she'd been near it, made her shudder.

He walked to her slowly, carefully. Then he grasped her shoulders in a comforting gesture that seemed a little awkward. Softly he said, "You don't have to go up. I just need the key. I'll go up and you can tell me when to stop."

She shook her head. "No, I can't let you do that. Not after what happened to the last inexperienced guy who used it. I'll go up with you or you won't go up at all."

He looked deeply into her eyes, seemed satisfied by the determination she hoped he saw there and stepped back. "Okay, let's go."

The key to the machine dangled from its hook under the seat where anyone who worked in the warehouse would find it easily. She started the motor and maneuvered the machine to what appeared to be the right place. Julian stood waiting nearby. "Right about here, I think," she said. She climbed down from the driver's seat and stepped up into the bucket, holding open the small door so Julian could join her.

"You're sure this is safe for two people?" he asked, pushing on the waist-high wall as if to test its sturdiness.

"I'm sure," she said, but she'd never considered how close they'd be as they rode together. She could sense Julian's heat enveloping her. Both her heart and head began to throb. She wanted only stillness from the moment, but that wouldn't be possible.

"Do you want me to work the controls?" he asked. His voice seemed hushed, as if he felt the spell, too, and didn't want to break it.

Inwardly, she gave herself a shake, hoping to evaporate her stupor. "No. They're very sensitive." *Like my skin would be if you touched me now.* "I'll just—" And her hand wrapped around the lever in a way that suggested things she had no business thinking about right now. Neither the time nor the place.

"Hold on," she warned. The bucket jumped slightly under her clumsy control. Julian's arm snaked around her from behind and didn't let go, protecting her from a fall of her own. Kelsey barely managed to breathe as he encircled her. His other arm braced his body while he gripped the railing to the bucket as if his life depended on it. Maybe it did.

That awful moment when she'd seen that young man plummet to his death screamed once again through her mind with blinding clarity. This was no time to be thinking of Julian's nearness or remembering the softness of his lips on hers. A death had occurred, serious crimes may have been committed. Her focus had to remain on that. Only that.

She cleared her throat. "I think this is about how high he was when I first saw him. This is level four," she said to the man pressed against her back. "There are only crates of spare parts here."

"Is it safe for me to walk on the floor of the shelves?"

"Yes. That's how we move boxes or take inventory. But you should use a—"

He had already climbed over the side of the bucket and onto the shelving—putting Kelsey's heart in her throat as she thought of how easily he could fall—before she finished her sentence. "Platform lift instead of this one."

"Can you tell if anything's missing?" he asked. "Do you keep count of the boxes?"

"I can't tell just from looking. But we do regular inventories. I could have this level checked when my crew arrives today."

"Go ahead and do that, but until we find out more," he said as he moved back toward her, "I want you to keep the events of last night between the two of us. If someone was here to steal something, I don't want him tipped off."

He edged closer. Her heart beat hard as he reached for the lip of the bucket in which she still stood. "Wait. Let me get the proper lift. Then you can just—"

Julian's leg came over the side, and the rest of him quickly followed. The agile maneuver barely took three seconds, but Kelsey's imagination conjured a hundred different horrors as he did it. And yet she knew that what he'd done wasn't so terribly dangerous. She'd had to do far worse things during various training exercises, particularly on grueling confidence courses. Had her experiences of the night before rattled her so badly that even the slightest thing sent her into a spiral of fear? She swiped away perspiration that had formed on her brow and once again realized how much her head ached.

"Are you all right?" Julian asked. Concern softened his voice, but his eyes searched and penetrated. Less than a foot separated their locked gazes. A mere ten inches of charged air vibrated between their lips. Kelsey was the first to drop her focus to that mouth of his, so sensuous and full of promise. His groan was nearly inaudible, but it was enough to tell her how close they were to behaving foolishly. Common sense reminded her to work the lever to bring them back down to earth.

She'd braced herself for the lurch of the bucket, but had forgotten to give Julian any warning. He jerked forward, right into her arms. She clutched him to her, terror clawing at her from head to toe. Letting go of the switch stopped the lift at level three. But her heart kept on pounding and her mind reeled with premonitions of sudden death.

"Thank you," he whispered into her ear as he held her close. But when he eased back ever so slightly, she could see in his eyes that he distanced himself emotionally. "At least you won't have another dead body on the cement below," he added. Cool amusement seemed to lace his voice.

Well, *that* certainly brought her fully out of whatever daydream she kept drifting into regarding Julian Fordham. She let go of the man and even set him away from her as much as the confines of the space would allow. She avoided his eyes, but heard him mutter an oath as if he realized how inappropriate his comment had been.

"Hold on to the railing. We're going down," she warned.

"Kelsey," he began, but she ignored the plaintive tone and pushed the control. The rise of her stomach attested to the fact that she dropped them too fast. When they hit the bottom of the extension arm, the percussion snapped her teeth together. She welcomed the jolt, despite the spikes of pain that seared through her brain near the bump on her scalp.

Now she remembered why she hadn't called Julian a year ago for another date. Major Julian Fordham could be heroic in his concern for others, he could be charming and funny, and he was certainly very sexy. But he had a startling inability to deal with deep feelings from others, let alone show any of his own. They may have had only a few dates, but his tendency to withdraw whenever things became emotional had been clear almost from the start. He was a very cool and controlled person. The complete opposite of her.

Kelsey had realized after that last evening they'd shared that Julian had been wounded deeply somewhere in his past. She hadn't been up to figuring out how or by whom. And adding his load of issues to her own considerable childhood baggage would have been sheer insanity. After the way she'd been raised, the last thing she needed was to find herself tied to a man as detached as Julian.

MECHANICALLY, JULIAN CONTINUED the search for clues in the warehouse even as his brain taunted him with his own words *another dead body on the cement below.* Could he have been a bigger idiot, he asked himself. He'd known as soon as the words were out of his mouth that they were all wrong. He'd wanted to take them back, or at least to explain that he'd meant only to ease the tension. He'd also hoped to regain some control over his rampaging libido with the morbid humor. But Kelsey seemed to be in no mood to hear his lame excuses, so he'd shut his mouth.

He searched meticulously. He even went outside with Kelsey to look inside both Dumpsters, surveying the ground for evidence that someone had dragged a body. There was nothing. Nothing at all.

He didn't want to be the one to tell her that there was every indication she might have conjured up the whole thing after hitting her head on something and passing out. Or perhaps something worse had happened to her and false memories had replaced the truth. The complete lack of evidence pointed to there being no dead body. He had to at least suggest this as a possibility before army resources were used to investigate a case that might be way off track—or even a figment of Kelsey's imagination. He turned to her as they stood in the cool evening air behind the warehouse where not even a footprint could be found.

He opened his mouth to speak, but snapped it shut as he looked at her with the moonlight gilding her hair and lending a fairylike quality to her features. The urge to kiss her resurfaced, hitting him nearly as hard as when he'd been thrown against her in the lift. Only a few steps separated them. He could take them. He could tell her with his caress rather than in words that he'd missed her. With his touch, he would explain that he'd been a fool when he'd stopped calling her. He'd feared she'd been half in love with him a year ago and he'd had to run away from her then. He was stronger now and knew that he had the capacity for deeper feelings. Maybe Kelsey would understand. Maybe she would welcome his kiss.

"You must think I'm crazy," she said as she scuffed her booted foot in the hard-packed dirt.

Julian's fantasies about taking her into his arms disappeared like smoke in the wind. "I don't think you're crazy," he assured her. Not crazy, but perhaps just very confused. But he didn't want to say that out loud when she looked so forlorn. Yet he had to say *something*. Doing his job the best he knew how, he forced aside sympathy and drew upon that cool, just-the-facts detachment he'd learned too well from his father, the air force general turned congressman. "We'll need to consider the possibility that something happened to you that you can't remember. Something that doesn't involve a dead body. You might have fallen and knocked yourself out. And then had a really bad dream or got your memories confused because of the blow you sustained. Head injuries can do strange things to people."

She snapped into a rigid posture so fast, he couldn't hold back a slight wince. "I did *not* make any of this up. It was *not* a figment of my imagination. There was no dream!" With each sentence her voice grew louder. Julian retreated a step as she said, "And I certainly would remember if I'd hit my own head!"

He held up his palms hoping to pacify her and said, "Hey, I'm only trying to help here. I'm not attacking your honesty or anything."

She relaxed slightly, but then raised and dropped her arms in exasperation. "I'm tired, my head hurts, I'm supposed to give a briefing today and there's no evidence to support what happened here last night." She gave a little laugh. "You'd be edgy, too, under those circumstances."

When they'd dated, her ability to be positive about almost everything had been one of the characteristics he'd found both enchanting and terrifying. Her good-natured outlook had seemed suspicious, unnatural, or at least exceptionally naive. She didn't appreciate the dangers of wearing her heart on her sleeve, couldn't see the pitfalls in always thinking the best of everyone. That's what he'd thought of her then.

Now, when she faced so much, he found himself admiring her pluck. It couldn't be easy to resist being dragged down by the situation she found herself in. He decided the best course of action was to accept her story at face value for the time being. "You've had a pretty traumatic experience, Kelsey. And you really need to go to the hospital and have your head examined— I mean..." He so dearly wanted to put that another way.

"I know what you mean," she said with a weary smile.

He couldn't let her smile make him forget the point he wanted to make. "You need to see a doctor. Get a complete physical. Promise me you will?" He wanted proof she hadn't been sexually assaulted, but she could have been traumatized without there being any physical proof at all. At the very least, she needed to be evaluated for a concussion.

"I will," she agreed. "But what happens now? Isn't there anything else you can do to help me figure out this mess? I mean, I can't just pretend it didn't happen when some young man is dead."

An odd little protest throbbed inside his chest as he realized she thought he might abandon her now. She must think him pretty damn cold if she believed he could do that. But, then again, most women thought the same of him. "I'm not going to drop your case just because I couldn't find anything on a single walk-through. There are tests we can perform, chemicals we can try. If someone died in this warehouse, we'll find some evidence."

She sighed. "You keep saying *if* someone died. But I can hardly blame you. I knew as soon as I came awake in my office and saw that everything had been cleaned up and put away I'd have trouble making anyone believe me. I suppose that's what the intruders wanted."

Julian nodded, glad she understood. He heard sounds coming from inside the warehouse behind them and glanced through the open door. "Is that your staff coming to work?"

She looked down at her watch. "Is it seven-thirty already? I've got to get ready or I'll be late for that briefing!"

On impulse, he grasped her shoulders so she would look up into his face. The flex of her muscled flesh beneath the cotton of her battle dress uniform made him want to run his hands over her. "Kelsey, you promised you'd go to the hospital. You're in no condition to give a briefing. I've kept you from getting medical attention long enough as it is. I should have insisted. You need… you should…" And then her warm fingers were pressed gently against his lips, putting an end to his wretched attempts to show his concern.

She stared at him for a few stretched seconds. Softly she said, "Thank you for caring. I promise to get checked out at the hospital as soon as I can." Then she withdrew her touch and gave him another one of her sweet-as-honey smiles. There was so much tenderness in this woman.

His father had taught him to avoid emotions like this, both in himself and others.

And yet he craved it.

He let go of her as if her body had suddenly gone burning hot to his touch. She staggered slightly and the morning light revealed a blush staining her cheeks. He almost reached for her again with an apology on his lips. But she regained her composure too quickly and got back to business.

"I have to get things settled inside and then go home for another uniform. Thanks for your help, Julian. We'll keep this all quiet until we figure out what's going on, right? I don't need to have people talking about the hysterical Captain O'Roark and her imaginary dead guy, okay?"

"There's a man in the office I trust to keep things quiet.

I'll tell him to make it all seem routine when he comes out here to do the tests I need."

"Why can't you do the tests yourself?" she asked. "I was hoping to keep this between us until we find something. Oh, wait." She went very still and her eyes went wide. "Should I tell my commander about all this, do you think?"

Julian didn't like seeing tension etched into her pretty face. "Don't tell anyone yet, Kelsey. If someone questions you later about your silence, I'll explain that I required secrecy until I figured out more details without tipping off possible suspects. If I open a case when I get back to the office, I'll be in charge of it and authorized to order your silence."

"You're going to open a case? The entire post will know all about it by this evening if you do that." She started turning in slow circles as if she searched for an escape. The tension he'd seen seconds ago had been replaced by a wild, hunted expression.

"I'll open a case, but I'll secure it. You have to trust me. And I'd do the tests myself if I had time. But I need to check some things that could have a bearing on your case as well as another one."

She stopped and glanced at him sideways. "I do trust you. That's why I came to you in the first place."

An unexpected spark of pleasure washed through him even as the possibility that he might fail her under these odd circumstances nibbled at his confidence. He hid his doubts behind the sure and commanding demeanor he'd perfected. "Could the soldier you saw have been from another military base?"

Kelsey's brows knit as she concentrated. "I don't think so. I remember…his uniform had a patch from a local unit I've seen here. I know I've seen it around. I can't remember exactly."

"That's a start. I'll let you know if anyone is reported AWOL. You start an inventory to find out if anything is missing."

She nodded, gazing up at him as if he were her lifeline. He didn't want to leave her alone, wanted to cart her off to the hospital himself, wanted to take her home to his apartment to keep her safe. But that wouldn't be very professional of him. And as an officer, she probably wouldn't appreciate being coddled.

Tapping the discipline his father had taught him, he made himself turn and walk away, heading around the side of the building. He resisted the urge to look back. If she stood staring at him with those big, troubled eyes of hers, he'd make a fool of himself. But once he rounded the corner, he stopped to wipe the sweat from his brow. Now he understood what people meant when they said they were conflicted. He could not possibly be more conflicted over Kelsey O'Roark.

Coffee. He needed coffee. Badly. Then he'd go back to the office, even though he'd had no sleep, and open a file on this strange mess. He hoped the luminol test would reveal the blood Kelsey said had been on the cement floor. Because if it didn't, he'd have to seriously consider the possibility that the episode she described had never happened.

He got into his car and headed toward the coffee shop as he thought over the situation. If there had been a break-in at the warehouse and if a soldier had fallen to his death, then someone had gone to an enormous amount of trouble to conceal those facts. That would mean that whatever the intruders had been up to must be worth a great deal. There had to be large amounts of money involved. And it would have to be an inside job. Pulling off something like this within the confines of a military post, there had to be an officer involved. But who?

"Note to self," he said out loud to the dashboard. "Kelsey's break-in might have something to do with the unsolved thefts at the post." If so, Captain Kelsey O'Roark may just have handed him the biggest break of his career.

And he'd be working very closely with her for quite some time to come. The thought made him feel nervous, but—consistent with his confusion—it also made him smile.

CHAPTER THREE

KELSEY GAVE HERSELF a few minutes after Julian disappeared around the side of the warehouse, then checked her uniform to be sure she'd put the sleeves back in order and that there were no telltale signs of her debacle. Looking over her shoulder into the thick forest of trees where the early sun hadn't yet reached, she shook off the feeling that someone was watching her and went inside. She would have to talk to her staff without revealing anything about the night before. And she'd have to decide what should be done next. Nodding to various staff members as she passed through, she headed for the office. Lieutenant Mark Sorrell already sat at his desk, at an angle to her own.

"Hi, Mark. I need you to do something for me." She picked up the day's work schedule and pretended to skim the details.

"Ma'am," he said as he looked up from his work. "You weren't supposed to be in today. Don't you have a briefing at HQ?"

"Yes. And I've got less than an hour to pull things together for that, not to mention change into my class B uniform. I stopped by to tell you that CID wants us to do an inventory. There's something going on and we need to be sure nothing's missing."

The lieutenant shrugged. Random inventories were getting to be somewhat routine. "Yes, ma'am. Not a problem. Which stuff needs to be counted and how long do I have?"

"Couple of days. But, listen, I want a complete inventory this time. Everything gets counted. No crate overlooked, and all that." She reached across the desk to get her briefing materials, glanced at the closed drawer that held the handgun she'd used such a short time earlier, felt a shiver run down her spine and turned to go.

But the squeak of Mark's chair as it swivelled around made her look back with raised eyebrows. Astonishment held his features. "You want a *complete* inventory? In a couple of *days?*" His eyes widened at the prospect.

"Yup. I think we need a baseline to work from. We haven't done one in nearly a year—"

"Seven and a half months," he interjected.

"—and I want a fresh start." She rubbed the back of her head where the swelling had gone down, but which continued to throb nonetheless. "I don't think I'll be back over here today, Mark. I have a vicious headache and I think I should go over to the infirmary to see if there's anything stronger than aspirin the docs can give me for it." She needed to make good on her promise to Julian that she'd let a doctor check her over.

"Right. I'll take care of things here." He'd recovered only slightly from his initial surprise. "You know I'll have to cancel some people's leave if we only have a few days to do this major inventory."

She thought about that a minute. "Well, use your judgment. But don't ruin any family reunions or anything. Call in people who can rearrange their plans and offer them three free days if they do it without complaint. You'll figure something out."

"Will do. Don't worry about a thing," Mark said. He always liked to be in charge when she was away. He did a good job, too. She mustered a pain-racked smile for him and headed out. Maybe she'd have time for a quick shower before her briefing.

"I TOLD YOU NOT TO come here where I work," snarled the man who had led Private Earlman to this dismal point in his life. "We're not supposed to know each other, remember?"

"Yeah, I know. But you told me to call in every few hours and you haven't been answering your cell," he said, wondering if that would reduce the evil gleam in the man's eyes. It was no wonder everyone called him the Wolf. And, of course, there was the dog—big as a horse and mean as a rattler—standing on the pavement beside the man. The parking lot had seemed like a safe enough place to meet.

The Wolf's eyes widened with surprise and he snapped his cell phone from his belt. In one swift motion, he flipped it open. Even from a few feet away, it was obvious the battery had gone dead. Not a single light or beep came from the unit.

"Damn!" The Wolf tossed the offending device onto the seat of his car before slamming the door shut. "Talk fast. I have to report in and I don't want to be seen with you." His tone implied he'd rather eat cockroaches.

"She's got Major Fordham working with her. He went to the warehouse to check things out." Surely this bit of news would be worthy enough to excuse catching up with the Wolf as he headed into his office.

"Okay. Noted. Anything else?" The man's wolfish eyes darted from side to side, continuously scanning the area for anyone who might observe them. The dog's eyes remained fixed on Earlman.

"Aren't you worried about that? Fordham is known for—"

"I know what he's known for. He won't find anything and that man is all about evidence. You worry too much." The Wolf smiled and the soldier half expected to see fangs. "Leave all the worrying to me. I've got everything under control."

THOUGHTS OF THE NOTES he would make danced through Julian's mind, distracting him as he entered the coffee shop. He nearly collided with his friend, Major Andrew Mitchum.

"Hey, buddy, what's got you so out of it?" Drew asked cheerfully, but he didn't wait for an answer. "Found something on those thieves we're trying to nail?" This time, he waited for a response.

"Not so loud, Drew," Julian urged. "And I need coffee more than I need to talk to you." He kept on walking to the counter where a smiling teenager greeted him. "Large," he said.

"Today we have vanilla hazelnut, chocolate latte, french caramel fudge," said the teen as her ponytail bobbed happily, "and raspberry kiss."

Mmm, that last one had him thinking of Kelsey again, but he shook it off. "Black. Plain," he said. The waitress stared at him, then blinked. Her smile never wavered as she repeated the list. About then, he remembered why he didn't come here very often.

Drew came up behind him and nudged his shoulder playfully. "He'll have a grande vanilla hazelnut," he said. "You're holding up the line, Jules."

Julian nodded wearily, paid for the steaming cup and followed Drew to a table. "I don't necessarily have anything new on these alleged thieves."

Drew's face lit with interest. "That 'necessarily' sounds intriguing. What's going on?"

Julian silently debated telling Drew anything related to Kelsey. The man was the commander of the 607th Military Police Group and Julian's friend, but Kelsey's claims weren't corroborated by any evidence yet. Maybe they never would be. "I don't have anything new. We've talked to units all over the post, alerted them to look out for missing stuff."

Drew leaned back against the seat, exasperated. "Nothing?"

"First it's a truck, then it's an incoming shipment that comes up short, then later it's something else. We just can't get a step ahead of these guys. But I've got a lead on a warehouse situation that might yield something. I'll keep you informed." He took a sip of his coffee and decided that this would be all he'd tell him, friend or no.

Drew looked closely at him. "Something going on with the G3?" He referred to Kelsey, the logistics officer, and Julian couldn't imagine how he'd put it together so fast. Drew's deductive abilities as a military cop were greater than Julian had thought.

Without flinching, Julian hedged, "I don't know. I asked for an inventory." This would be well-known by this afternoon anyway. He took another sip and lingered over its taste a moment to give the impression he hadn't been surprised. "If something's missing, we might work from there. But don't hold your breath."

"Well, that abandoned crate we found lying broken in the woods last week had to come from somewhere. And it fit right in with the anonymous calls we've been getting about this theft ring." Drew eyed Julian as if for a reaction.

Julian kept his expression neutral. "Could be," he said as he got up from the table. "I'll let you know. I've got to get back to the office."

"No, you don't," Drew said with a laugh. "You just got off a night shift. Go home. You look wrecked."

Julian gave him a wan smile. "Gee, thanks."

"Hey, only your good buddies will tell you the painful truth, Jules."

As he walked out to his car, Julian wished he could talk to his brother Nathan—one of the few people who really *would* tell him the painful truth. Nathan might be able to help him sort through his confusion regarding Kelsey. But Nate was newly married, newly promoted to major and newly transferred with his wife to Fort Dix. The last thing the man needed was to have his lonely older brother intrude on all that happiness, even if Nathan positively relished the job of giving Julian the painful truth right between the eyes.

Julian came to a stop just before he pulled the handle to open his car door. Where the hell had *lonely older brother* come from? And if that was some sort of Freudian slip, then maybe he *should* call Nathan sometime soon. Maybe Nate could help him figure out how to overcome whatever held him back from going after what he wanted most.

As the younger of the two, Nathan had been spared some of the childhood lessons Julian had learned too well. While their father had demanded emotional fortitude from Julian as a teenager, refusing even to allow open grieving over the sudden death of their mother, Nathan had been able to cry on Julian's shoulder. When their old man had left them in the care of various housekeepers at the many different places they'd lived around the globe while he pursued his military and political ambitions, Julian had taken care of Nathan in all the ways that mattered—attending his soccer games, praising his successes, assisting with homework and advising him as best he could. When Julian escaped his father's control after college by joining the army—shunning the air force just for spite—his brother had followed in his footsteps. But in every other way, their lives were completely different. Their differences were most notable when it came to relationships with women.

Yes, Nathan might be able to help Julian figure things out. He'd call as soon as he could have such a conversation without sounding pathetically weak and overly emotional. Or lonely.

DESPITE KELSEY'S THROBBING HEAD, the briefing went fairly well. At least she knew the answers to most of the questions and she found ways to seem relatively intelligent even when a question stumped her. She'd only had an hour to study the material before her world had turned upside down, so things could have gone quite a lot worse. All she wanted now was a much-needed soak in a bathtub filled to the brim with steaming, fragrant water.

But first she had to see a doctor. Reluctantly, Kelsey turned into the parking lot of DeWitt Army Community Hospital, a place she only visited when she was ordered to stand for her physicals. Never before had she put up with the tedium of checking in and going through triage. There seemed to be a score of lines in which she was required to wait. Progress seemed glacial in each. A nurse insisted that a head injury called for a complete examination, which required the removal of her clothing and the donning of an open-back hospital gown. Half the day had disappeared before she found herself sitting on crackling paper spread over a high examination table. Her bare feet dangled, making her feel ten years old again. At least she'd retained her underwear and bra so she didn't feel completely naked, too.

The doctor turned out to be a petite female with a warm

smile. Her kind expression defused Kelsey's explosive nerves, brought to the brink of detonation by the interminable wait with nothing to do but swing her feet and stare at the container of tongue depressors on the counter. "I'm Dr. Britt. And it says here that you've had a bump on the head. How long ago did that happen?"

Kelsey did not want to explain the true circumstances under which she'd come to be cracked over the head with a blunt instrument, so she implied that she'd done it to herself on the edge of a desk after fetching a fallen pencil. Julian had inadvertently given her that idea when he'd suggested she'd imagined the events after knocking herself out. She'd rather have the doctor think she was clumsy enough to smack her head on the desk than to have her wondering about her patient's sanity after hearing the true story that had no corroborating evidence.

"Yes, you have quite a knot back here. Does this hurt?" the doctor asked as she poked around. Then, when Kelsey winced, " Sorry. How long did you say you were unconscious?"

"I'm not sure. Maybe an hour."

"That's a very long time to be out. You should have come straight to the emergency room. Head injuries can be dangerous. Any dizziness? Nausea?"

"I was a little dizzy when I first stood up after I awoke, but that went away. Now I just have a headache." She blinked as the doctor shined a light into each of her eyes.

"Well, you're lucky. You've been walking around all this time with no ill effects, so I can only conclude you escaped without serious injury. But if—"

Beethoven's Fifth began to chime from somewhere inside the pile of clothing Kelsey had left on the chair. "I just need to—" Without thinking, she ducked out from under the fingers prodding at her skull, hopped off the table and dug out the cell phone.

"You really shouldn't—" the doctor began, but Kelsey had already flipped her phone open to say hello. She shot the doctor an apologetic expression.

"Hi, hi, hi, Kels!" came the voice of her sister over the phone.

"Shannon!" She smiled at Dr. Britt and mouthed "my sister," then held up her finger to indicate she'd get off the phone in a minute.

The good doctor smiled and waited.

"I'm visiting you!" her sister said.

Kelsey hoped she didn't mean what it sounded like. But she couldn't find out more right away. The doctor stood by and deserved her attention. "Shannon, I'm in a meeting right now. I need to call you back. It'll just be a few minutes."

When her sister reluctantly agreed, Kelsey snapped her phone shut and gave Dr. Britt an apology. "I shouldn't have answered. Sorry. It's just been a stressful day."

"I understand," said the doctor. Then she delivered a litany of things to watch out for, the dangers of a concussion, the signs of trouble. Kelsey could only give half her attention. She was worried about the missing body, about spending time with Julian and about what her sister had meant about visiting.

"Here's a prescription for pain medication." Dr. Britt handed her a sheet. "And I'll leave instructions for you at the checkout desk about how to deal with a concussion. Follow the directions, Captain. They're important." She looked Kelsey in the eye when she said this.

"Yes, I'll read and follow the directions," she assured her. The last thing Kelsey needed was complications from her head injury. She'd be careful.

The instant the doctor left the examination room, Kelsey recalled the last incoming number and hit Send on her cell phone. Shannon answered almost instantly.

"Where are you, Shan? You're supposed to be in California with that guy named Calvin or Kevin or something." Kelsey never could keep track of Shannon's boyfriends.

"It was Kelvin and he's an asshole. Come home right now and I'll tell you all the sordid details, which involve fishnet stockings and black lingerie—for him."

Suddenly Kelsey's stomach fell to her toes under the weight of suspicion. "What do you mean by 'come home right now,' Shannon?"

Her sister's gleeful reply squeezed her around the chest until she could hardly breathe.

"I mean, I'm standing on your doorstep at this very minute! I've come for a visit! Isn't that great?"

A groan nearly escaped her, but she clamped a hand over her mouth to stifle it. She wondered if it was too late to ask Dr. Britt to admit her to the hospital. For a split second, Kelsey wondered how long she could string the doctors along so she could stay for the duration of her sister's visit. Not that she didn't love her sister, Kelsey reminded herself as guilt washed through her. As her only close relative besides the mother she so rarely talked to, Shannon meant the world to her. Really.

No, she couldn't lie to the doctor to escape Shannon. As sisters went, there could not be a more opposite pair, despite their closeness in age. They loved each other, but sometimes Shannon could get on Kelsey's nerves. Somehow she'd find a way to make the visit enjoyable anyway. That was her duty as the elder sister.

Then another thought struck her. "Shannon, did you bring your dog?"

"Of course! I couldn't leave my bitty baby Bella-kins," she uttered in that ridiculous baby talk she used when addressing the yappy little monster. Sounding as if she had her face in the creature's fur, she added, "My wittle puppy dog is right here with Mommy, aren't you. And she wants to see her aunty Kelsey really, really soon. Isn't that so, baby Bella."

"God save me," Kelsey muttered.

"What was that?" Shannon asked through the phone.

"Nothing, Shan." Kelsey reached for her clothes and tried to dance into her dark green uniform slacks while holding the phone to her ear. "I'll be home in a little while," she promised. "There's a key under the medium-size rock to the left of the outside steps. Just let yourself in and…" She did *not* want to tell her sister to make herself at home. But what choice did she have? And there had to be some chance that this visit would go better than all the ones before. "…Make yourself, um, comfortable."

"'Kay," Shannon agreed cheerfully. "Ciao!" Then the connection went dead.

Forgetting about her sore head, Kelsey drooped against the wall of the examination room. Her head connected with the surface and artillery fire roared through Kelsey's skull, followed by a battalion of bass drummers. She winced, wishing she could just live here in this tiny room for a few weeks.

Knowing that she couldn't avoid it, she started putting on her class B uniform. She took a long time buttoning the light green blouse and fastening the black tie at her throat, delaying the inevitable. She loved her sister, she kept telling herself. She loved her. Shannon was a dear person, warm and easygoing and carefree.

And that was it in a nutshell. Shannon seemed to be as

perpetually free of worries as any human being could ever
be. Not even their mother could match Shannon in this regard. Widowed young with two girls to raise, Mary
O'Roark was a good person. But now that Kelsey and
Shannon were on their own, she was content to live in her
little house on the meager disability pension she'd somehow squeezed out of her former employer after a minor factory accident. She spent her time watching soap operas. But
she had enough motherly sense to fret over her daughters.
Shannon's only worry was her little dog. Because she left
everything else to her older sister.

Kelsey wanted to go back to work. Or to the gym. Or
to Alaska. But she had to go home. And when she walked
through the door, she was greeted with exactly what she'd
expected. Chaos.

Her usually sweet and docile cat, Jasper, hissed and spit
from the top of a bookcase, while Bella yapped incessantly
from below. Magazines and books lay scattered across the
floor. A toppled pet carrier and several suitcases sat randomly throughout the living room. A teakettle whistled
with piercing clarity. She could hear her sister singing in
the bathroom. Steam poured out from beneath the door.

"Stop it, Bella!" Kelsey yelled. The dog turned and ran
toward her without even taking a breath between barks. She
made three circles around Kelsey's ankles, giving Jasper
time to make an escape in a streak across the living room
and down the hall. Instantly, Bella gave chase. The pair
ended up in the spare bedroom where Shannon should
have put her suitcases. Kelsey shut the door on the animals,
figuring Jasper ought to be able to hold his own against a
ten-pound froufrou dog like Bella. Besides, she suspected
Jasper secretly enjoyed the excitement. And with the door
shut, she could barely hear the yowls and yaps from within.

On her way back toward the kitchen, she rapped on the bathroom door. "I'm home, Shan," she called to her sister.

The rock concert ceased long enough for Shannon to say "'kay!" then began anew. For a thirty-year-old woman, Shannon could seem so much like a teenager sometimes.

Kelsey closed her eyes a moment, fighting the headache that seemed to be growing too big for her skull. Then she went to the kitchen to turn off the stove under the shrieking teakettle. Pivoting, she saw a cellophane-wrapped basket holding a beautiful porcelain teapot and two large matching cups sitting alongside an assortment of specialty teas. A bow adorned the package and a note dangled from the ribbon. A gift for her? From Shannon? Should she peek at the note? Absolutely. That way, if it wasn't for her, she wouldn't upset Shannon with any hint of disappointment.

"To my dearest, sweetest, generousest (and only) sister. Love, Shannon."

Aw! Kelsey's headache abated, despite the occasional thump and bark she heard from the spare bedroom. Surely this was a better beginning than some of Shannon's other visits. The rest of her stay would be good, too. They would enjoy each other's company. They would catch up and laugh about old times and be…well…sisters.

Feeling better already, Kelsey set about throwing some food together for dinner. She'd have to get to the commissary for groceries now that Shannon was here. But she heated up slices of roast chicken, fried some fresh green beans in butter and garlic with some pine nuts thrown in for show. Then she popped a batch of biscuits into the oven.

"That should hold us awhile," Shannon said from the doorway. She wore Kelsey's bathrobe and a towel adorned her head in a sweeping pile. "I forgot how much you like to cook."

Kelsey smiled and then hugged her sister. "It'll be more fun cooking for two," she said. And she meant it. There were definitely some good things about having Shannon here. If only she hadn't dropped in on the heels of an accidental death in Kelsey's warehouse, the visit might even be welcome. A resounding thud from inside the guest room weakened Kelsey's smile slightly, but she quickly recovered. "Sit. Tell me what's been happening with you."

They spent a truly lovely hour eating a peaceful dinner, punctuated only now and then by frenzied movement and high-pitched barking. Shannon explained that she'd loved California, but did not love Kelvin. She planned to get a job locally and a place of her own, but that would take a few weeks.

"I'd stay with Mom, but you know how hard it is to find work out there," she said. "I figured any job here would be better than the factory back home."

Kelsey had to agree with that assessment. Their rural West Virginia town had little to offer. Right after high school she'd enlisted. The army had been her best chance to get out of there and she'd taken it. And once she'd completed basic training and three years as a grunt getting her bachelor's degree in her spare time, she'd scored well enough on the test to be sent to Officer's Candidate School. For the first time in her life, Kelsey had felt smart and capable. And she loved the army for giving that to her.

Shannon had found a ticket out of West Virginia on the coattails of a man who'd turned out be a loser. That was the story of her life.

"I don't want you to go back home. You know you can stay here as long as you want," slipped out of Kelsey's mouth before she knew what she'd meant to say. But despite her sister's less-than-tidy habits and more-than-annoying dog, it really was good to see her.

"Oh! I almost forgot. This is for you." And Shannon pushed the basket with the teapot and cups toward Kelsey.

She made a show of reading the note that she'd already read. "You are so sweet. Should we try them out? I think I have some cookies for dessert."

"Homemade, no doubt."

"Of course. Is there another kind?"

Shannon laughed. "Not in *your* household. Yes, let's have tea."

As Shannon got up to put the kettle back on, Kelsey reached for the gift, unable to remember the last time anyone had given her a present. But just as she began to unwrap the cellophane, the phone rang. "I'll just be a second," she said. Then, into the phone, "Hello?"

"Hi, Kelsey." The voice had the deep and serious tone of Major Julian Fordham.

Kelsey's heart skipped a beat.

"I have some news and I thought you'd like to know right away."

"Yes," she whispered so Shannon wouldn't overhear. "Has the body been found? Are the intruders in custody?"

"Well, I checked all the rosters and even called around to most of the units today to be sure," he said gently.

"And?" She turned her back on Shannon and hunkered closer to the phone, trying to ignore her sister's theatrics of asking who was on the other end of the line. Kelsey sensed that Julian's news wasn't necessarily good and she didn't want her sister to see her reaction. She'd never been good at keeping a poker face. Better to keep presenting her back even though Shannon moved repeatedly into her line of vision, grinning and asking if the caller was a man,

enunciating the word as though the very idea of Kelsey
having a boyfriend was beyond belief.

"Um, well, the thing is…" He hesitated, then blurted,
"There isn't a single person missing from Fort Belvoir. No
one was reported AWOL today. No one."

CHAPTER FOUR

KELSEY SLEPT FITFULLY, dreaming of dead bodies from which she tried to run but could never escape. When dawn finally gilded the trees outside her small apartment, she decided there would be no sense to staying in bed. She padded toward the kitchen to put the kettle on for tea, thinking about the fact that no one had been reported missing on post. That made no sense. The man had fallen well before reveille. He should have shown up on an AWOL report.

Unless, of course, the guy had been on scheduled leave at the time. She'd have to get in touch with Julian right away to suggest that. If only she could recall what unit the young guy's uniform patch had been from.

On the way down the hall, she nearly tripped over Jasper who sat like a sentinel outside of the guest bedroom. Behind the closed door slept Shannon. The dog had to be in there, too. Soft snuffling sounds told Kelsey the animal was awake. Perhaps Bella needed to relieve herself. Did she dare let the little canine monster out? Jasper's yellow eyes, so full of anticipation, followed the shadows that moved through the dim light peaking from under the door.

As Kelsey stood there contemplating how she would keep Jasper from leading the chase with Bella the instant the two locked eyes, the door flew open. "Oh, oh, oh!" said

Shannon as she lurched from the room holding the dog at arm's length. From Bella dripped a continuous stream that left a thin, wet trail along the path Shannon took to the sliding door that led to the balcony.

Kelsey watched them go, too stunned to react. The hallway and living room floors were wood and Shannon carefully avoided the rugs. But the bedroom was fully carpeted in beige plush, which now sported a bright yellow dampness near the threshold.

"Shit!" Kelsey mumbled.

"No, just pee," corrected Shannon as she came back inside, leaving the dog to scrabble piteously at the sliding door in her effort to come back inside with her mistress. "Sorry about the mess. I'll clean it up. You'll never know it was there. She does this once in a while. But she'll get used to things here and it'll all work out."

Kelsey shuddered at the thought of Shannon and her dog staying long enough to get used to things. "There's carpet cleaner under the sink. I have to make tea."

"And muffins?" asked her younger sister hopefully.

She glanced at her watch. "Sure. Why not? I have a couple of hours if I skip my run."

"Great! I'll just throw on some clothes and take Bella out on the leash for a bit in case she has to poopoo."

"Good idea." And then she'd have time to feed Jasper in peace and wonder exactly how long her sister planned to stay. She'd have to raise that issue with Shannon soon. But not yet. She'd only just arrived.

The peace lasted only as long as it took Shannon to walk her dog. Kelsey couldn't wait to leave the madness behind and head for work, even if going to the warehouse meant reliving the nightmare she'd experienced there.

But once she got to work, she found she didn't have time

to dwell on the horror of the night before last. Mark Sorrell confronted her the instant she stepped inside.

"We might have hit pay dirt on our initial inventory efforts," he announced. "Looks like there could be some crates of spare parts missing. Of course, it'll take us a few days to confirm that. Those crates could just be misplaced."

"Crates of what?" she asked.

"Repair parts for rocket launchers and the like."

Kelsey felt the blood drain from her head and she decided she better sit down. Trying not to let Mark see how this news affected her, she eased around to her own desk chair. "Well, keep on with the inventory. We want to cooperate with the CID." She thought of those parts potentially falling into the hands of terrorists and shuddered. If any Americans or allies were hurt from weapons that came from her warehouse, she'd never forgive herself.

"What are they looking for exactly?" asked Mark.

"I think they're worried someone is fencing stolen government property. I just wish it hadn't been from *my* warehouse." She wished that pretty fervently, along with wishing no one had died in her warehouse either.

"That guy who came here and did something to the floor in aisle seven was from CID, too, right?"

"I guess so," she hedged. "We just need to cooperate." She shuffled some papers, hoping to look busy so Mark wouldn't keep pestering her with questions she didn't want to answer. But she couldn't concentrate on anything. After an hour or so, she gave up. "I'm going over to CID to tell them what you found."

"Shouldn't you wait until we have something more concrete?"

"I think they'd want to know. I'll make sure they understand that it's still not a sure thing." She grabbed her beret and headed out, relieved that she would soon be enveloped in the sense of security Julian always gave her.

As she drove, she worried that she'd already succumbed to the old feelings she'd had for Julian. For a whole year, she'd done fine without him. But now that her world seemed to have tilted on its axis, she found herself rushing to him for comfort. That seemed vaguely pathetic, but she kept heading toward his office anyway.

JULIAN SAT BEHIND HIS DESK and reviewed his notes. Something wasn't right about Kelsey's case and he needed to get it sorted out as quickly as possible. He'd have to see her again today and he wanted to be prepared. He ran his fingers through his hair and wondered if he'd ever really be prepared for seeing Kelsey.

Frustration drove him from his desk chair and into the outer office.

"Sergeant McKay, I need a picture of every unit patch worn on this post."

Julian's assistant nodded.

"And I need the names of everyone who was on leave yesterday."

The usually unflappable sergeant glanced up at him with surprise in his dark eyes. "All of them?"

"All of them," Julian said without apology. "As soon as you can."

"Yes, sir," McKay said. "And here's that report you asked for from Lieutenant Bates." He handed over a large, sealed envelope.

Bates was the guy who had done the luminol test on the warehouse floor. Good. This should at least give Julian somewhere to start. He went back to his office, closed the door and applied his letter opener. The report slid from the sleeve and fluttered onto his desk. Julian stared at the thing in disbelief.

"Negative" was stamped across the document. Bates's signature had been scratched across the bottom. Julian bolted from his chair again and yanked his office door open.

"McKay, tell Bates I want to see him ASAP!" Julian shouted.

"Sorry, sir. Lieutenant Bates is on leave. He just stayed long enough to do your test."

"Where did he go? Can we reach him?"

"I'll find out, sir," McKay said as he picked up the phone to begin his inquiry. If anyone could find Bates, McKay would.

Julian retreated to his chair and looked at the report again, half hoping he'd misread it. But it hadn't miraculously changed in the last few minutes. There was no trace of blood on the warehouse floor. To be on the safe side, Bates had checked two more aisles to each side of the one he'd been told to test. All negative. How could that be?

The most likely possibility came immediately to mind. Kelsey needed the services of a shrink, not of the CID. Disappointment skulked around the inner corners of his mind. He wouldn't be working on a case with her, would have no excuse to spend time with her, would have to convince her to see a doctor. Not a prospect he looked forward to.

Feeling weak but unable to help himself, he dialed his brother's office phone number. Nathan answered on the second ring. "Hey, Jules!" he said as soon as Julian said hello. "You sound as if someone died."

More like someone *hadn't* died. But that was too complicated to say out loud. "Yeah, well, things have been weird around here lately. And I haven't slept in too many hours because of a night shift I took on. I just called to see how you and Rachel and the kid are doing."

"We're fine. Adam is doing okay, too. Marriage is good. You should try it."

"Been there, done that," he said.

"No, you didn't, Julian. That woman wasn't right for you. I don't know why you picked someone who was so high maintenance. She wasn't your type."

That was certainly true. Kelsey was his type. Maddie had been more his father's sort of woman. And didn't that say a great deal about how he'd ended up marrying her. Would he never get over the desire to please his unpleasable father? After talking to a psychologist a couple of times, Julian knew he'd also chosen Maddie because he was used to taking care of people. He'd substituted taking care *of* her in place of actually caring *for* her. He knew that, but wasn't sure he could change. "Well, it's over, so I don't dwell on it," he said to his brother.

"You've got some twisted idea that one bad marriage makes you no good for another. But that's not true," Nathan said.

"Women want to know how you feel inside. I've never been good at letting that kind of thing out, Nate."

"That's not true either. You're perfectly capable of expressing your feelings when you trust the person you're with. With all the moving around we did, you learned not to trust easily. And then there's the way Dad treated you. But you can overcome the head trips he laid on you."

"You can't possibly remember the extent of those head trips. You were too young." The three-year difference in their ages shouldn't have been such a wide gulf, but their father had made it so by treating Julian like an only son who didn't measure up. For reasons no one understood, Nathan had hardly existed at all in their father's world.

"Maybe," Nathan said. "And I had you to protect me from him. But, for God's sake, Jules, you deserve to have a life. Someone to love. Kids someday." His brother made those things sound wonderful.

The very thought of someone to love made Julian sweat with worry that he'd screw it up. Again. The idea of taking on kids and all the emotional responsibilities that went with them made his head ache. "Yeah, right. Have you taken Rachel and Adam out to see Dad lately?"

"Yeah," admitted Nathan, sounding reluctant. "We saw him last week. He's the same."

"Which means he's just as cruel and cutting as he ever was. Not even Alzheimer's could strip him of his mean streak." Julian's words were razor sharp and he wished he could take them back. "When are you going again? I should go with you."

"I honestly don't know. Depends on how he's doing. And, yes, you should go with me."

"Yeah. I talked to his doctor last week. The drugs aren't helping other than to keep him quieter. He's not likely to recover from his dementia, Nate."

"So why does he still scare the shit out of me?"

Julian thought that was a very good question that applied more to him than to Nathan. "You go see him more than I do. And the last time you went to see him, he had that shrieking fit and called you every name in the book." Julian gave a rueful chuckle. "He must have thought you were me that time."

"He had no idea who I was. He doesn't know either one of us anymore."

"Oh, how the mighty have fallen," Julian said as images

of his father walking along in his full uniform and then in his expensive business suit on the congressional campaign trail came flashing through his mind. "Look, I just wanted to see how things were going. And…" He hesitated to mention Kelsey, thereby encouraging his brother's obsession with getting him married. But that was why he'd called and he wouldn't let himself take the easier road by avoiding it now. "I guess I've been thinking about spending more time with a particular woman. Nothing serious, of course. Just maybe something more regular, maybe sort of on an ongoing basis."

His brother laughed out loud. "Jules! That's great! You could make it work! You just have to lighten up, buddy. Get the old man out of your head. And that bitch of an ex-wife. Stop hearing them criticize and berate you all the time."

"I'm working on it," Julian said. But talking to his therapist had done little to make Julian think he could carry his end of a relationship. If he couldn't make a relationship work with Kelsey, a woman he found nearly irresistible, how would he ever make one work? "The thing is, she's told me something that turned out not to be true. I like this woman, but I'm going to have trouble getting past her fabrication."

"Jules," said his brother softly. "Are you sure she lied to you? Or are you leaping to that conclusion based on something you shouldn't put so much faith in?"

Julian sat still, startled that his brother had figured him out so easily. "I put my faith in the evidence."

"Try putting your faith in the person. A real flesh-and-blood person," Nathan advised. "They keep you much warmer at night. Maybe this woman was misinformed or misled or confused. People get things wrong sometimes for reasons other than a desire to lie. You have to just let go of all those defenses you've built up over the years. You can do it, Jules."

Could his brother be right about Kelsey being misled? Obviously no one died in her warehouse, but perhaps she really believed the story she'd told him. Maybe she was just confused or her subconscious had taken over regarding what she thought she saw. Could he help her with that, care for her, love her?

He shook his head against that overly optimistic line of thinking. He looked down at the damning luminol report. "I've probably already destroyed my chances with her. But thanks for the vote of confidence. It's what I needed right now."

As he closed his conversation with his brother—which had been both frightening and uplifting at the same time—he wondered if he could try again to have a meaningful relationship with a woman. He sat at his desk for long moments, thinking about what his brother had said. He hoped it was true. He didn't want to be lonely all his life.

"Hey, pal, anything new on our thieves?" asked Drew Mitchum as he came into view at the doorway of Julian's office. Drew was ever vigilant in his effort to snare the bad guys. He took his job as the senior MP officer very seriously.

"Maybe. I don't know yet." Julian casually turned the luminol report so it faced down, then he rubbed his eyes. His thoughts weighed upon him and he'd only managed to get a few hours of sleep since the last time he'd talked to Drew. "Have you heard about anyone going missing since yesterday?"

Drew looked off into space, concentrating. "No, I don't think so. Why?"

"Just something I'm working on," he evaded. "Looks

like a dead end, though." And in his weariness, he almost laughed at the unintended pun.

"Let me know if you need any help. I want to close down that pilfering ring as much as you do. And the guy who's leading them."

Julian's mouth spoke before he had officially decided he should say anything. "What makes you think it's a guy?" A woman could lead a merry band of criminals as easily as a man. Maybe easier.

Drew shrugged, "Just more likely from a statistical perspective. Do you know something about some female suspect?"

Did he? No. Absolutely not. Kelsey was no thief. None of the facts pointed in that direction, even if her story made no sense. "No. It's just my job to look at things from all angles, no matter how remote. I'll let you know if I find anything worth reporting."

Drew left the office and seconds later Kelsey walked in. She stood on the threshold and gave his tired eyes a moment of pleasure as she stared after the departing chief. Then his heart began to beat too fast and he searched for something to say to her.

"Do you know Drew?" he asked her as he worked at slowing down his pulse.

She shook her head. "I think I know who he is—the MP commander, right? I've never been introduced, but something about him seems familiar. I can't quite figure it out." She stepped into the room, but didn't sit down. "Do you have a minute?"

He would always have a minute for Kelsey, he realized. But he wished he could put off this meeting. If she stayed, he'd have to tell her about the luminol report. And she wouldn't like the results or the implication that she'd fabricated the story of the dead man. And then he'd lose any chance he ever had of seeing her again.

KELSEY COULD SEE that Julian wasn't entirely comfortable around her. He was one of those men who couldn't handle emotion in any significant quantity. But she was one of those people who had a hard time keeping things locked away inside. Most of the time, her thoughts and feelings bubbled out of her, even when she tried to hold back. They were opposites in some very important ways. So why did she still find him so attractive?

He didn't give her a chance to think about that or even to tell him the inventory. Instead, he came around his desk to close his office door as he began to explain how a head injury could do strange things to people. She listened, bewildered, as he talked about trauma to certain lobes and the intricacies of the mind. He seemed to be making it up as he went along in a nearly incomprehensible manner, but his earnest expression held her attention.

"So, hitting your head could have altered your memories," he said. "There's no way for us to tell what's real and what's not. But maybe a doctor could help."

She sat, stunned to silence, in his guest chair—the same one she'd been in when she'd first come to him for help. He leaned his hips against the front edge of his desk, white-knuckled hands clutching the lip of the surface on either side. She looked up at him. "I don't understand what you're trying to tell me, Julian. Are you saying that it's all in my head? Already? You're giving up?"

His gaze dropped away and he gave every indication of carefully studying the pattern in the linoleum flooring. After a long moment, he said, "It's not that I'm not going to continue to investigate the situation." He lifted his eyes and focused on her again. He took a deep breath and let it out slowly. "It's just that the luminol test came back negative. There was no blood anywhere the warehouse floor. No blood, no missing soldier. Nothing."

"I told you, they cleaned it all up afterward." Inside, anxiety took hold of her stomach and began to squeeze. "And the dead soldier could have been on leave so he wouldn't show up on an AWOL list."

"Maybe," he said, and to his credit he appeared to think about that for a moment. "But luminol finds traces of blood, no matter how minute. If there had been blood on the floor within the past year, we would have found it."

She couldn't think what to say to that. So she held his gaze, hoping he'd throw her some sort of flotation device to keep her from drowning in the confusion and fear that seethed all around her. But all she got was a softening of his eyes. "I'm sorry, Kelsey," he said gently.

"Do the test again. There must have been a mistake," she said, sure that this was the only logical explanation.

He shook his head. "Doing it over wouldn't make blood suddenly appear. It's either there, or it's not. The test isn't difficult. But even so, I sent an officer, not some private fresh out of basic, to do it for me. There's no chance that the test could have been wrong."

A sense of dread rose like a huge ocean swell inside her and she found herself getting to her feet, facing the man she'd trusted to help her. "It *has* to be wrong this time," she insisted. "I saw the man fall. I saw him on the concrete. I saw all that blood." She had to fight hard against the urge to cover her eyes in the futile hope of blotting out the awful memories.

"That's why you need to see a doctor. I'll go with you, if you want. We'll find out what really happened—"

"I *know* what really happened! And I need you to believe me." She searched his eyes for some sign that he wanted to.

He looked back steadily, unwavering and giving nothing away about his feelings. At last he said, "I want to believe you. But there is no evidence."

"Yes, there is," she said, suddenly remembering why she'd come here in the first place. "Besides my concussion—which would be very hard to get by merely hitting my head on something—Lieutenant Sorrell found some boxes missing from the warehouse. They were parts for rocket launchers." She bit her lip, feeling like a liar for not saying that the boxes could simply be misplaced. But she couldn't bring herself to give Julian more reasons to dismiss her case as the ravings of an overactive imagination and a self-inflicted blow to the head. Especially when she saw uncertainty flicker across his face.

"Okay," he said as his expression shifted from pity to respect. "You might just be on to something."

Seeing his eyes light with interest and knowing he would remain her champion meant a great deal to her. She closed the space between them and wrapped her arms around his neck in an embrace of gratitude. "Thank you," she said against his shoulder as she fought back tears of relief.

His arms lifted slowly, hesitantly. But soon they held her close. "You know I want to help you," he murmured into her ear. "I don't want to make any of this harder for you."

"I know," she said, wishing she could stay like this with him for a long time. Holding him, being held by him, erased all the months since they'd last been together and reminded her of all the reasons she'd been infatuated with him in the first place.

He was warm and strong, confident and intelligent, handsome and kind. And she would be in love with him again in no time, if he kept on holding her against his heart. Unfortunately, he'd given no indication that he would return her feelings, any more than he had the last time. If she didn't tread carefully, she'd be brokenhearted once more.

So, she eased back from him with an apology on her lips. "This isn't very professional, I'm afraid. Sorry if I—"

But instead of listening to what she would have said, his mouth came down to hers and he kissed her.

SOME PART OF JULIAN'S MIND told him he shouldn't be kissing Kelsey. Certainly not now, certainly not here. But that part of his mind didn't currently command any part of his body. Not since she'd first slipped her arms around his neck and pressed herself against him.

She made him feel alive. She made him *feel*.

He couldn't have known until this moment how much he hungered for this—her warm lips and intoxicating scent, her fast-beating heart against his. And he wanted more. Craved it. Needed it. So he slid his tongue along her lips, urging her to accept him. She did. Julian's whole body rejoiced and his dormant emotions soared.

But then an insistent buzzing came to his ears, as if from far away. In another second, the sound registered and he forced himself to disengage from the woman in his embrace. Doing so was about as easy as separating his arm from his shoulder.

She didn't open her eyes when he withdrew. Instead, she went up on her toes as if in search of more. He would have liked nothing better than to give in, but his intercom buzzer continued to sound off and if he didn't answer it, his secretary would be marching down the hall within the minute.

"I have to—" he began, but she pulled his head down a few inches to bring him within reach. Heat surged through him at her eagerness. And he gave in to a few staccato kisses before he held her at arm's length.

She opened her eyes and stood before him with a slight smile on her lips. "Why did you stop calling me a year ago?"

Whoa! That conversation would need to happen another day. "I have to answer this or—"

But the buzzer had already stopped and he could hear the click of heels marching toward his door. In another second, Sally rapped loudly. Without waiting for him to respond, his secretary opened both the door and her mouth, then snapped the latter shut as she glanced from one officer to the other and back again.

"Sorry," she said as sheepishly as he'd ever heard her. "I didn't know you were with anyone. But the general is on line two." Eyeing Captain O'Roark with interest now, she asked if she should take a message. Both women blushed.

"No, I'll take it," Julian said. The call seemed a perfect excuse for escaping what could be some very awkward moments with Kelsey.

Sally retreated to the reception area where she would resume her position of supreme commander of the entire CID office. Kelsey didn't move. Her smile was gone. The stricken expression in her eyes made his heart feel constricted. Her blush deepened.

"I'm sorry, Kelsey. It's the general," he said as he lifted the receiver and pressed line two. "General Wilkes, what can I do for you, sir?"

Kelsey mouthed to him that she would wait outside for him to finish. This was the last thing he wanted. He shook his head, but she ignored him. He did not want to discuss what had just happened between them. He needed time to think. But he couldn't say anything to dissuade her from waiting as he listened to the man on the other end of the line explain his concern over the arrest of an officer's teen-age son.

Even as he commented on the details of what the general said, offering encouragement and support, Julian began to wonder what good could ever come of the kiss he'd just initiated with the irresistible Kelsey O'Roark. The instant she was out of sight, he deflated into his chair. But his edginess remained. She always did this to him.

She made him want things. She made him *want*.

But no matter what his brother said, he knew this would lead to no good—especially for Kelsey. He didn't want to hurt her, but he didn't know how *not* to. So he had to keep his distance.

KELSEY PACED in the hallway outside his office. She had a sus-picion that the infuriating man was relieved to have to take the phone call so he wouldn't have to deal with what had just happened between them. It gave him the perfect excuse to avoid an honest conversation with her. And wasn't that the Julian she remembered from when they'd spent time together before? The man went well beyond commitment-phobic.

And yet, when they were together, the world seemed to stop around them and there was only the two of them. Just the memory of kissing him could make her skin heat and her insides go all liquid. Besides, she wanted to know what had made him this way. She wanted the chance to see if she could help him. Intellectually, she knew she'd be set-ting herself up for heartbreak. She knew she should leave all wounded men alone and find some nice, ordinary guy whose biggest defect was an addiction to Monday Night

Football. Those kind of guys were out there if you looked hard enough for them.

But could they kiss like Julian? Could they make her heart pound and her blood zing through her veins? She didn't think so.

So where did that leave her?

Standing in the hallway outside his office, waiting.

For what? Would he suddenly turn into the kind of man who would be there for her in the morning? Or could she have the sexual relationship with this man that her body craved without any expectation of something deeper? Neither seemed likely.

Even so, the power of that kiss would have made her stay until he finished his call. Unfortunately, her cell phone chimed its Beethoven symphony and Mark Sorrell said he needed her back at the warehouse.

"There's this officer here asking a lot of questions," Mark said.

"What's the guy's name?"

"Major Mitchum from the MP unit. He wants a list of everyone who's been in the warehouse for the past two weeks. I can't deal with him and do this inventory, too." Mark sounded exasperated.

"I'll be right there." She went out to Sally and asked her to tell Major Fordham that she had to get back to work. "Tell him to call me," Kelsey murmured as she retreated toward the exit. She knew her cheeks were flaming. People watched her with interest as she left. The humiliation of what felt too much like a dismissal from Julian—in the aftershock of that kiss—was nearly more than she could bear. But she was wearing the uniform of the United States Army, so she held her head high and strode with purpose. With every step, she wished she could completely avoid the man.

Except, of course, to pursue the mystery of what had happened in her warehouse.

"DO YOU WANT US TO go back to the warehouse again tonight, sir?" the Wolf asked.

"I was very clear that you are to take a couple of men inside every night, wasn't I?"

"Yes, sir, but it seems like such a waste of time and a huge risk. What good is it for us to go in there night after night just to rearrange the inventory?"

"It's what I want and that's all you need to know," said the officer. "And after what happened to her the other night, Captain O'Roark isn't likely to show up at the warehouse at night again anytime soon. And you said you knew the people that the CID agent posted to watch the building each night. So, what's the problem?"

"No problem, sir. We'll do exactly as you said, sir." The Wolf knew better than to argue with this dangerous man. He'd put a bullet in him as easily as shake his hand. The officer might be young, but he could be deadly.

CHAPTER FIVE

HER YOUNGER SISTER WAS her only sibling, so she cherished the time they could spend together. Truly, she did. But fantasies of Shannon departing with her little dog for her own place somewhere kept playing through Kelsey's mind. The chaos inside her small apartment had taken on a life of its own. That, mixed with everything else, made Kelsey short-tempered. During the next few days, she found herself spending extra hours at her warehouse, telling herself that the inventory required her supervision.

And maybe it did. Although Major Mitchum hadn't been back to the warehouse to bother them with any more questions, things were moving more slowly than she'd hoped. Crates would appear to be missing only to show up in some other location where they should not have been. Sometimes boxes would contain something other than the label indicated. For someone as orderly as Kelsey, this was hard to take. So she'd been spending most of her time watching over things there.

"How could everything have become so confused?" she demanded of her deputy. "There's no way so many items could have become mixed up unless our practices have been slipping for a long time! How could that be?" She sounded overly loud even to her own ears, but she couldn't help it. She had always demanded strict adherence to standard operating procedures and to find out that her orders had been ignored made her screaming angry. Still, she knew she had to calm down. Pacing through their shared office to blow off steam, she ran her fingers through her short brown hair.

Mark had the sense to keep his mouth shut. He couldn't possibly have answered her questions and any attempt would have only made her angrier. So he continued to examine the pencil in his hand as he sat dejectedly in his desk chair.

"I know everything was in order two months ago," Kelsey said. "I did a spot check myself and nothing was out of place. It's as if someone deliberately messed with everything." She stopped in her tracks. Turning to Mark, she asked, "Could that really be what's going on here? Could someone have created the disorder?"

"Why would anyone do that?" Mark asked with a puzzled expression.

"To confuse us. To throw us off the track. To slow us down."

The lieutenant's brow knit. "Well, I'm certainly confused now. What track would we be thrown off of, exactly?"

Too late, Kelsey remembered she hadn't yet confided in her deputy regarding the strange events that had taken place in this very warehouse several nights earlier. The only one who knew that story was the major with the killer kiss. Self-preservation had made her avoid him these past few days, but this twist in the inventory would certainly have to be reported to Julian.

The notion of seeing him again sparked a strange combination of anxiety and anticipation that caused her to pace some more. She should not be wary of the man. Just because he had the power to turn her into lust-flavored Jell-O with a single touch, she shouldn't quake at the thought of seeing him again. But she shouldn't look forward to it so much either.

"Captain? What track?" Mark asked, bringing her back to the here and now.

"I don't know," she said. She'd never been very good at coming up with convenient lies. Or any lies at all, for that matter. "I guess I'm not making any sense."

She noted his confused and worried expression, but nothing came to mind that she could say to reassure him. "Just get it all sorted out!"

"Yes, ma'am. We're already working on that. I have two teams reorganizing as we speak."

"Well, I want everything back where it's supposed to be within the next twenty-four hours!" she barked. Once that unnecessary order had been delivered, she stormed out the door and into the cavernous area where soldiers scurried about like ants, trying to bring order to the chaos among the crates and pallets.

Kelsey didn't trust herself to remain in the vicinity of anyone under her command. She prided herself on being a steady, reasonable officer. If she stayed, she would surely destroy that image she'd worked so hard to convey. Out into the summer sunshine she strode, with absolutely no idea as to where she might be headed.

Halfway to her car, her cell phone toned melodically from its holster at her waist. Snapping the thing open, she answered with a curt, "What!"

"Kelsey?" Shannon inquired. And Kelsey wondered if her sister had ever heard her use such a tone of voice before.

"Yeah, Shannon. It's me." She did what she could to moderate her voice, hoping that the younger O'Roark wouldn't hear the blade-sharp edginess just beneath the surface.

"Oh, thank God! I need your help. Bella is missing! She ran away when we went out for our walk! I went after her, but she was too fast. I don't know the streets or whether there's traffic in your neighborhood. She could be far away by now. I have no idea where to start looking."

Shannon seemed to be on the precipice of hysteria. Ironically, this had a slight calming effect on Kelsey. "Slow down, Shan. I'll come home right now. We'll go look for her. Don't worry." So much for seeing Julian. And maybe that was for the best.

"You'll come now? That's such a relief!" The gratitude in her sister's voice made Kelsey regret every ill thought she'd harbored since the arrival of her human and canine guests. "But I'm already out looking. Sort of aimlessly, I admit. Hang on a second…I'm on Beauregard Road. Can you come get me there?"

"Yes. I'm on my way," she said as she turned the key in the ignition. "We'll drive around until we find her."

"Thanks, Kels," came back to her over the cell phone. "Hurry."

"I will." Kelsey snapped the phone shut and paid attention to pulling the car out of the parking lot. When she realized how hard she gripped the steering wheel, she took a few deep breaths and relaxed her fingers.

She'd been as tight as an overwound spring for days and the insanity just seemed to keep on coming. Was it any wonder she'd snarled at her deputy?

THOSE WOLF EYES DARTED from one object to another in the storeroom until they finally landed on Private Earlman's face. The young man blanched, wondering why he should suddenly be the object of that evil stare as the Wolf listened to his phone. "I'll make sure he takes care of that. Yes, sir, that won't be a problem." When the Wolf closed his phone, his gaze still rested upon the trembling private.

"Did you deal with the locker like I told you to?" he demanded as he paced the small room in the back of the mess hall.

"I...I...did what you said. I talked to the roommate. I think we're good. The locker hasn't got anything in it but clothes." At least he hoped it didn't because he hadn't been able to get into it. But he wasn't about to admit that to this partner in crime. The roommate had come back from getting a soda from the machine just as Earlman had been about to break into the locker.

There'd been no chance to go back and finish the job. And it had occurred to Earlman that he'd somehow been given all of the risky tasks lately. Ever since that awful night, there was no one else to dump the trickier jobs onto. He wasn't certain how he felt about that. Sure, the rewards would be bigger now, with one less person to share the loot. But if he got caught, he'd be the only one going to jail. The others would just take off for their destination in Mexico a little sooner than planned.

"That's good," said the Wolf. "Because we can't afford any more problems. We're almost finished. One more big job and we're there. We just have to keep the bimbo and the CID idiot off our backs." The Wolf grinned and slapped the private on the shoulder heartily. "We're almost there, my friend!"

Earlman smiled back because that was what was expected of him. But somehow, the younger man didn't feel as if he had any friends at all anymore.

DREW MITCHUM HAD left Julian a voice mail message. A Specialist Ryan Rigley had been listed as AWOL that very morning. Julian drove to the A Company building to see what he could find out. On the way, he acknowledged that the only reason he bothered was so that he'd have an excuse to call Kelsey. He didn't actually believe this AWOL would have anything to do with the dead body she'd reported but couldn't produce. And yet, he couldn't ignore the thread of doubt that the AWOL had sewn through his thoughts. He also couldn't forget the way Kelsey had looked when she'd first come to him on that fateful morning. If no one had died that night, why had she been so roughed up? What terrible thing had happened to her?

If he thoroughly investigated this missing specialist, he'd have to tell Kelsey about it and he desperately needed an excuse to contact her. He·deeply regretted taking the coward's way out after their kiss. If he could find a reason to talk to her again, perhaps he could manage to apologize. Whether for the kiss or for the way he'd avoided her afterward, he wasn't quite sure. Somehow, he didn't think he'd find it in himself to speak regretfully of holding her in his arms again and tasting her.

The very memory of it made his blood move a little faster through his veins. He shifted slightly in the driver's seat and tried to think of other things as he approached the place. His efforts led him to line up the questions he would need to ask about the missing soldier.

Who were his friends?

Had he talked of leaving?

Did anyone know where he was?

Julian had already reviewed the young man's personnel folder. He'd had an uneventful military career, until now. And his disappearance would probably be explained within the hour. A few questions to his roommate and his sergeant and the mystery would be solved. Julian would ask Drew to send an MP to go fetch the boy, wherever he was. And then Julian would call Kelsey.

Full circle with his thoughts back on the woman again. He tried to think of nothing at all as he parked the car and walked to the building. Fortunately, he found the staff sergeant in Rigley's chain of command almost as soon as he arrived. A few minutes of conversation with the man had the expected results.

"So Rigley put in for leave and was denied. He talked to you about how important it was for him to go home at this particular time, but you couldn't spare him. Is that right?" Julian asked as he glanced down at his notes.

"I didn't know he'd take it so hard or I would have kept an eye on him. He didn't seem all that broken up about it. He'd just been home last month and I had other people wanting to take leave. I can't let them all go at once, sir."

Julian looked at the sergeant and tried to reassure him. "No, you sure can't. And you did everything by the book." He smiled his encouragement and got the expected results when the staff sergeant began to spill information without being questioned.

"The surprising thing is that he asked for next week off, not this week. So I thought he was just out sick or something. I didn't even report him until today."

"How long has he been gone?"

"A couple of days," hedged the sergeant. "Maybe I should have paid closer attention. But in an all-volunteer army, we don't get many guys who go AWOL anymore."

Julian nodded his commiseration. "You had no reason to suspect. We all do the best we can with these kids. Would I be able to talk to any of his friends, maybe his roommate?"

"Okay, but I already talked to them. They don't know anything."

Julian smiled. "I have to try anyway."

The sergeant shrugged and gave him directions to where Rigley's roommate worked. The office was right around the corner, so Julian walked. As he turned onto the next street, a little white ball of fluff came hurtling out from between two parked cars, nearly tripping him. A glimpse of a leash trailing the animal encouraged Julian to give chase, but the dog—or whatever—quickly dashed beneath a fence and disappeared.

Seeing no owner in pursuit, Julian shrugged off the incident and retraced his steps until he once again headed for the roommate's office. He found the soldier easily.

"Rigley kept pretty much to himself, sir," responded the young man who bunked with the missing soldier. "I can't say for sure where he went."

It was the "for sure" that tipped off Julian. And the eyes that wavered left and right, but never held eye contact for long. This specialist knew more about Rigley than he wanted to say. Probably trying to protect his friend. The youth's next comment confirmed Julian's suspicion.

"He'll be back in a day or so, I bet. He's not the kind of guy to quit the army."

Julian nodded and made a note. "This is very helpful," he said, knowing the kid would be even more cooperative with a little praise. "Why do you think he'll just come back? He'd have to face disciplinary action for the time he went AWOL even if he returned on his own."

"I'm just guessing. He's just not the type to run off permanently. He loves the army." Now he shifted from foot to foot. "He'll get a few days in the stockade and be back at work in no time. The flag on his record from the disciplinary action gets taken off after a while, if he stays out of trouble."

"Sounds like your roommate gave this a lot of thought." Julian knew when to stop pushing for answers. He could come back to this point another time if Rigley didn't actually show up in a day or so. "Does Rigley hang with any other guys? Any other friends besides you?"

The long pause put Julian on alert. He watched uncertainty flicker across the man's face. Finally, he seemed to make up his mind.

"Sometimes he hangs with some guys I don't know. One of them has a dog. I've seen 'em coming back from town a few times, but I've never met 'em."

The image of a white streak of fur flashed through Julian's mind. That leash-dragging creature he'd seen earlier had probably been a dog, though it hadn't looked like any dog *he'd* ever seen before. But an albino long-haired rat didn't seem likely either. He made a note to find out more about Rigley's friend with a dog. *White fluffy thing?* he wrote. The likelihood of the dog he'd seen being the same dog whose owner knew Rigley seemed remote. There had to be a hundred dogs on post. But possibilities shouldn't be overlooked just because they were amazingly coincidental.

"What kind of dog?" Julian asked.

"Kinda medium size. Barked some. I don't know much about dogs."

"What color?"

"Sort of brown, maybe."

Okay, so that wasn't going to be very helpful. "Can you describe any of these guys?"

"Naw," said the roommate. "Besides, they don't have anything to do with him going off this time."

Julian eyed him closely and watched him blush. He'd said more than he'd intended. And if Julian was any judge of character, the specialist was about to give up the whole story in one big rush out of sheer frustration with himself. With pencil poised above his notebook, Julian waited.

"Okay! It's like this. He has this girlfriend. She's in Florida where he grew up, see? I think he went to see her."

"Why would he do that? His leave wasn't approved. Why did he have to go right now, do you think?"

"I heard him on the phone to her one day and it sounded like she was nagging him for something. Then another day, he came back to the room grinning and saying his baby was going to get her wish. I don't know more than that, sir." And his eyes were steady this time.

Julian closed the flap of his notebook. "Okay. But if you think of anything else, you'll call me?" He handed over his business card.

"Yes, sir," he said. "I don't want Rigley in any more trouble than he's already in."

"I'm sure you don't. So if you think of anything else, you let me know." Julian gave him a conspiratorial look. "Maybe we can get him back here before things get any worse for him."

"Yeah, that would be good. Thank you, sir."

Julian went back out into the heat and wished he didn't have a quarter-mile walk back to the air-conditioning of his car. He needed to think and the thick, humid air made that nearly impossible. Rigley had run off to be with his girlfriend. He'd have to follow up on the AWOL, open a file on the case, try to locate the kid so he could be brought back to face charges. But that unpleasantness paled next to the chore of telling Kelsey that the single incident of AWOL wasn't her dead body.

He'd have to go talk to her. And if she persisted in her convictions, he'd have to convince her to see a doctor. If he failed to coax her to do so, then for her own safety and

for the good of the army, he might end up having to report
the whole thing to her superior officer. He probably should
have done so already. Questioning his ability to remain objective, wondering if he could already be holding back for
Kelsey's sake, Julian headed toward his car once again.

Turning the corner, he smacked right into a woman
walking in the opposite direction. "Sorry," he said as he
held her upright with his hands to her shoulders. "This corner is downright hazardous!" came out of his mouth. When
the woman focused on him, he saw both confusion and
tears in her eyes. "Are you hurt?" he asked.

She sniffed and made an effort to pull herself together.
"I'm fine. You haven't seen a small white dog around here,
have you?"

Julian almost laughed. Where had she been before when
his sighting might have been helpful? "As a matter of fact, I
chased after a white dog dragging a leash about an hour ago."

Her face lit up as if she'd just won the lottery. "Did you
find her? Where is she?"

Oh, how he hated to burst her bubble. "Sorry, she
slipped under a fence and got away." Predictably, her shoulders drooped. "But I can show you where I last saw her."

"Yes, that might help. But the truth is, she could be anywhere by now. I've been looking all morning." She fell into
step next to Julian as he headed for the alley where the dog
had gone.

"Well, first, let's call the animal control center and put
those folks on alert," Julian said as he pulled his cell phone
from its case.

"That's a good idea," she said, looking at him as if he
were a superhero come to the rescue. "Why didn't I think
of that?"

He smiled at her as he dialed the number. "I'm in law

enforcement, so this is second nature to me. And I know these guys, so maybe I can get you some extra help." But no one answered the line. "I'm getting the voice mail message right now. Can you give them a number where you can be reached?" He offered her the phone.

She listened a moment and then said in a rush, "This is Shannon O'Roark and I've lost my Maltese, Bella. If you find her or if someone reports seeing her, could you call me on my cell phone?" She said the number and then added a home number for good measure. The number was the same as Kelsey's.

It hit him then that although this woman was round where Kelsey was lean, and cute where Kelsey was pretty, they were clearly related. Cousins or, given the similarity in the eyes and the same last name, more likely they were sisters. It bothered Julian that he hadn't known Kelsey had a sister. In fact, given the effect the captain had on him these days, it seemed completely wrong that he knew almost nothing about her. How could that be?

Shannon handed back his phone. "You're sisters," he blurted.

"What?" she said, quite understandably.

"I know Kelsey O'Roark," he said. "You must be sisters."

"Yes, Kelsey is my sister. How did you know that?" She gazed at him with something akin to awe. Julian took a step back, uncomfortable with the interested look in her eyes.

"Um, you said your name to the answering machine. And you gave out Kelsey's number. You look like her, too."

"Really? No one thinks we look much alike. It would help if she'd go blond or I'd go back to brunette. But *that's* not likely to happen." She squinted slightly at him, as if trying to figure something out. "So, you know Kelsey's phone number by heart."

Oh, hell. Was she going to make something out of that? "Yeah, well, I remember everyone's phone number. It's part of the job," he lied. He had an excellent memory for numbers, but after a year apart, he shouldn't have been able to dial Kelsey's the other day without thinking about it. What did this say about his ability to put Kelsey out of his mind?

"Yeah," she said doubtfully, "part of the job. Hey, I'm meeting Kelsey in another minute so she can help me look for Bella. She's going to pick me up right over there on that street corner. You want to say hello?"

This didn't seem like a good time to attempt to have his difficult conversation with Kelsey. "I've got to get back to work. Tell her I'll call her soon."

"I'll tell her. If we find my dog quickly, we'll be home. Kelsey will probably make something great for dinner. Did you know she's an awesome cook? Maybe you could join us."

Julian smiled politely but didn't respond. He'd heard about Kelsey's culinary skills, but he had enough trouble figuring out how to deal with the woman without having her sister trying to get them together over dinner. Which was the only motive she could have for praising Kelsey's abilities in the kitchen at this particular moment. And when he next shared dinner with an O'Roark, he hoped he would be alone with the one in uniform.

"But if we can't find Bella that won't work. We could be out looking a long time." She shrugged and the sad, worried shadow fell across her face again.

"I saw your dog go down that alley and under the fence," he offered, pointing. "I'll keep an eye out for her. And if I spot her, I'll call you. Now that I know her name, maybe I'll be able to catch her."

Shannon nodded and reached into her pocket. "Here,

take some of these. She'll go to anyone who has her favorite dog biscuits." She dropped a few small bone-shaped things into his palm. "Thanks for thinking of contacting animal control."

Hoping to lighten her heart a little, he touched his fingers to his beret, Dudley Doright fashion, and said, "All in a day's work, ma'am." That got her to smile again, even if only for a moment.

As he walked away, he heard her call after him, "I hope to see you again soon, Major!"

He kept on going, unwilling to say more out of fear she would see that his interest in Kelsey was more then he wanted to let on. He'd seen the way she'd looked at him, sizing him up, speculating as to whether he was good enough for her sister. That was the last thing he needed right now.

But it was nice that Shannon seemed to approve of him. Maybe she would be an ally, if he needed one. Not that he knew exactly what he was going to do regarding Kelsey. Other than his determination to talk to her again about seeing a doctor, he remained as confused as ever.

Besides, the chances were slim to none that Kelsey would even be speaking to him afterward. Even so, he still yearned for more.

CHAPTER SIX

"THIS MAN SAW Bella go through that alley," Shannon said the instant she got into Kelsey's car. She pointed the way. "He was a nice guy. Said he knew you."

"I know a lot of guys on this post, Shan. The population is overwhelmingly male, as I'm sure you've noticed. Did he say his name?" Kelsey pulled out from the curb and headed in the direction that would take her to the other end of the stipulated alleyway. Might as well start looking where the dog had last been seen.

"Didn't have to. It was on his name tag. Major Fordham."

Kelsey wasn't surprised her sister could tell someone's military rank just by looking at his uniform. She'd made a study of ranks when Kelsey had joined the army. Shannon had wanted to know as much as necessary about all those handsome, fit young men.

But this particular rank and name made Kelsey's face heat all the way to the tips of her ears. She knew she must be blushing eight shades of red. Shannon wasn't likely to let that go unnoticed, if her interested stare was any indication.

"Uh-oh," said Shannon with amusement in her voice. "There's a story here with this Major Fordham. Ooh. Tell all."

"No, there's nothing to tell." Kelsey clamped her lips

shut, determined not to spill her guts to her sister. Besides, Shannon wasn't any sort of expert on love to dole out reasonable advice. Quite the opposite.

Shannon harrumphed meaningfully.

"Seriously. He and I dated a few times and that was over a year ago. He's not a relationship kind of guy." There was no point in worrying Shannon with the story about what had happened at the warehouse.

"Well, he said he'd be calling you. You want to give a man like that a second chance."

Kelsey shifted uncomfortably in the driver's seat.

"We could be roaming around for a while. I don't want Bella left out all night. So we have to find her no matter how long it takes." Those statements were calculated to return Shannon's focus back to her missing pooch. It worked.

"Go up this street. She might have headed back toward the apartment. She's a very smart dog."

If she was so smart, why had she run off in the first place? Kelsey wanted to know. But she didn't ask out loud. That dog meant the world to Shannon. The micro-canine had seen her sister through some tough times. Which reminded her…

"So you never finished telling me about that Kelvin guy you were living with in California? What was that about the black lingerie again?" Surely, between this topic and searching for the dog, the conversation wouldn't turn back to Julian.

"Oh, he just wasn't right for me. Too kinky. I may be weird, but I'm not *that* weird. I wrote you an e-mail about it."

"Didn't get it. But I thought you were head over heels in love."

"Yeah, well, what do *I* know. You said he wasn't good for me that time you met him and you were right. I dumped the creep. When he kicked Bella, I knew I had to get out of there." She called out the window to her dog.

Kelsey winced as she recalled the occasions during the past few days when she'd had uncomplimentary thoughts about yappy little Bella. No dog deserved to be kicked.

After a while, Kelsey said, "Have you called Mom to tell her you're with me? She'd want to know where you are." Lately, Shannon had moved from one place to another and it was hard to keep up. But their mother tried her best.

"I can't think about calling her until we find Bella. Mom's a lot of emotional work for me. One crisis at a time, okay?"

"I'm glad you knew you could come here," she said, meaning it this time, because Shannon had gotten herself out of a bad situation. But Kelsey also began to calculate how she could help Shannon find a job and a place of her own. Shannon had a lot of good qualities, but her taste in men held her back. If she could shake herself loose of them all for a little while, she could pursue some sort of career, maybe go back to college. She was nine tenths of the way to an associate's degree.

"Yeah, well, I tried crashing with my friends, but they aren't very tolerant of Bella. I didn't want to be a burden to you. Again. But I couldn't think of where else to go. I seem to always end up back with you and you've got to be sick of it."

"No, that's not true. We're sisters. We can rely on one another for support."

"Except that I do all the relying and you do all the supporting. I'm sorry about that. I swear I'll get my act together. No more loser boyfriends."

"Sounds like a plan," Kelsey said as she glanced into her rearview mirror for the hundredth time. Shannon looked over her shoulder and out the back window.

"Is that big black truck following us?" she asked. "Stop the car! Maybe whoever's in it has found Bella."

"The truck is not following us," Kelsey lied. "We're not stopping so you can go talk to strangers in badass vehicles." She had an uncomfortable feeling about the truck, which seemed to have tailed them for quite a distance now. But she couldn't figure out why. She had absolutely no reason to connect the truck with the events in her warehouse. Still, she had the overwhelming need to protect her sister if she could. So she was not going to stop and ask the truck driver about Bella.

"Well, it looks like it's following us."

And next thing Kelsey knew, Shannon had her head hanging out of the window and was hollering back at the truck as to whether anyone inside had seen a white dog. Predictably, the truck made a hasty turn at the next intersection and sped away.

"Shannon! Stop being an idiot and sit back down. You took off your seat belt, for God's sake!" Kelsey tugged on her sister's arm until she'd come all the way back inside the car. "Buckle up or I'm taking us home this instant."

"Yes, Mom," Shannon said as she clicked the belt. But they both knew that their own mother had always been far too distracted to worry about whether her daughters had practiced safety rules. "That was weird the way that truck just took off, don't you think?"

"Yes, very weird. Hey! Was that a flash of white over there?"

What with her worry over her sister's dog compounded by the idea that someone had begun to follow her around, Kelsey turned the corner a little too abruptly. With wheels squealing, the chase was on.

PRIVATE EARLMAN WANTED to go home, take a shower, sleep for a day and a half and forget about the mess he'd gotten himself tangled in. Instead, he dutifully made a call. "They're driving all over post. I can't keep following them without getting caught," complained the private, who was pretty full up with the detective work. He knew better than to mention that the women had noticed his truck and had taunted him from their own vehicle.

"They're still looking for that dog?"

"Yeah. At least that's how it looks to me when they get out of the car and start calling out some name or other and looking under bushes and porches. I think they're heading for the MP station now."

For once, the Wolf was reasonable. "I see. Well, no sense in you following them all over the place. You go get some sleep. I'll send someone else to her apartment to watch for her there. We don't want to lose track of her, just in case she suddenly gets smart about things."

Earlman gave a sigh of relief. He could just about taste the hot meal he'd get at the mess hall before he headed for the barracks and his bunk. There would be time enough to get even with those two women who'd been such a thorn in his side.

THEY'D BEEN AT IT for hours and Kelsey could hardly see straight. They were on the far end of the post now because the people they'd asked had led them in this direction. The dog had been spotted at various times by different people throughout the day, but no one had been able to catch her.

"This is hopeless, isn't it," Shannon said. Kelsey thought she detected the threat of tears just beneath the surface.

"No, it's not hopeless. Maybe we should circle back and talk to the guys at the MP station. I don't know if the animal control office would alert them to grab Bella if they see her."

"That's a good idea. The MPs are always patrolling around the post, right? If they saw her, maybe they could give me a call. It'll be getting dark in a little while anyway. Poor Bella."

Her sister's voice hitched on the last syllable and Kelsey gave her a few minutes to pull herself together. Shannon had done well so far, holding back tears. But every hour that passed made the situation a bit more dire. Little Bella could be gone forever. Kelsey regretted every single bad thought she'd ever had about that dog.

"We can look some more tomorrow," Kelsey said. "It's warm all night this time of year. She'll be okay." But in her heart, she knew that the chances of finding Bella would diminish precipitously by tomorrow.

It would take Shannon a long time to recover from such a loss if they didn't find her. But they were out of leads and out of ideas as to what to do next. She turned the car around and headed for the more populated section of the installation.

As she parked in the lot nearest to the MP building, Kelsey's heart sank. The lot was almost empty. Glancing at her watch, she realized it was well past fifteen hundred hours. Late in the work day by army standards. MPs took their physical training seriously. Most of them were probably out running. But someone had to be on duty. This was one place that never closed. She and her sister got out of the car and headed for the entry. Maybe they'd get lucky and find out someone had already picked up the dog.

As they walked, Kelsey put her arm around her sister's shoulders. "We'll find her, Shan," she promised. But they both knew this was one of those things that Kelsey had no power to fix. They went inside and approached a young MP manning the reception desk.

"May I help you, ma'am?" His name tag said Blanchard.

"Yes, Sergeant. We've already talked to the animal control people about our lost dog, but we were wondering if your soldiers could keep an eye out for her, too." Kelsey gave him her best smile.

"Well, um." He looked like a man who wanted to help but knew he shouldn't.

"We don't want you to do anything special. Just let the MPs on patrol know that if they see a little white dog, she's got an owner who's looking for her," said Shannon. She didn't smile, but she moved a little closer to the guy and looked so much like a damsel in distress that Kelsey felt pretty certain Sergeant Blanchard didn't stand a chance.

"I guess I could do that. Sort of word of mouth. I can't put out an APB or anything."

Shannon beamed at him, then wiped a tear away. Had she done it on purpose to garner sympathy? If so, this was a side of Shannon Kelsey hadn't seen before. Oh, sure, she knew her sister was a flirt. But this seemed more like a performance. As Kelsey eyed her sister with new admiration, another man entered the office.

"Afternoon, Sergeant. Anything new on the charge sheet since I was last here?" asked Major Mitchum. Kelsey had spent time with him recently, but she still couldn't decide what it was about him that worried her.

"Yes, sir," said Blanchard as he handed over a clipboard with a sheaf of paper attached.

As he took the sheets, the major recognized Kelsey. "Hello, Captain. How's the inventory coming along?"

She didn't really want to tell this man anything. Something about him continued to put her on red alert. For reasons she couldn't identify, she didn't trust him. So she didn't give him the whole story. She'd save that for Julian. "It's going. Inventories are always difficult. But we're getting things in order and can get a report to you soon."

"That's great," he said with a congenial smile. "Is there anything I can help you with today?" He glanced at Shannon and she gave the man a sad smile. The damsel in distress to the hilt.

"I lost my dog," she said to the major. "I was hoping your MPs could let me know if they see her."

"Sure," the major said. "I'll ask them to keep a look out. It's the small white one, right?"

"Yes, that's right. How did you know?" Kelsey asked. The fact that this man knew those details before they said them gave her the creeps.

"Julian asked me to watch for it." The major smiled and Kelsey felt bad about her suspicious thoughts. "I have a dog of my own. A beautiful husky. I know how I'd feel if she ran off."

"Thank you, Major," Shannon said. "I really appreciate anything you can do."

He nodded. "Call me with your inventory results, Captain O'Roark," he said as he walked by them and through an interior door.

As he passed, the reason for her wariness of him hit Kelsey square in the nose. His cologne wafted to her and the scent was one she would never forget. It was the same fragrance she'd detected just before she'd been knocked out in her warehouse.

Shaken, she went out into the summer heat again with her sister and hundreds of questions streamed through her mind. Why hadn't she realized it was the cologne that bothered her on her previous meetings with Mitchum? Was Mitchum connected with the black truck that had been following her? Was Mitchum involved somehow? Or was her mind playing tricks on her?

"Who's Julian?" Shannon asked.

"Major Fordham," she responded automatically.

"Well, that was nice of him. To call the MPs so they would look for Bella. We need to invite him over for dinner or something." She stopped talking and eyed Kelsey. "Are you okay?"

"I'm fine." Kelsey wanted nothing more than to talk to Julian. But she couldn't leave her sister to search for her dog alone.

She heard someone approaching along the sidewalk on which they'd paused. When she turned, she saw a tall, good-looking guy. From his uniform, she noted that he was Sergeant Steinhauser. And he had an enormous dog by his side, the largest German shepherd Kelsey had ever seen.

"Afternoon, ma'am," he said as he took in Kelsey's rank. "Are you the two women looking for that white dog?"

Kelsey wondered if Julian had alerted the entire post about Bella. If so, how was she supposed to resist him if he continued to be so sweet?

Shannon's face lit with hope. "Did you find her?"

"No, I didn't find her. But maybe I could be of some assistance," said Steinhauser with a grin that revealed one slightly crooked left cuspid. "Buddy here is a K9 officer and I'm his handler. Sometimes it takes a dog to find a dog."

Shannon beamed at him. "Do you think so? That would be so great! She's been gone since this morning. She's not used to being on her own."

Kelsey looked at the well-behaved dog at the man's side. "You're sure you don't have better things to do than help us find a lost pet?" she asked. "Don't you have bombs to sniff or criminals to chase?" She smiled as she said it, but she wanted to be sure he wouldn't get into trouble by helping them.

Steinhauser laughed and somehow the crooked tooth didn't detract from his appealing looks. Shannon just about drooled. She was a sucker for the hero types, though she never actually seemed to end up with any.

"We're not actually expecting any bombs today," Steinhauser said. "We're supposed to help people. That's our job." He glanced at his watch. "And it's almost quitting time for us anyway." He smiled warmly toward Shannon. "We could spend an hour or so helping out a lady in need."

Kelsey would have found amusement in the interest he seemed to take in her sister, but right now, she had other things on her mind. Suddenly, she realized that Steinhauser could end up being the answer to many of her prayers. "We'd really appreciate your help." She managed to smile even as she thought about the conversation she needed to have with Julian about Mitchum's cologne.

"The first thing we should do is to let Buddy sniff something that belongs to your little dog. Some bedding or a blanket she might have slept with."

"I'd have that back at the apartment."

"Buddy and I could follow you in my SUV. It's set up especially for a big dog like him." He patted the K9's shoulder and Buddy looked up at his handler with trusting eyes and happily lolling tongue. Kelsey's estimation of the guy rose another notch. She might not be much of a dog person herself, but she knew that anyone with a great dog like that had to be a decent human being. "Would that be okay with you, ma'am?" he asked Kelsey.

Kelsey's opinion of him went up still more. He might

have eyes only for Shannon, but the sergeant knew how to show respect nonetheless. "Yes, that would be great."

Shannon remained surprisingly quiet during the fifteen-minute drive home. And Kelsey was simply too wound up to talk. At least her rearview mirror gave no hint of someone following her now. Or maybe Steinhauser's SUV was in the way. When they arrived at the apartment complex, the sergeant pulled in right next to them.

Before Kelsey had snapped off her seat belt, Shannon reached over and held her back with a light touch on her arm. "Listen, Kelsey. You've been so great, traipsing all over the post helping me look for Bella. But you must be tired. I could go out with the sergeant by myself, if you want. He's an MP, so I'm sure I'll be in good hands. And you must have a million things you need to do after I stole your afternoon from you."

Kelsey sighed with relief. Not only was she more than happy to give up the hunt in favor of pursuing her own secret agenda, but she could see that Shannon might have designs on the K9 handler. Wouldn't it be cool if her sister could find a nice guy for once?

"Sure, Shan. You'll be safer with an MP than you'd be with just about anyone else. I do have a bunch of things I need to take care of. Thanks."

By the time she and Shannon were out of the car, Sergeant Steinhauser and Buddy were already standing on the sidewalk waiting.

"This way," Kelsey said as she led them to the building's entrance. Man, woman and dog followed her inside her apartment and Jasper stopped dead in his tracks, abruptly aborting his usual mad dash to greet her. He took one look at the monstrous German shepherd and transformed into a Halloween cat with his back arched up high and his hair sticking out all over. He hissed and yowled as he backed up slowly. Buddy lowered his head, his eyes alight with interest, and took a step toward the cat. But Steinhauser made a quick hand gesture and Buddy sat down immediately. Then the big dog yawned hugely. One look at those enormous pointy teeth and Jasper bolted for hiding in the depths of the apartment.

"He hates dogs," Shannon said and although Kelsey wanted to defend her pet, she had to agree that Jasper seemed to dislike all the dogs he'd come into contact with—one yappy white thing and one enormous K9. "I'll just go get Bella's little pink blanket that she sleeps with every night."

"That'll work," said the sergeant. When Shannon reappeared from the bedroom, Steinhauser put the blanket in front of Buddy's nose and the big tail began to whap loudly against the wall as the animal tried to wag it. "Let's go."

"Take a jacket," Kelsey found herself saying like a mother hen to her chick. "It might get chilly after sunset." She handed over one of Shannon's sweaters that had been tossed onto the back of the couch.

And off they went. When she shut the door, Kelsey sighed and leaned against it for a moment. "You can come out now, Jasper. They're gone." But the cat did not reappear.

Kelsey glanced at her watch. If she hurried, she should be able to catch Julian at work. And if he wasn't there, she would track him down at his apartment just outside the post. She changed quickly out of her uniform, disliking the fear that nibbled at her stomach. As she headed back to the car, she glanced all around her before she got behind the wheel. She found no sign of the black truck from earlier in the day. And she had no choice. The things she needed to talk with Julian about were too important for a phone call.

JULIAN HAD SPENT a few hours in his office, planning his approach with Kelsey. He'd decided that if he told her that he'd seen a shrink himself, maybe she would find his suggestion more palatable. He hated to reveal this fact about himself. What self-respecting military officer ever wanted to admit he'd been to a therapist? But if it would help Kelsey, he would tell her.

He'd been agonizing over exactly what to say all afternoon, without actually coming up with anything he felt would have a hope of convincing her. He succeeded only in making himself pace inside his office—something he rarely did. To make matters worse, he hadn't been able to reach Kelsey by phone. She wasn't at her office, she wasn't at home and he kept getting voice mail on her cell.

His frustration mounted until he finally decided her unavailability gave him permission to put the whole thing off until tomorrow. He'd go home now and get some much-needed sleep and deal with Captain O'Roark in the morning.

That plan went down the drain as soon as he walked out the door of the office building and saw Kelsey's car just pulling in next to where he'd parked.

She opened her window and called to him. "I need to talk to you."

A blast of cold air wafted toward him from the interior of her car. "Ditto. But I already locked up my office. Can I meet you at your place in an hour?"

She thought about that a moment. "How about I follow you to your apartment?"

He noticed she wore civilian clothes. She always looked

great in almost anything she wore—even camouflage—but he liked her best in jeans and a T-shirt, just like she wore at the moment.

"Have you eaten yet? If it's Tuesday, I get Chinese food delivered."

"I'm starving. I could eat Chinese."

"Let's go then." He got into his car and felt the sweat begin to drip down his brow from the intense heat inside. He, too, cranked up the air conditioner and then drove off, checking in the rearview mirror to make sure she was keeping up. He couldn't help but think about the fact that he'd have her in his apartment soon. They'd eat together, almost like a date. He wanted to kiss her again, wanted to hold her. Hell, he wanted a whole lot more than that. But he promised himself he wouldn't succumb to that fantasy. Instead, he would focus on what he had to say to her. That would surely end any chance he may have ever had of getting even a cordial hello from Kelsey again, never mind a kiss.

That would be for the best. They were colleagues and needed to remain professional. The fact that he longed for something personal didn't change that. He thought of all the reasons for not attempting anything so foolish as a sexual overture of any kind with Kelsey. He figured if he kept repeating them over and over as he drove to his apartment, perhaps he'd be able to recall one or two once they were alone.

She parked next to him and he found himself standing beside her in the darkness with only a distant streetlight illuminating their surroundings. And he thought once more about kissing her. She must have sensed his predatory instincts rising, because she lowered her gaze and started walking toward the building.

Julian followed, repeating the mantra of reasons not to start anything with her.

"We didn't find my sister's dog yet," she said.

Dog? What dog? And how did a dog figure in to the objective of him pinning Kelsey to a wall and kissing her breathless?

But then it came back to him all at once. Oh, yeah, the little white *dog!* "I'm sorry about that. I hope she turns up soon," he managed to say.

"We appreciate that you've been asking everyone to keep a look out for Bella. Major Mitchum said you asked him."

Had he mentioned the dog to Mitchum when they'd talked about a routine case today? He couldn't recall one way or the other. That wasn't like him. Normally he had an exceptionally sharp memory. But at the moment, his brain seemed to be at ease, while his libido had gone to battle stations.

She glanced at him as they walked next to one another. "Shannon is still out looking with a K9 guy, Sergeant Steinhauser. Do you know him?"

"Can't say that I do," he said. "But if you convinced one of those MPs with the dogs to help you, then it should be no time before you find…Bella."

"That's what we're hoping."

They climbed the stairs to the second floor. He dug out his keys, fumbled with them for longer than usual out of sheer nervousness and finally opened his door. He held it so that she could pass through first and as she did so, he caught her scent and breathed it in deeply.

Her stay in his apartment would be an exercise in frustration. And yet, he wanted her here. He wanted to share a meal with her. Because when she'd said they were friends that morning in his office when she'd come to him for help, he'd been honored that she thought of him that way. He wanted her friendship almost as much as he wanted her body. So eating dinner together would be nice. And the possibilities that might present themselves after that appealed even more.

Even though he shouldn't let himself think of any of those possibilities.

"Spartan," she commented as she moved into the living area.

He looked around as if seeing his place for the first time. She'd picked exactly the right word to describe it. There was a futon for a couch and a small entertainment center with a seldom-watched TV in it. There was a desk with his computer on it. A floor lamp stood near a nondescript end table, placed so he could read by its light. A pile of books—some already read, others yet to be delved into—sat on the equally nondescript coffee table.

And that was all.

He had a bedroom, of course, and it contained a real bed, a dresser and even a chair on which he mostly draped clothes before they went to the cleaners. But if he had any sense at all, she wouldn't be seeing that room. And she would have described it the same way in any case. Spartan. It was almost as if he thought of it as a temporary home. He'd learned that from his life as an air force brat, moving every couple of years with his father. He'd hated those many moves, the need to make new friends, the uprooted feeling. Had he ever really had a home?

"I'm a bachelor. I don't need much," he said, hoping he didn't sound defensive. "I'll call for the food. What would you like?"

She told him and he placed the order. "It'll be here in about fifteen minutes," he told her, wondering if he should wait until after they ate to broach the subject of a visit to a psychologist.

"Sit down," he said. And when she did, he realized he'd have to sit next to her on the futon. There were no other seats. He didn't even have a kitchen chair he could slide into the room. Why bother getting kitchen furniture when you're going to eat in the living room anyway, he'd always figured. "I have a couple of beers in the refrigerator. Maybe some juice." He hoped she didn't pick the juice because he couldn't remember how long it had been sitting in there.

"I came to tell you some things that might help your investigation," she said without choosing a beverage. "First, the inventory is showing that my warehouse is a mess. Things are misplaced, stuff is missing. I'm beginning to think someone is messing with the place to keep us from figuring out what's missing."

Julian fetched his notebook from his briefcase—delaying the moment when he'd have to sit too close to her—and wrote down what she'd said. "I'll put a twenty-four-hour watch on the place, then. We need the full inventory as soon as possible."

"That's what Major Mitchum said and he…"

"Drew is asking about your inventory?" Julian didn't remember discussing Kelsey's warehouse with him. Did Drew know something he hadn't shared yet?

"Yeah. He said there's been a series of thefts and he needs to know if anything's missing from the warehouse. Are you working with him on my case?" There was an accusing note to her voice.

"No. I haven't shared your story with anyone. As promised. But he and I have been working the black market theft ring for a while now. We've had zero luck finding out who's involved."

"Well, don't trust Drew."

That made him look up sharply from his notes. "What?"

"I ran into him today. And I finally remembered why he seemed familiar to me. He wears the same cologne as the guy who knocked me out."

CHAPTER SEVEN

"YOU DIDN'T TELL ME you smelled cologne that night." His mind raced over the implications. Drew was his friend. The thought of him being involved in this made Julian queasy.

"I didn't remember it until I got a whiff of the same scent again today. It came back to me all at once. I think the fragrance is what made me think someone was behind me. I started to turn to look when I got hit on the head."

Julian stared at her and couldn't help wondering if this was another manifestation of her imagination. But scents were excellent memory triggers. "Do you remember anything else?"

She thought a moment, then shook her head. "It all happened exactly the way I told you."

He had his doubts about that. Stalling for time until maybe they could at least eat together, he said, "I didn't get you anything to drink. Would you like some orange juice or the beer?"

Confusion registered on her face. "Did you hear what I said about Drew? He can't be trusted. He's probably the guy who knocked me out in the warehouse."

"Kelsey, you're leaping to unfounded conclusions. Drew might wear a very ordinary scent that lots of other guys wear. Maybe it's just a popular aftershave or something. It's a lead we can follow up on, but it's far from conclusive." And he didn't want to believe his friend was the officer who led this ring of criminals.

"I'll take a beer," she said as she sank against the back of the futon in weary frustration.

Julian went to the kitchen to fetch two beers and spent an extra couple of minutes out of sight to think about how he should begin. But no matter how he might start it, he was pretty certain how it would end up. He popped the tops of the bottles, then leaned against the counter with his head bent forward. Even before he got to the part about her going to see a shrink, she'd want to know why he'd seen a psychologist. Could he make something up? No, he'd have to tell her the truth. And he really didn't want to do that.

"Are you okay?" she asked from the doorway. "I thought you got lost."

He'd taken too long and she'd come to check on him. Just like a girlfriend would. Or a wife. Someone who cared for him. Those concepts made him want to run full tilt away from her. They also made him glance at her mouth.

The doorbell sounded. Just in time. After exchanging a twenty for the food, he brought the bag over to the coffee table and cleared a spot by way of sweeping everything off of it at once.

"I could have moved the books for you," she said as she bent to sort them out.

"It's okay. I've already read most of them anyway. I'm just going to give them to the library in a few days."

"All the more reason to keep them in good shape," she said, but she smiled up at him and that sweet expression eliminated any hint of reproach he might otherwise have heard in her comments.

She stayed on the floor next to the newly stacked books, so he sat on the floor, too, as he rummaged through the bag.

He handed her a set of chopsticks and a carton. "I think that one's yours."

She held the carton in one hand and the chopsticks in the other for a few seconds. Then she shrugged and opened the flaps of the little box. "Yup, this is the lo mein. Ever try to eat this with chopsticks?" she asked.

He chuckled. "Nope. Have you?"

"Not yet," she said.

She made her first attempt and Julian could barely take his eyes off her mouth and tongue as she struggled to eat the slippery food. She couldn't have looked sexier if she'd tried.

"I suppose there's no chance you'd have a fork in your kitchen drawer," she commented.

"I think there's one in the dishwasher, but it's probably not clean. In fact, I'm not sure how long ago I put it in there, so I wouldn't go that route, if I were you." And besides, he liked watching her eat with chopsticks while her eyes sparkled with amusement and her lips puckered to suck at the strands of lo mein.

"You really *are* a bachelor," she said with a laugh. "I guess I'll have to persevere."

He smiled, but part of him thought of how quickly she could rectify things in his apartment if she lived here. The forks would all certainly be clean. And not because he'd let her do all the work, but rather because if he lived with her here, he'd take more care with things himself. Living alone gave him the freedom to indulge very bad habits.

Did he need a cure for bachelorhood? Did he want to be saved from his Spartan home life? Only if Kelsey did the saving, his heart said. But his brain retreated in quickstep from the very notion of committing to her enough to live with her. Although his therapist said he'd come a long way, Julian didn't believe for one second that he could be what Kelsey deserved.

His appetite left him as he recalled what he needed to discuss with her. He watched her for another few minutes, then decided he'd put it off for long enough.

"Kelsey, I want to tell you something."

She looked up at him with interest, her chopsticks halfway to her mouth. Pausing made the slippery food slide right back into the carton. "Okay," she said instead of attempting another bite.

"About your case." All of a sudden, he could not remember any of the careful sentences he'd constructed during the long hours of silent rehearsal. He searched his mind and nothing came forward. Mild panic began to take hold. "I…" he began. "I've been seeing a psychologist off post. He's been helping me with…things."

She appeared to be rapt with interest. "What kind of things?" she asked before he could go on.

He sighed. He'd known he wouldn't be able to say something like that without explaining. Officers in the army, and especially members of the CID, didn't run off to tell their troubles to a shrink without serious provocation.

"Actually, I started going there after I stopped calling you." He let that sink in for a moment. "I wanted to know why I'd stopped calling you."

In nearly a whisper, she asked, "Why *did* you stop calling?"

"Because you scared the hell out of me." Now, there was an admission he hadn't intended to make. But he knew if he had any chance of helping her, he'd have to make sure she knew he cared about her. He wanted her to know that he truly wanted to help.

She blinked once, twice. Then she chuckled. "I don't

ever scare anyone, Julian. My commander tells me that the only thing I could improve in myself as an officer is to toughen up on my staff and be firmer with the troops."

"I've seen you with your troops. They respect you just fine."

She smiled. "Thanks, but sometimes I can't bring myself to really command them. I tend to ask nicely and sometimes I don't get the desired results that way. So, why do I scare *you?*"

"It's not so much you, as it is the feelings I have for you." Uh-oh. He hadn't meant to say that. "I mean…did I tell you I was married?"

She reeled back as if he'd slapped her. "You're *married?*" she yelled.

"No, no." Would he never find the right words? "I *used* to be married. Years ago. And it ended bitterly with lots of accusations. I probably deserved every single one of them."

"No, that's not—" she began, clearly preparing to defend him.

He cut her off with a wave of his hand. "Look, I'm not good with romance or emotions or anything else that makes a relationship work. I can't seem to say what I feel. In short, I'm a cold son of a bitch."

She opened her mouth, as _if_ to protest, but he stopped her. "I'm working on it. That's why I see the therapist. Maybe someday, I'll erase all the nonsense my father packed into my head when I was younger."

Ever ready to protect those she cared for, she sat up straighter and her eyes filled with anger. "Did he abuse you?"

"Not physically. He was just a tyrant. Did I tell you he was a one-star general in the air force? When he figured out he wasn't going to get his second star, he retired and ran for office. Of course, he succeeded and became a congressman."

"No, I don't think you mentioned that. And you up and joined the army?".

"Yeah. He wasn't happy about that, to say the least. But it doesn't matter anymore because he's in a nursing home with Alzheimer's. And I hate that he still rents space in my head and affects my ability to have any real relationship." He looked down at his food, disgusted with himself. He needed to get back to why he'd admitted his therapy sessions to her. "I'm only telling you all this because—"

"You have a good relationship with your brother," she said. "I remember that you said you were close. Do the two of you get to see much of each other these days?"

He shook his head. "He's happily married and stationed at Fort Dix now. Look, none of this is important. I don't want to talk about me. We need to talk about you. About your case."

"Okay," she agreed. But he could see she was reluctant to leave the enlightening conversation about what made him tick.

"First, I need to tell you that someone did, in fact, show up AWOL today," he said.

Her face immediately lit up. "Who? How long has he been missing? What unit is he from? What did his superiors say?"

He held up his hands in defense against the onslaught of her questions. "Slow down. I have to tell you that I don't think this is your dead guy. I think this Specialist Rigley is in Florida visiting his girlfriend. His roommate seems pretty sure he'll come back soon."

"But you're going to make some calls, right? To see if he's there or not. He could be the guy in my warehouse."

"I want to give him a day or two to come in on his own.

If I start calling his parents and friends I'll just upset them," he said, hoping she would see the reason in this. She didn't.

"So upset them! This could be his life we're talking about. If he's not actually in Florida, he could be a dead body somewhere. I think his parents would want to know that as soon as possible."

"Before I'd be willing to do that, we'd need something more to go on than what we have. There's no physical evidence to back your story."

"So now it's my *story* is it?" She looked wounded. Her big brown eyes were full of hurt and he thought his heart would break at the sight of it.

"I'm sorry, Kelsey. I wish I had better news for you. But the only thing we have is some missing warehouse stuff. I already knew Fort Belvoir had a theft ring operating within it. It's a long road from theft to murder."

Very softly, she said, "It wasn't murder. His death was an accident. But someone tried to cover it up and *that's* a crime, isn't it?"

"Yes, it is," he agreed, feeling bleak. If her memories were accurate, then a serious crime *had* been committed. The question was, could her recollections be trusted? He closed his eyes briefly and ran his fingers through his hair. God, he wished he could help her. But there just wasn't anything to work with. "I'm still investigating the missing materiel and I need you to keep going with the inventory. But I can't spend much more time on the dead-body angle unless something else turns up."

She stared at him a moment and then her shoulders fell and she looked so dejected, he longed to move around the coffee table to give her a hug. Instead, he had to get the rest of his speech said.

He took a deep breath and let it out, knowing her reaction would not be pretty. "So, I've been seeing this thera-pist, right? And he and I sometimes talk about how psy-chologists can help with criminal cases. One thing I learned from him is that hypnotism isn't just something to amuse an audience. It can really help unlock repressed memories for witnesses. I got to thinking about your situation and—"

Her gaze had already begun to harden. He blundered on, knowing no other way to help her. "Well, your memories seem potentially unreliable, given the lack of evidence. So maybe you're blocking the true memories for some reason. A good regression therapist or hypnotist could help you with—"

"Now you're saying I need a shrink!" Her expression had turned flinty. "You think I've made it all up, that no one died right in front of me, that none of it really hap-pened!" She stood up abruptly, fists clenched at her sides and cheeks flushed. "Julian, I need you to believe me!"

He scrambled to his feet, too, hoping she wouldn't bolt out the door before he made her understand the importance of finding out the truth. "Kelsey, you came to me for help. And I'm convinced something very bad happened to you that night." Suppressing a shudder, he remembered the horrified look in her eyes when she'd come to his office. Her clothes had been rumpled and dirty, her sleeve torn. "But what clearly didn't happen was a death on the floor of that building. There would be traces of blood if that had happened."

All at once, she covered her face with her hands and for a moment he feared she was crying. He took a few steps closer, reached out, put his hands on her shoulders in com-fort. But then he heard a soft low growl emanating from her. The growl grew in volume and pitch until it became a full-blown roar. In the next instant, she'd smacked his hands from her shoulders and yanked herself away. She walked in small angry circles between his futon and entertainment center. Then she turned and pointed an accusing finger at him. "I don't need this from you! You know, I hadn't gotten around to mentioning that someone in a big black truck has been following me all day. Does *that* give you some of the precious evidence you need? I couldn't get all of the license plate—maybe M95 something. But you know what! Just forget I ever asked you to help me! Don't bother to find out about this Specialist Rigley. I'll deal with this whole thing myself!" She headed for the door.

He followed close on her heels. "Kelsey, you have to listen to reason. I only want to help you. If we could just uncover what really happened to you, then I could find whoever hurt you—"

She whirled about to face him so suddenly, he had to back up a step. "You're all about evidence, aren't you, Julian. Intuition just can't be factored in at all. Or faith," she said. She stared at him and he thought he saw tears shimmering in her eyes.

He had no idea what to say to her. Evidence *was* all that mattered in his line of work. You couldn't prove a case on intuition. And what did faith have to do with any of this? Faith had no place in criminal investigations. He made one last attempt at making her see reason. "I promise I'll look into the lead on the black truck, but tell me you'll consider seeing a psychologist. Please. Anyway, if your memories are true, then the hypnotism will prove that."

Her gaze shifted sideways and doubt washed over her face. "I'll let you know," she said. And with that, she opened his door and stormed out. He couldn't ever remember seeing her so angry. In fact, he'd never seen her angry at all. She seemed so even-tempered, so sweet, so caring.

And those were exactly the qualities that made her terrifying.

THE HEADLIGHTS THAT FOLLOWED her home seemed far too close for comfort. She tried slowing down, but the lights just came up on her even closer, making her heart beat faster. She didn't dare stop. She didn't dare speed up. All she could think to do was to put on her flashers and continue at a pace that would cause any other driver to go around her.

Instead, the vehicle on her tail suddenly nudged her car. She lurched against her seat belt and heard the grind of the two bumpers. And then her heart began to race in earnest. She reached for her cell phone, but another jolt from the car behind made her rethink taking either hand off the steering wheel. What she needed to do, she decided, was to drive to a populated area. She turned at the next intersection, away from her neighborhood but toward the Commissary.

To her relief and frustration, her tormentor raced off ahead instead of turning with her. She could see it was a dark-colored truck, but no more than that. She hit the steering wheel with the heel of her hand in anger. She'd never find out who this maniac was if she couldn't get a good look at the vehicle or tags. For a moment, she considered the possibility of following her follower. But she quickly dismissed the idea as foolhardy, given that she was alone and the streets were dark.

Realizing that she was shaking from head to toe, she pulled her car over to the curb in a well-lit area. There were still a few people walking through the parking lots around her. But the hour was late and the stores would be closing soon. She needed to get home. But suddenly the walk from her car to her building made her quake.

If she weren't so mad at Julian, she might consider calling him to tell him what had happened. He would come to make sure she got home safely. But even if she hadn't been mad at him, she realized she wouldn't have dialed his number. She wouldn't call anyone. Because if she couldn't take care of herself on a military installation on U.S. soil, she had no right to call herself an officer.

By the time she got back to her neighborhood, she'd won her battle against the threat of tears. Crying would do no good. But her heart ached over Julian's defection at a time when she needed him the most. She could no longer count on him to stand by her. She was alone in this. And alone in her walk through her parking lot. Vigilance was her only weapon and she listened carefully for the sound of footsteps behind her or for an unusual rustle in the shrubbery along the sidewalk. Once inside, she let out the breath she hadn't realized she'd been holding.

At last, she entered the safe harbor of her own apartment and bolted the door behind her. For once, she wished with all her heart that Shannon were with her instead of only Jasper. But Shannon wasn't back yet and Kelsey didn't know when she'd be home, if at all, given the way Shannon had looked at that K9 handler. Jasper rubbed around her ankles and this went a long way to soothing her nerves. But she could have used a little conversation that went beyond her cat's purring and the nonsense words she cooed in response.

With a sigh, she went to her bedroom to change into her pajamas. She thought of how she would have to take action in her own case if she were ever to find relief from the fear and nightmares that had plagued her since the incident in her warehouse. Julian obviously had no plans to pursue the AWOL specialist angle, so she'd take matters into her own hands. And at least she'd be doing something for herself instead of standing idly by while the heroic CID officer supposedly took care of her problem for her. Enough of that. First, she'd need to get a copy of Rigley's official photo. Then she needed to get a look at his personal stuff. By the time Shannon came home an hour later, she had an idea.

"I can see that you don't have Bella with you," Kelsey said to her sister. "Did you find anyone who's seen her?"

"No, but Ken thinks something will turn up. He said he'd help me look some more tomorrow. And we put up a few signs. That should help."

"I take it that Ken is Sergeant Steinhauser, right?" She watched her sister closely for signs of interest in this man. Despite her own worries, Kelsey couldn't help but hope that Shannon's life would turn itself around.

Although she looked worried, Shannon's small smile gave her away. "He's been so nice. He said I could come over to the K9 unit tomorrow and help with the dogs until he goes out on patrol again. We can look for Bella again then, unless someone calls about finding her."

A disappointed "Oh," came out of Kelsey's mouth before she could stop herself.

"What does 'oh' mean? Did you need me for something? I can delay going over to the K9 if you need me."

"I've been thinking about ways to learn more about this guy I just found out about. He's gone AWOL," she began. "I want to look around in his room, take a look at his uniform, check out his stuff to see if it tells me anything about what happened to him. But I need to finagle my way into the guy's room at the barracks. And I might need someone to distract his roommate."

"Why is it your job to check on a missing soldier? Is this someone who's under your command?" Shannon asked.

Kelsey didn't want to tell her sister the whole story. But she didn't want to lie to her either. And Shannon had handed her the perfect excuse. "Yeah, something like that. I can't give you the details yet. But when I can, I will. Trust me."

Shannon gazed into her eyes for a few moments as if to gauge the seriousness of the situation. "You're not in trouble, are you? I'd want you to tell me if you were." Both sisters had had their share of troubles when they were growing up in West Virginia. That was one of the reasons Kelsey had needed the discipline of the army. "I'd do everything in my power to help," Shannon said. "We'd find a lawyer or a—"

Kelsey held up her palms. "I'm not in any trouble." That much was technically true. No one had accused her of anything—other than dreaming up her whole story. "I just need to do this for my own satisfaction. I swear." She hoped that would be enough.

It was. Shannon reached across the table and put her hand on Kelsey's arm. "After all you've done for me, I'd be glad to help you. Just tell me what you want me to do."

"I don't know exactly. Just talk to the guy so I can have a quick look around the room." The truth was, she had only a vague idea of what she was looking for. But she knew she had to do *something*. And she had this nagging suspicion that if she could see his personal stuff, she'd somehow know whether Rigley was her dead guy in the warehouse.

"I'm good at distracting men, at least," Shannon said with a grin.

"No, no! Don't flirt with him. Just talk to him." Kelsey did not want her sister doing anything she wouldn't be willing to do herself. But she knew she wouldn't have much success if she went alone. She just didn't have the knack of making casual conversation with men she didn't know.

"Okay. Relax. I'll just talk to the guy. You'll look around. It will all work out. When do we do it?"

"You know, it would probably be best to wait until after work to try this. The roommate is likely to be away from the barracks until then. So maybe evening would be best. So, tomorrow, you should go on and do what Sergeant Steinhauser suggested. Maybe you'll find Bella before I even call you."

"Yeah," Shannon said, but her eyes filled with tears. "I know she's just a silly little dog and most people don't even like her. But she's mine—or maybe I'm hers—and I just hate to think of her outside all night all alone." She sniffed, clearly trying hard to hold back her grief.

"It's okay to cry, Shan."

The floodgates opened and the tears fell in great big grief-stricken drops.

"But let's try to think of what else Bella might be doing right now. I bet some nice family found her over by the on-post family housing. And she was so cute, they took her inside their home. And she's probably all warm and cozy and well fed as we speak."

Shannon made an effort to regain control. "You think that's possible?"

"Actually, I think it's pretty likely. She's a smart dog, like you said. She knows people are the source of comfort. If she couldn't make her way back to you, she'd find shelter with some other nice person."

"And maybe that person will see one of the signs we posted today?"

"Absolutely!"

"And even if they don't see a sign, at least Bella will

be okay. She wears a name tag, you know. They'll know her name."

Kelsey smiled at that. "I have this strong feeling she's going to be okay. You just need to take it on faith that she'll be fine."

Shannon nodded. Kelsey couldn't help but wonder why some people had no trouble with the concept of faith. And why some people couldn't get there even with a detailed road map.

"I'VE GOT THE little dog," said the Wolf into his cell phone.

"What are you talking about?" came the caustic reply from the officer on the other end.

"I have it hidden. As long as the little mutt is missing, those two will be too busy looking for it to bother us. They're chasing their tails, searching all over for it." He snorted with derision. "They even have someone from the K9 unit helping them."

"Are you kidding me, or what? Just get rid of the stupid dog. And put a muzzle on those women, too. We're too close to finishing this gig to be messing around."

"I'll get rid of the dog when I know it won't be any use to us," the Wolf said.

"All I want is for that officer bitch to stay out of my way. So far, she's been pretty stupid. But if she causes any more trouble, snuff her."

"Don't be ridiculous. We're not going to snuff anyone unless we're forced to." The Wolf began to pace back and forth on the sidewalk.

"You need to remember who you're talking to!" snapped the officer.

The Wolf closed his eyes and searched for patience.

This guy was younger and less experienced, but he was an officer and needed to be coddled. "Sir, I'm just trying to do what you said about keeping my focus on finishing the job. We don't want to take the risk of elevating security. We almost have the whole shipment together now."

"And that's why I want you to stop messing around. Extract the rest of the materiel and get it outside the fence." One of the hardest aspects of stealing from the army was getting the stuff out of the enclosed installation. There seemed to be guards patrolling all the exits all the time. And that's why the Wolf was part of the operation. He knew what it took to get out without detection.

"Yes, sir," said the Wolf. "I'm taking care of it." And one way he was taking care of it was by ensuring the sisters, and their friend from CID, stayed busy looking for the dog. As long as they remained distracted, they wouldn't have to die.

WALKING INTO THE BARRACKS a little after seventeen hundred hours, Kelsey could feel nervous sweat beginning to accumulate at strategic locations on her body. She took a deep breath and reminded herself that she wasn't doing anything illegal. What could be wrong with getting Rigley's bunkmate to let them in the room for a minute? And if she happened to get a peek inside Rigley's locker, who would know?

"So who are we here to see again?" Shannon asked as they cruised the hallway on the second floor. Considering that she hadn't found her dog, Shannon seemed more in control of her emotions. Maybe this was just the distraction she needed to take her mind off Bella.

"Specialist Rigley. But he's not here, remember? We're looking for his roommate. I want you keep his attention on you so I can get a quick look around."

"Got it. Okay, so if you want me to go into action, just say, um…Starbucks, and I'll do my thing."

Kelsey stopped in her tracks. "This isn't a movie, Shan. We don't need code words."

"Oh, really? Then why didn't you wear your uniform and just order a room inspection? Why are you dressed all young and sexy?"

Kelsey looked down at her T-shirt and jeans. She had dressed to be appealing and unthreatening. She hadn't meant to look sexy. She tugged the snug little T-shirt down from where it had crept up to show an inch of midriff. "Let's just knock on the door," she said.

Two light raps brought a young man to the entry. "Well, well, well. To what do I owe the honor of a visit from such lovely ladies?" said the soldier with a wide grin.

"Is Specialist Rigley here?" Kelsey asked.

"Nope, but I'm here. Bill Cohen at your service." He placed his splayed fingers over the center of his T-shirt-covered chest as if to affirm that he was talking about himself and no other.

"Well, do you know where Rigley is?" Kelsey asked in her sweetest voice. But the smile she offered him didn't prevent a worried expression from creeping over his features.

"Lot of people looking for Rigley lately. He's just not here right now."

Kelsey could tell he was hedging. He knew full well that Rigley was AWOL and probably knew a lot more than that. But she had no idea how to get him to talk to her, much less to get a look around the inside of the room. Maybe she shouldn't have been so direct, maybe she—

"You know, we just asked about Rigley because we met him a while back and thought he was kinda cute," Shannon interjected. "We were just in the area, you know? We thought we'd look him up."

"Well, he's visiting his family in Florida right now," Bill admitted, turning an interested look to Shannon. Kelsey dared to hope that her sister might wheedle her way into Bill's good graces, after all.

"Bill Cohen," Shannon said as she tapped her finger thoughtfully at the side of her mouth. "I could swear I've heard that name somewhere before." She gave him a sly, sexy smile.

Flirting. She was definitely flirting. Kelsey stifled a groan.

Shannon moved just a bit closer to Bill. "Have I seen you around town before? Or did I hear some people talking about you?"

As Shannon spoke, Bill's serious expression slowly eased back to the grin that seemed a more natural look for him. "Well, I'm pretty well known around the local pool halls. You ever play pool?"

"Ooh, I just love pool," cooed Shannon as Kelsey stood by watching in awe. "But I'm not very good. Maybe you could give me a few pointers sometime."

"I could give you a lesson or two, if you want. There's a table at the club that's usually open about now."

"Is there?" Shannon said, as if this was the most intriguing revelation she'd heard in a long time. "Do you have time to go there now?" She glanced at her watch. "I bet it wouldn't be crowded at the club yet."

"Only if you'll tell me your name," Bill said with a wink.

"Charlotte," Shannon said without a moment's hesitation. The two of them shook hands. "And this is my sister, Kendra. She's an E-5 already!"

Kelsey wasn't sure how she felt about the lies pouring from Shannon's mouth. Could they get in trouble for giving false names? Was there a penalty for impersonating a sergeant?

But there was no stopping the woman now that she was on a roll. "I'm just visiting my sister for a couple of weeks. To tell you the truth, she's the one who was interested in Rigley. I just came along for something to do. But just because he's off on vacation doesn't mean we couldn't hang out, right?"

Kelsey frowned. Her sister's performance was impressive, but how was she supposed to get in to see Rigley's stuff if they trooped off to the club to play pool?

"So, Kendra, do you still have that headache or can you come with us to the club?"

Playing along without feeling completely sure where this line of conversation would end up, Kelsey rubbed her head. "It seems a little worse, actually."

Shannon gave Bill a disappointed look. Then her face lit up as she asked, "Hey, do you have a couple of aspirins she could take before we go, Bill?" Kelsey's sister had all the makings of a professional con artist.

"I could probably find some. And I'll grab my shirt." He led them inside his room.

To Kelsey's complete disappointment, the place was spotless. Not a single article of clothing or personal item sat out where she could look at it. The only sign of life was Bill's slightly mussed bed where he'd been sitting to watch TV.

"I think Ryan has some aspirin in his locker." He approached a narrow door that looked locked. Bill looked over his shoulder at Shannon. "Don't tell anyone about this trick, okay?" But without waiting for their agreement, he smacked the locker door hard, above the latch. The door popped open, just the way they used to back in high school.

"Aspirin's on the top shelf. Help yourself. There's a cup

for water in there," Bill said, pointing to the bathroom. He began to shrug into his button-down shirt as Kelsey took the aspirin bottle and went where he directed. She closed the door behind her, figuring he wouldn't mind if she pretended to use the facilities while she was in there. Staring at herself in the mirror, she stretched her mind toward some way to get Bill out of the room while she remained to poke around. But no matter how hard she tried to pretend she was Julian, sleuthing on a case, no solution came to her.

Feeling like a criminal, wondering if Bill's actions would count as breaking and entering and if she and Shannon would be accomplices, she decided she could use two aspirin, after all. Her head throbbed. Too late for doubts. And the results were worth the risk.

Because inside, hanging neatly on a hanger, had been one of Rigley's uniforms. The right sleeve faced out. Kelsey had seen exactly what she'd been looking for. The unit patch on the sleeve was the same one on the uniform of the soldier in her warehouse.

CHAPTER EIGHT

THE DAY AFTER Kelsey stormed out of his apartment, Julian ran harder than usual at PT after work. Even so, Drew caught up with him halfway around the perimeter of the golf course, where there was a track for running. The man didn't seem even slightly winded and Julian suspected he had crossed the field to get to him.

Not much in the mood for talking, Julian responded with noncommittal grunts for a while. His mind went over and over his conversation with Kelsey. He second-guessed himself, wondering if he could have handled things better. He'd gotten an "I'll think about it" out of her about seeing a psychologist, but at what price? He suspected he'd cost himself any chance at another kiss. Or for any of the other half-formed wishes he had toward the captain.

"Has anything unusual or unexplained happened this past week?" Julian asked Drew without preamble. He didn't want to doubt Drew's loyalty to the army and the country, but he couldn't completely discount what Kelsey had said about his cologne. He waited for the man's reaction.

"What?" Drew managed to say between huffs and puffs. Julian felt a twinge of gratification that the man had certainly become winded now that he'd been keeping pace awhile.

"I just want to know if there's anything weird going on, any rumors, any hints of something bad happening," he said as he ran on.

"You know," Drew said between huffs. "You're going to…have to tell me…what's bothering you…before I can…help."

"You tell me why you're so interested in the G3's warehouse lately and maybe we'll get somewhere," Julian said, glancing at Drew.

The MP chief didn't hesitate at all. "Just worried about these stories we keep hearing about those thieves. What better place to pilfer stuff—" he paused to huff a few times "—than our largest warehouse?"

That sounded reasonable to Julian, but he didn't let his guard down. "I told you I asked for a full inventory there a week ago," he said. "So I guess we had the same thing in mind. I can't tell you more than that yet."

Drew slowed his pace, then came to a panting stop before Julian realized he'd lost his companion. Doubling back, Julian almost laughed at the sight of Drew bent forward, with his hands on his knees, wheezing.

"You been smoking again?" Julian asked, noting Drew's high color.

"No, I swear. I quit for good months ago. But I can't talk when I'm running." He straightened up and eyed Julian the way only the military police can. "We used to be friends. But lately you're keeping stuff from me. My guess is there's a woman involved. There always is. Maybe one of those babes with the lost dog."

Julian's eyebrows shot up in surprise at Drew's guess until he realized it had been a joke. He gave a short laugh. "You watch too many cop movies. I'm simply not at liberty to tell you everything. I wish I could." Julian wished he didn't have to carry around the burden of his suspicion, too. He hated not trusting Drew.

Drew sighed. "Hey, I caught that look on your face just now. At least tell me there *is* a woman mixed up in this somehow. Give me that much satisfaction."

"Okay, there's a woman." And Julian's guts tightened a little as he said it. The words sounded like an admission and way too close to some kind of commitment.

"Yeah, see? Like I said!" Drew grinned from ear to ear. He'd heard the story of Julian's marriage and knew full well that the experience had left Julian completely relationship shy. "'Bout time, too, pal."

"So what have you heard around post?" Julian pressed.

Drew shrugged. "Honestly, there's nothing we haven't heard already. Mysterious sightings of people hanging around outside the fence. That missing transport truck hasn't been found. No one seems to be able to put any names to the people involved. I'm beginning to think we're being led to a dead end on purpose."

Julian recalled that Kelsey had said something similar about the mixed-up inventory in her warehouse. It did, indeed, seem as though someone was out to confuse the hell out of them all.

The trick was to sort out what was real from what was not.

"And as far as that AWOL," Drew continued, "I didn't find out much. He bought a couple of park passes into Disney World, but those could be used anytime for something like a year. The parents haven't heard from him in weeks and they didn't know much about the girlfriend except that he's always with her. I couldn't even get a name. I'm not detecting a great in-law relationship if that girl marries Rigley."

Julian fervently hoped Rigley was marrying her at this

very moment, or at least having a good time with her, because the alternative Kelsey suggested was grim.

"You want me to send someone to go look for him in Florida?" asked Drew.

"If you don't mind," Julian said. "I think I'd like to go there myself and see if I can find him."

Drew's expression darkened. "This must have something to do with our elusive thieves if you want to go tailing after an AWOL yourself."

"I hope not, but that's what I'd like to go find out." Besides, maybe Kelsey would be more willing to talk to him again if she knew he'd turned over even the most unlikely stone in his search for her dead soldier.

"Suit yourself," Drew said. "I'll watch the fort," he added with a grin.

Julian gave the man a nod and then took off running again and Drew didn't bother to try to keep up. As he rounded the last curve in the track, Julian made a mental note to ask his paralegal how far he'd gotten in finding out all the people on post who owned black trucks. He had a partial license number to go on and Julian wanted to pursue every one of them, given that Kelsey's safety could be involved. No matter what actually happened to her in the warehouse, someone could be following her. He would make sure he knew everything he could find out about anyone who might intend her harm.

The other task he had for his paralegal would seem rather bizarre. And he hadn't yet decided how he would go about the inquiry. What he needed to know was the name of Drew Mitchum's cologne and how much of the stuff was sold on post and in the surrounding area. But figuring that out wouldn't be easy. Somehow, he'd have to find a way even if doing so implicated the man he'd come to think of as a good friend.

"I CAN'T BELIEVE YOU actually went to the pool hall with Bill when I gave you every excuse to come with me to help nurse my headache. What were you thinking?" Kelsey asked as soon as she caught up with her suddenly very busy sister late in the afternoon the day after their potentially criminal activities. Shannon stood washing a very grungy-looking mutt in a huge sink at the animal control office where Kelsey had tracked her down.

Shannon looked up and sighed, then went back to scrubbing. "He was kinda cute. And I didn't have anything else to do. I thought maybe I could get more information for you. Which I did," she said proudly.

"What do you mean?" Kelsey worried that Shannon had involved herself too deeply in the whole ill-conceived plan.

"Well, your Ryan Rigley recently bought his girlfriend a huge, expensive diamond ring. Bill thought that he'd gone back to Florida to pop the big question. Rigley bought Disney World tickets, too. Not that it would be a surprise to the girl. She'd been nagging him to get married for a while now."

"Wow, that's really great to know," Kelsey said. As much as she wanted to protect Shannon, she couldn't help but admire her information-gathering skills. "So what happened with Bill in the end?"

Shannon made a face as she untangled a knot in the soggy dog's fur. "I realized pretty quickly he had issues. I let him win at a couple of games of pool. Then I told him that the redhead on the other side of the hall had been making eyes at him and encouraged him to go on over. I got out of there the minute his back was turned. No more troubled men for me! I figure it's progress that I could spot this one's problems so quickly and take myself out of the situation."

"Yes! That's great! How did you get home?" This was

her way of finding out if Shannon had actually made it home at all. The guest room door had been closed when Kelsey'd awakened this morning and she'd gone straight to work without checking to see if Shannon slept behind it. Later in the day, as the inventory had progressed at the warehouse, Kelsey admitted to herself that she hadn't been ready this morning to find out that Shannon had been out all night with someone she had met only hours before.

Shannon deftly skipped over the question. "Yeah, I'm making progress on the male companionship end of things. Too bad those skills don't transfer so well to the workplace, right? I mean, what should I put on my resume? 'Able to dump troubled men in a single game of pool' or 'Extracts herself from difficult situations involving the opposite sex with speed and agility.' No one really thinks those are worth much in an office environment."

Kelsey heard the humor in her sister's voice and laughed out loud. "But how about 'Easily extracts critical information from obscure sources.'"

Shannon smiled at that. Then added, "Ken picked me up when I called him. Now, there's a decent sort of guy."

The humor left Kelsey instantly as a bad feeling crept over her. "How did you explain being at the pool hall in the first place?"

"I told him I'd helped you with Bill, but now I was ready to go. He was very nice about it."

Kelsey's heart seemed to flip over inside her chest. "You told him about me wanting to get inside Bill's room?" The legality of what she'd done remained a question. Images of a view through jailhouse bars flashed across her mind.

Shannon stopped lathering the dog long enough to focus on her sister's face. The dog squirmed, but Shannon kept a firm grip on the slippery beast. "No, I didn't tell him that.

I'm not stupid, you know. If what we did last night had been something you could broadcast, you wouldn't have been so nervous."

Relief washed over Kelsey. "I know you're not stupid. And I'm very grateful for your help. I just forgot to mention to you that we probably don't want our activities to get back to anyone." She found herself barely resisting a furtive glance around the kennel.

Shannon had the audacity to laugh. "My suspicion is that you don't want a certain major, last name sounds like Fordham, to find out what you were up to."

Kelsey felt herself beginning to blush. How had her sister figured that out with so little to go on? But she would admit nothing and she knew how to turn the tables on her sister's probing.

"Did you stay over at Ken's place all night?" There it was. Direct and to the point.

It was Shannon's turn to blush. "No."

"Then why are you blushing?"

"Because I wanted to. He and Buddy are very good at taking my mind off Bella," Shannon admitted. "And I'm not good at sleeping alone." She sighed and began to rinse off the soapy dog in the sink.

She looked up at Kelsey. "I don't recall the last time I was with a guy who didn't want to jump me as soon as we were alone. But Ken is respectful. He treats me like a lady. So I couldn't disappoint him by inviting myself over to his apartment, could I?"

"I can see how that would have been difficult," Kelsey agreed, gaining a new respect for Shannon. And for Ken.

"But I spent this morning at the K9 office helping him with paperwork. We made some calls to see if anyone's seen Bella and then we put up more signs. But I can't just hang around him all the time. He's got an important job. So I decided to do some volunteer work here at the animal control office until Ken gets off from work."

"Wow, sounds like you had a full day already."

"I need to stay busy, you know? If I don't, I get all teary-eyed, thinking about Bella. When I have time on my hands, I keep going over and over in my head that if I'd only kept a better hold of her leash or if I'd just been able to grab it as she started to run away…"

Kelsey reached over and patted her sister's shoulder. "Don't beat yourself up over it, Shan. It could have happened to anyone."

"Not to you," she said flatly.

"What do you mean? Of course it could happen to me." A shining example of that was the fact that she'd somehow lost a dead body and about an hour of her life to unconsciousness a few days ago.

"I just wish I could be more like you, that's all. You're always so sure of yourself."

"Except for last night when I couldn't have managed without you," she pointed out.

Shannon smiled again. "I supposed that's true. And I'd like to know if you found whatever it was you were looking for in Rigley's room."

"I got to look around and that was my goal. But I'm still not sure of the significance of what I got to see. And I wanted to talk to you about that." Kelsey hesitated.

Shannon looked at her with concern in her eyes. "What?"

"I just wanted to know if you'd be okay on your own for a day or two even though we haven't found Bella yet. I've requested leave so I can go to Florida where this Rigley guy is supposed to be. He didn't have leave to go and maybe I can get him to come back here before he gets into too much trouble." She waited to see if this would sound plausible to Shannon.

Shannon didn't respond right away, but Kelsey felt the weight of her sister's gaze on her. After a long moment, the younger O'Roark released her from scrutiny. But then she said, "I still don't understand why this soldier is your problem. Don't you have MPs to go looking for the AWOLs? Or what about that Major Fordham? Shouldn't *he* be the one to go tracking this missing person?"

Well, yes. But Kelsey didn't want to have to explain. "I'm just trying to keep Rigley out of trouble if I can help it." She hated lying to her sister, but she could find no purpose in involving Shannon any deeper than she already had. Shannon would only worry.

Kelsey felt sure she could do enough worrying for the both of them.

Shannon shot her a disbelieving look. "Fine. Don't tell me, if you don't want to. Go off to Florida, if that's what you want to do. I'll be fine." The words were conciliatory, but the tone was completely the opposite.

"Shannon," Kelsey began, exasperation putting an edge to her voice. "I promise I'll tell you everything as soon as I can." And she meant it. There would come a time when this mess would be sorted out and then she'd tell Shannon the whole story. Kelsey very much wanted to believe that time would come soon.

Shannon picked up a blow-dryer—Kelsey had never thought about dog grooming before, but now she was getting a full tour—and applied it to the sodden mutt. "I can't help worrying about you when you're behaving so mysteriously," she said. "At least tell me it all has something to do with that man."

"Which man?" Kelsey heard herself say before she realized that this was not where she wanted the conversation to go.

"Fordham, of course. You blush every time I mention his name. And there you go again!" There was a wicked gleam in Shannon's eyes.

Did she blush at the mere mention of Julian? Good heavens! Kelsey barely resisted the urge to put her palms over her heated cheeks. "Okay, it all has to do with Julian Fordham—in a strange sort of way."

Shannon smiled. "Then you can go to Florida for a few days," she decreed as if Kelsey had required her permission before departure. "I'll be fine."

"Just promise you'll call me the instant you find Bella. I'm worried about her, too." And to Kelsey's surprise, that statement was true. Maybe absence made the heart grow fonder, after all.

"SHE BOUGHT A TICKET for where? Well, that ought to keep her out of our business for a while," declared the Wolf. "Too bad she didn't take her boyfriend with her."

"What do you want me to do now?" asked Private Earlman. "I can't follow her to Florida."

"I guess you get some leisure time until she gets back."

This was the best news he'd heard in days. But his happiness came too quickly. The Wolf came up with another idea.

"On second thought, I need you to do something else for me. Do you know anything about dogs?"

The private stifled a groan. "I'm allergic," he said, hoping for a reprieve.

"Go buy some antihistamine because I need you to take the creature off my hands for a few days. I've got another fish to reel in and the dog is in the way."

THE FLIGHT SOUTH HAD been uneventful, but Kelsey's conversation with Rigley's parents proved fruitless.

"I do not approve of that girl," said Mrs. Rigley for the hundredth time. "She's no good for my boy. And now you say he's gone missing because of her."

"Are you certain you haven't got an address for her?" she asked one last time. Neither the mother nor father had seen their son in many weeks. They were as certain as Julian that he was with that girl about whom they knew so little.

"He's with her. He's always with her," complained Mr. Rigley in the same monotone he'd used during the entire conversation. "Talked about taking her on a fancy trip for her birthday. Like he could afford such a thing."

"Like he could afford such a thing!" said Mrs. Rigley with more feeling. "She is forever wanting him to buy her things."

Kelsey had reason to agree with the Rigleys as she thought about the expensive diamond ring and Disney tickets their son had purchased. The young man clearly seemed willing to spend lots of money on his girlfriend and Kelsey wondered how a lowly private could afford such extravagance.

"If you could just give me the girl's name, that would help a great deal," she said, giving up the effort to glean more from the interview.

"Her name is Virginia, I think. He calls her Ginny," said the father. Abruptly and without explanation, he heaved himself out of his easy chair and walked away. Kelsey heard him trudging up the stairs a moment later.

"That's another thing that isn't right. Shouldn't I know her last name and who her people are? Shouldn't she have come for a visit by now, if she thinks she's going to marry our son?" exclaimed the mother.

"Yes, I'm sure she should have," agreed Kelsey.

"You'll let us know when you find him, won't you?" Mrs. Rigley asked.

"Of course I will. And I'm sure I'll find him very soon. We'll get this whole thing straightened out." Kelsey's words were meant to allay the woman's fears, but none of the reassurances were likely to be true in the long run if Ryan turned out to be the man who'd fallen that fateful night.

Mrs. Rigley stood. Kelsey took her cue and gathered her purse and beret. "If this girlfriend calls you, would you give her my numbers?" She held out a piece of paper with her phone numbers on it. The woman nodded and led the way to the front door of the cozy Florida home.

As they were saying goodbye and promising once again to contact each other if they heard anything, Mr. Rigley clomped back down the stairs.

"I remembered he had a picture of the two of them tacked to his bulletin board in his bedroom. Here."

He handed her the photograph and she smiled gratefully. This could make all the difference.

Back in her car, she pondered her next move. She was on a difficult mission to prove that Rigley had not come to Florida at all, but lay dead somewhere after falling from her lift. It seemed like a hopeless task. But since she was here, she might as well show the picture around a few places. There was a hotel owned and operated by the Department of Defense right on the Disney grounds that enjoyed all the privileges of the ones run by the enormous entertainment company. The prices were low, by Orlando standards, to make vacations affordable for soldiers like Rigley. If someone recognized Rigley from a recent visit, she'd know she had to go home and talk to a psychologist as quickly as possible. If Rigley was alive and well and hanging out with his girlfriend, he couldn't be her dead soldier. And then maybe Julian was right that there had never been a dead soldier at all.

JULIAN DECIDED to check in to the Florida hotel first and then make some phone calls from his room. He would talk to the parents. Maybe the kid was taking it easy at his childhood home by now. That would make things simple. If not, he'd have to try to hunt him down, wherever he might be. Julian's other cases would just have to take a back seat.

He got a cab to take him straight to the Shades of Green hotel. It was convenient and inexpensive, set up by the Department of Defense so military members could afford to vacation at Disney World. He'd heard it remained financially independent of taxpayer dollars, even after its renovation. And there was always a possibility that if Rigley wasn't with his parents, he'd be there. Rigley's roommate had insisted the Specialist's girlfriend wanted to vacation at Disney.

At the check-in desk, the perky clerk in a summery green polo shirt smiled at him warmly. "I can see by your uniform that you're in the army, but I'm afraid I'll still need to see your DOD ID card," she said.

He fished it out and handed it over to her. Then he watched her tap on a keyboard.

"I don't seem to have a reservation for you, sir."

"I didn't make one. I just need a single night's stay. I'm investigating a case. I'm with the Criminal Investigative Division," he added, since his army ID card didn't specify that.

Her smile went a little sorrowful and Julian could feel bad news coming. "I'm sorry, sir, but we're booked solid. No room at the inn, so to speak. It's always very crowded in the summertime. We're usually booked up six months in advance, unless there's a cancellation."

He closed his eyes and searched for patience. "Where else can I get a room for the night around here?" he asked.

"I can put you up at the Contemporary for the same price."

"That's fine. Listen, can you tell me if you've seen this man?" He held up Rigley's picture.

She blinked rapidly a few times. "My, my, there sure are a lot of people looking for that young man! But as I told the nice woman a little while ago, I've never seen him before."

Julian's senses went on red alert. "What do you mean?" he asked gently so as not to frighten away a possible lead. "Who else was looking for him?" But he had a terrible feeling he knew.

"Well, the lady who took the very last room we had, for one," she said, her smile back in place. "She had a different photograph, but I'm fairly certain it was the same man."

Inside, he began to burn with anger. She'd gone too far now, interfering in his work.

"An officer, brown hair, about this high?" He held up his hand about eye level.

The woman nodded.

"Captain O'Roark." He said it as a statement, but the receptionist took it as a question.

"I'm not allowed to give you the names of our guests," she said, looking a little worried. Perhaps she could sense his fury.

"You don't have to," he bit out. "Just tell me what room she's in."

"I can't do that either, of course," she said, backing up a step.

"That's fine. I'll just knock on every single door until I find her," he said in a low, menacing voice.

"And I'll call the police," she countered, raising her chin a fraction.

"I *am* the police," he said just short of a bellow.

She cocked an eyebrow at him. "Not in Florida, not in Orlando and certainly not in Disney World."

Okay, what she said was true. He needed a different strategy. He sucked in a deep breath and let it out. "Yes, of course. I apologize if I sounded surly. It's just that Captain O'Roark isn't an investigator and she's interfered with an ongoing investigation. She could get into trouble doing what she's doing," he said in a much milder tone. He added a smile that had been known to make stubborn women yield in the past.

She relaxed slightly. "I understand. But she seemed very nice."

"She *is* nice." He wanted to get on the receptionist's good side and agreeing with everything she said might help. Besides, Kelsey *was* nice. She knew the names of all the people she came into contact with, from her superiors to the night janitor. If he tried to say another negative thing about her, people who knew her would rise to her defense and he'd never get anywhere. "I didn't mean to imply she was anything but nice. In fact, I'm really just trying to protect her."

"You mean she could be in danger?" The receptionist glanced around as if the danger lurked in the wings of the hotel at this very moment.

"There's no danger here," he said reassuringly. "But she's messing around in something that could get her into hot water. I don't want to see that happen. Do you?"

"No, of course not." Her resolve to keep him from Kelsey seemed to waver.

"Maybe you could just connect me to her room by phone. You can do that without breaking the rules, right?"

Her face brightened. "Yes, of course! We do that all the time. The house phone is right over there."

Too far, he saw dejectedly. If he stood at the phone, he wouldn't be able to see what room number the receptionist punched in to connect them. He'd have to hope that luck would put Kelsey in her room and answering the phone right now. "Thank you," he said. Then he went to the indicated phone.

The line rang and rang, then a message service picked up. "What the hell are you doing in Orlando, Kelsey?" he barked into the phone. "Call my cell phone immediately." He gave the number and used a good amount of will power to keep from slamming down the receiver.

Maybe she had her cell with her and he could reach her that way. Scrolling through his phone book, he realized he'd deleted her number, probably a year ago when he'd decided she was more than he could handle, though he couldn't remember doing it. He hadn't put it back in when she'd waltzed once again into his life. Frustration seeped into him through his pores. It was all he could do not to start throwing things.

Instead, he called Sergeant McKay back at the office. "I need a picture of Kelsey O'Roark sent to my cell phone ASAP. And her cell phone number."

"You need a photograph of Captain O'Roark?" repeated the paralegal as if he didn't believe it.

"Yes. How long will that take?"

"Um, let's see," he said, apparently recovering from his surprise. "If I can get her photo to come up on the computer, I should be able to paste it right into an e-mail. You can access your mail from your phone, right?"

"Yes. That's good. Really, good work," he said. "Just send it off as quickly as you can."

"Give me five minutes," the sergeant promised. "I'll call you with the phone number when I get it."

And sure enough, after a couple of laps pacing the lobby area, Julian heard his cell make the tone that indicated he'd received mail. And there it was. Kelsey's official photo on the tiny color monitor of his cell phone. Ah, the wonders of modern technology! He smiled grimly and marched over to the concierge.

"Have you seen this woman?" he asked as he held out his phone and his CID badge. "I need to find her."

"Um," said the young man at the desk. "I'm not sure if I'm supposed to—"

But he didn't need to say more. Walking along the hallway toward a first-floor hotel room strode Kelsey O'Roark, wearing a towel wrapped just beneath her armpits and presumably a swimsuit underneath. As Julian stalked forward to intercept her, his mouth watered at the thought of Kelsey in nothing but a bikini.

CHAPTER NINE

SHE SAW HIM coming toward her and stopped dead in her tracks. Water dripped down her skin in lazy rivulets and the indoor air-conditioning had begun to make her shiver. This is what she got for dashing out for a quick swim to clear her head when she should have continued making phone calls to try to track down Rigley. Too late to rethink her choices now.

The towel she'd wrapped herself in seemed entirely inadequate at this moment. She wondered if she could flee in the other direction, but then he was suddenly right in front of her.

"What are you doing here!" he demanded.

She didn't want him to mistake her shivers for any kind of trepidation, so she squared her shoulders. "I don't have to tell you why I'm here, Major Fordham. But, if you must know, I'm on leave. So, if you'll excuse me…" She tried to step around him.

He blocked her way. If he'd been the wet one, there would be steam coming off of him, he was so angry. "Don't give me that vacation nonsense, Kelsey. You're here looking for Rigley. I want to know why you would do such a thing."

"I'm on leave," she insisted, knowing all too well that she could be accused of interfering with an ongoing investigation if she didn't tread very carefully.

"Damn it, Kelsey!" he shouted, then he turned away from her and ran his fingers through his hair. When he glanced back at her, he added, "You're shivering."

"I'm wet," she agreed, realizing too late that her choice of words could sound suggestive. She closed her eyes in frustration, trying to block out the bad turn of luck that had this particular man standing in front of her while she dripped water onto the carpet. "I'd like to go to my room now and change into clothes." That sounded a little suggestive, too, somehow, but she couldn't seem to help it. She held up her room key as if to prove she had no intentions of going on the lam and only wanted to get dressed.

Before she could react, he plucked her key from her fingers. "Which room?"

"One twenty," she said, noting once again that words had slipped out of her mouth before she'd fully considered the consequences. It had to be the shock of having him show up like this, because she saw now that it might have been smarter to keep her room number to herself.

Without another word, he marched the additional fifteen or so feet to her door and unlocked it for her. He held it open so she could pass through before him. She sidled by, wary of touching him, yet aware that she could feel his heat as she passed. He followed her inside, as she'd known he would.

"Change into something warm before you freeze to death," he commanded. "Your teeth are chattering."

She knew they were. She'd like to think it was only because of the chill air. But this man in her room would have made her quiver under the best of circumstances. In the current context, she couldn't seem to find any control over what she thought or felt. A gnawing edginess suffused her and she wanted to shout and curse and kick things. Instead, she collected a sweatshirt and jeans from where they'd been flung over the arm of a chair.

"I don't need your permission to be in Florida, Julian," she said as she passed him again. She managed to stop short of saying something childish, like "you're not the boss of me."

"You do if you're asking people about Specialist Rigley. Which you are, in fact, doing!"

She kept on going until she was in the relative safety of the small bathroom. He'd followed her so closely, she nearly slammed the door in his face. Nevertheless, she couldn't help but rejoice that Julian was showing so much emotion. Finally!

He just shouted right through the door, "You're interfering with an ongoing investigation!"

Kelsey groaned at that because she had no retort prepared. She'd hoped to get away with her interference by not getting caught at it. Again without thinking, she said, "Is that a crime?"

"Yes! It could be. You have no business being here. I'm sending you home immediately." He seemed to be working himself into a real fury now.

She decided to concentrate on drying herself off, a somewhat more sensual experience than it ordinarily might have been if Julian hadn't been standing just outside her door making her imagine possibilities that were completely inappropriate. Trying to put order to her wayward thoughts, she hung up her dripping swimsuit and tugged on the sweatshirt. Then she realized she hadn't brought any underwear in with her. She'd have to go commando in the jeans. The very thought of doing so in front of Julian made her skin tingle and her blood sing through her veins.

He might be annoyed with her right at the moment, and she with him, but that did little to thwart her ever-present desire for the man.

As HE SPOKE to her through the bathroom door—or perhaps he shouted—Julian's gaze fell upon Kelsey's personal stuff strewn all over the room. He'd noticed her things without judgment when he'd first entered, but now the individual items began to register. There on the floor sat an open suitcase filled with civilian clothes. A short, silky nightgown lay across the top and a bottle of scented body lotion stood on the floor nearby. He lifted his face as if he could smell it from here, so well did he remember her fragrance. That scent wafted through his memory, light and tantalizing. And the sound of her voice coming from beyond the door retreated into the background. All his senses turned themselves over to the visual stimuli around him.

On the foot of the bed sat a sexy pair of shorts and a tank top that he just knew would show off her figure to its finest. Nearby, a discarded pair of lacy panties, so recently on her body, suggested thoughts that didn't belong in his mind at the moment. His mouth suddenly began to water. He vaguely knew she said something else from inside the bathroom, but his brain had shifted gears and his pulse throbbed in his ears.

He tried to look away, tried to think of other things, tried to get a grip on his libido. But there, draped over the back of the chair, lay a bra in light blue lace to match the panties. Did his sweet and no-nonsense Kelsey actually wear these sexy undergarments? The proof was before his eyes. He felt certain she'd look very good in them. An image streamed through his mind. And the air suddenly seemed thicker and warmer.

He wiped his brow and with a surge of willpower turned away and faced the exit. Nothing but the instructions for fire escape there. Nothing that should remind him of just how much he wanted to make love with the woman in the bathroom.

"Are you listening to me?" she asked as she flung open the door so hard it bashed against the side of the tub. "How was I supposed to know you'd be doing *anything* about Rigley? Last I heard, you didn't want to ask any questions. You didn't think he was my dead soldier. You—"

In a shout borne partially of sexual frustration, he said, "I *still* don't think he's your dead guy! I only came out here to make you happy. No stone unturned, and all that! Anything to please you. Your wish is my command!"

Okay. That was *not* what he should have said, he suddenly realized. But when he saw Kelsey's expression soften, he couldn't regret it. He wanted to kiss her, to hold her, to sweep her toward the bed that sat so conveniently near at hand. His blood pulsed through his veins a little faster.

A smile tugged at her lips. "You came here for *me?*"

Drowning in a confusion of basic needs and complex emotions, he could only think of retreat. Something to bring back the anger seemed like a good idea if it would replace the almost painful need he felt.

"I still don't think Rigley is your dead guy," he insisted. But he'd lost his fire for the argument. And he'd thought of another way to deal with his yearning. He could take a step closer, draw her into his arms…

"Well, then where is he?" she asked evenly.

Her eyes were a very appealing chocolate brown, he realized as he managed to come up with an answer that sounded at least marginally coherent. "I haven't had a chance to find out. The first question I asked led me to realize you'd been here ahead of me." He looked away, down at his shoes, sideways to the wallpaper, forward to that sexy demi-bra draped across the chair. Argh!

His cheeks felt as if they were on fire. His blood burned, too, and seemed to be heading rapidly and in large quantities to southern portions of his body. Any minute, she would notice.

"Did you talk to his parents already?" he managed to ask even though he barely recalled the topic of conversation. Would she let him kiss her? His gaze drifted to her mouth.

"We can talk about that later," she said with a sweet, sexy smile. "Right now, I want to hear more about you doing anything to please me."

And then he noticed that she'd been studying his mouth, too. The hunger in her eyes made his own desire surge. He didn't need an engraved invitation.

Especially when her wish seemed to match his own so perfectly.

When he stepped closer to her, she mirrored his move. In the next instant, he'd pressed his mouth to hers, slid his tongue along her lips, delved within. She wrapped her arms around his neck, welcoming him into her embrace. He splayed his hands across her back, instantly noted she wore nothing beneath her sweatshirt and pulled her closer. Not close enough. Their clothes were in the way. But he couldn't stop kissing her to do anything about that just yet. She tasted so good, he just needed to keep on exploring her with his tongue as the world seemed to shrink away to nothing. There was only Kelsey, her body snugly against his, her mouth beneath his own.

But then she began to take matters into her own hands. He felt her slip his tie from its knot, undo the buttons of his shirt, unbuckle his belt. All the while, she let him kiss her, let him take his fill of her mouth until he needed more than that. Greedily, he slid his lips to her jaw and throat and that delicate place just beneath her earlobe, tasting. She moaned, inciting him to a blood-pounding pitch of desire. And suddenly he needed everything from her, all of it, now, now, now.

All at once, she pulled away and he would have murmured his protest except that in the next instant, she swept the sweatshirt over her head and tossed it aside. Every muscle in his body froze and he stared, transfixed. She was perfect. He was in heaven. But she wouldn't let him be still to savor the sight of her. Instead, she walked backward, tugging him by his opened shirt as she went. In seconds, they were at the foot of the bed.

He looked into her eyes then, because somehow a vague doubt had crossed his mind. He wanted her desperately, but he knew that making love with her would mean something. His libido refused to get out of the way to allow him to figure out what that something might be. But he sensed that he was on the precipice of…something.

She tumbled back onto the bed, taking him down with her. Full length, his body pressed to hers. And no doubts could stand under the onslaught of her seduction.

KELSEY HAD NEVER FELT so frenzied with desire in her entire life. Not that there had been an inordinate number of times when she'd given in to desire. Mostly, she'd been too busy with her education and her career to take up with men. But this was Julian. There was something about him that drew her.

As she helped him out of his unbuttoned shirt and then his T-shirt, she saw that his body was everything she'd imagined. Taut muscles hugged his torso and his arms were strong, his shoulders broad. As he hovered over her, she couldn't keep herself from running her palms over his flesh. She felt him quiver beneath her touch.

"You're perfect," she whispered. "And I want you."

His response was to kiss her again while his hand slid over her skin from hip to breast and back again. Then his mouth skimmed down her throat and across her collarbone until he captured one hardened nipple between his lips. She heard a soft moan escape from her throat as she writhed with pleasure beneath him.

"Please, please," she found herself saying.

"Yes," he agreed. And he unbuttoned her jeans and tugged them down her legs. He flung them aside and then knelt beside her.

She could see him panting and a sheen covered his skin. His erection strained against the cloth of his slacks. Those should come off, she thought, and she reached to help.

He put his hands over hers, stopping her.

She could hardly believe it. She stared at him, holding her breath while she waited for him to explain.

"I'm sorry," he said. "I just realized I left my bag by the front desk."

She stared. How could something like that intrude into his consciousness at a time like this? But she saw that his cheeks were flushed and his breathing labored.

Before she could inquire, he added, "I'm not sure I'd even have anything in the bag that we could use." Scooting away from her, he turned his back, dropped his feet over the side of the bed, ran his fingers through his hair. "I mean, even if I had a condom in there, it would be old." Then he laughed ruefully. "Obviously a lack of planning on my part."

Ah, so *that* was the problem! She found herself amused, even in the face of delayed gratification. She crawled to him and wrapped her arms around him from behind. "Well, I'm not going to save the day by saying I have condoms stashed in my overnight case. I'm not a one-night-stand kind of woman." She saw his spine straighten at her words, but he needed to hear the truth. "But the night isn't lost yet," she murmured into his ear. "I bet there are condoms for sale at the hotel store. And you can retrieve your suitcase on your way. What do you think?"

With a light touch of his fingers, he stroked along her arm where it draped across his chest. Then he tipped his head in her direction, putting them temple to temple. "I think I'll go see what there is at the hotel store," he agreed.

She gave a surreptitious sigh of relief. She wanted tonight in this man's arms—and a lot more than just tonight, if she could get it. But knowing Julian the way she did, the following days would have to take care of themselves.

He stood and the muscles of his back bunched and flexed as he slid his T-shirt once more onto his sleek body. Kelsey just knelt on the bed and watched him. Somehow, she didn't feel the slightest bit self-conscious about her own lack of clothing. And she hoped that if his last glimpse was of a naked and hopeful woman, he would actually come back to her. Because there was every possibility he'd think too much on his way to the store. Then he might decide he should get his own room. And that would really hurt.

"I'll be right back," he said as he hitched his pants back together and buckled his belt.

"Promise?" she said, unable to stop herself even though she knew she sounded needy.

He turned his head to look at her for the first time since

he'd stopped kissing her. His gaze went from her eyes to her body and then slid slowly back to her eyes. "I promise," he said. "I'll leave the rest of my uniform here for collateral."

With that, he pocketed her room key and took himself off wearing only his army pants and white T-shirt. The darker green stripes down the outer seam of the slacks gave him away as an officer, but he didn't seem to care. Kelsey scrambled off the bed, turning off all but one dim light and picking up her clothes. Then she straightened and folded back the covers, leaving fresh white sheets exposed.

Standing by the bed without a stitch of clothing on, she had a moment of feeling both giddy and wanton. It had been a long time since she'd been with a man. But in her eagerness to be with Julian, she worried that she'd seemed too easy. And yet, she didn't want to pretend to be demure just for the sake of appearances.

She slipped into her nightgown anyway, feeling a little less wanton, but no less giddy, as she awaited Julian's return.

HE HADN'T BOTHERED to put on his light green shirt and now he wondered if he should have. Glancing down, he saw with relief that his erection would no longer draw anyone's gaze to the front of his trousers, at least. But he felt half dressed and disheveled. To go buy condoms in this condition seemed the epitome of bad taste.

Too late. He'd just have to muddle through in the T-shirt and slacks. Because no matter how many doubts now converged within his mind, he had promised her he'd be back. A rash promise, perhaps. But an oath he wouldn't break. Most of him didn't want to break it. Some of him wanted to run as fast as he could toward the airport.

It wasn't that he didn't care for her. He did. He cared

for her more than he wanted to admit. It was just that he didn't know if he could give her what she wanted. What she deserved. She wasn't a "one-night-stand kind of woman." So what would she expect of him after tonight?

Could he give it?

Did he dare to try?

As he retrieved his bag from the woman at the front desk, he gently shook his head as if to dislodge the uncertainties that plagued him. His therapist had encouraged him to embark on a new relationship now that so many years had passed since the breakup of his marriage. He wanted to do that embarking with Kelsey.

He got directions to the hotel store and headed that way after slipping the strap of the suitcase over his shoulder. As he approached the wide window front, his steps slowed. He could see from here that the person at the cash register was a female who looked to be about twelve years old, though he knew she had to be at least sixteen. Just great.

Glancing heavenward as if to question the sense of humor of the gods, Julian went forward. Feeling like a teenager, he chose two bottles of cola, two packs of chips and a bag of chocolate chip cookies. Then he approached the register, behind which were kept the medicinal items like aspirin and, of course, condoms.

As he walked forward, at the pace of a condemned man, he thought back to other times he'd purchased this particular item. He couldn't recall ever doing so under such difficult circumstances. They'd always been a small part of a larger group of purchases at a grocery store, nothing noticeable, nothing to draw scrutiny. But now he was going to have to ask this fresh-faced girl to hand over a pack of them. And he knew his own face had to be some deep shade of red.

"Hello!" chirped the teenager. "Is this everything, then?"

"Nope. I'll also need some condoms." There! He'd been a man about it. Just spit it right out while he fished his wallet from his back pocket. He hadn't quite been able to make eye contact while he'd said it, but maybe that was best. He didn't want to embarrass *her*, too.

Her smile never wavered. "Okay. What kind?" She turned to where the various items were hanging on a rack behind her and eyed the selection.

Kind? "Um. It doesn't matter."

"Really? I always thought guys were sort of particular about this kinda thing."

Okay, now this was beginning to seem funny, even to him. But she appeared to be earnest and he held back his nervous laughter. Still, he heard the joke leaving his mouth before he could stop himself. "Well, I'd like to say extra large, but that would just be wishful thinking. Just any kind will be fine."

She seemed amused rather than offended, thank heaven. "You don't care if they're ribbed or lubricated?"

He was about to say he didn't care, but then noted that this young person seemed to know an awful lot about condoms. "Will *she* care?" he ventured, figuring this youthful female knew more about it than he did.

She gave him a kindhearted smile and reached for whatever she deemed appropriate. "Just one? There's only two to a pack."

"Uh…" He hesitated.

Without waiting for an answer from him, she threw four packs onto the counter. "There you go. I've given you a variety. That should hold you awhile."

"Ambitious," he said dryly, as his brain suggested he ask if she got paid a commission on her sales. He stopped himself, however, and decided to close his mouth and keep it that way.

"You're going to wine and dine her, I see," she commented as she scanned the colas and cookies into the register.

He nodded mutely and handed over enough cash to cover the total.

She gave him his change, smiling sweetly the entire time. "Hey! Good luck!" she called as he made a hasty retreat.

From the doorway, he flashed her an embarrassed smile and bolted into the hallway.

But now came the more difficult part. He had to reenter Kelsey's room. He had to walk in there with his stash of junk food and his four packs of condoms, two per pack, and see if she'd had second thoughts.

What worried him most was that if he could have so many doubts in the few minutes he'd been gone, then so could she.

CHAPTER TEN

HER HEART HAMMERED as she heard the card key rasp in the lock. The click of the door as it opened made her want to shout with happiness. For the past several minutes she'd been trying to convince herself not to be disappointed if he didn't come back.

But then, like a hopeful bride, she'd slipped between the sheets and awaited him there, wanting to make him comfortable about reigniting their mutual fire. The single light gave off a limited glow, setting a mood as conducive to love as she could create in a hotel room usually inhabited by children and their parents.

"Hi," he said as he put a bag too large to contain only condoms onto the bed.

"Hi," she answered softly. "What did you get?"

"Snacks. For later." He smiled at her, warming her to her toes.

"Good thinking."

"I'm just gonna duck into the bathroom for a second."

"Okay." Just come out soon, she resisted saying. She needed him, wanted him.

He took his small suitcase with him and in another second she heard the water running in the sink. Once again, her heart skipped in anticipation when the door opened. And out came her Adonis, bare-chested and looking like one of the guys from those excellent commercials for boxer shorts.

He walked to her and she patted the space beside her where she longed for him to be. But he surprised her and kneeled at the bedside instead. He put his chin on his layered hands and looked at her. "Are you sure you still want me to stay?" he asked.

Now her heart just about melted, so sweet did he sound asking her permission in such a tender voice. She could really end up loving this guy. Really, really loving.

"I'm sure," she answered, gazing into his dark eyes so he'd see she had no doubts.

He didn't move right away, but continued to look at her, tipping his head slightly so their faces were more even with one another. "You're very beautiful," he whispered.

No one had ever said she was beautiful before. Cute, yes. Pretty, sometimes. But not beautiful. "You're sweet." She leaned forward and kissed him gently.

In the next moment, he slid between the sheets and she sighed with pleasure. What had seemed like a disaster when she'd first seen him in the hotel hallway now seemed like an incredible turn of luck as she shifted her body closer to his.

THE INSTANT JULIAN TOUCHED HER again, the flames inside him rekindled and burned away any lingering doubts. This was where he wanted to be—with this woman, in this bed, touching her, tasting her, making her writhe. Every arch of her back, every moan, made him want her more.

When she offered to sheath him in a condom, his admiration for her grew in proportion to his desire. Her blush made his heart ache with an unfamiliar yearning that had only a little to do with how beautiful she looked naked. He could hardly believe that this woman, this sweet and kind and wholesome woman, would do him the honor of making love with him. And all at once, he wanted more than just tonight with her.

But even as she concentrated on the latex, even as he throbbed and sizzled with the intensity of feeling her fingers slide down his length, even as she smiled at him in triumph and threw herself into his arms to kiss him passionately when the job was done—he knew there would be a price to pay for making love with Kelsey tonight. He didn't want to think about the price. His body didn't want him to think about it either.

"Now?" he asked, knowing that he'd probably owe his soul to her by morning.

"Now," she agreed, sliding down onto the sheets with him so they could once again be pressed together, pelvis to pelvis.

Passion and longing and love shined from those eyes of hers, taking his breath away and making his blood pump fiercely through his veins. Oh, how he wanted her love, no matter what the cost! Even if he had to breach the carefully constructed walls around his heart and find a way to love her in return.

With that acknowledgment, he made love with Kelsey, thrilling at her hushed cries of "Yes! Yes! Yes!" Time slowed as his heart rate accelerated. A seething, roiling tension filled him, turning into a need so raw and primal he wanted to howl. When he heard and saw and felt her reach that same ragged crest and then spike to that elemental pinnacle of rapture, he took those last few strokes and experienced the final quivers of exquisite pleasure.

IN THE MORNING, Kelsey was glad they were in a hotel room, because she wouldn't want to have been responsible for straightening up the place after the night they'd shared. The sheets and blankets were only partially on the bed. The empty cola bottles and snack bags were strewn everywhere. And the plastic from three of the condom packages lay crumpled on the nightstand.

"I bet you wish you could brag that you'd used all of these," she said to him as she indicated the remaining condoms. Sometime during the night before, she'd laughed when she'd seen that he'd bought four packs of two. He'd grinned wolfishly and promised to do his best to use each and every one.

"I think we did pretty well," he retorted with a chuckle.

"Yes, we did," she agreed as she stretched. "But it's already nearly noon. Time to get back to business." She leaped out of the bed before he could seduce her into the kind of business his expression indicated he'd like to get back to. She slipped her nightshirt over her head and let it cover her body while she gathered fresh clothing. "I'm taking a shower. Then I'm going to the parks with my picture to see if anyone remembers seeing Specialist Rigley."

"What?" He sat up, suddenly very alert. "You can't do that! It's *my* job to find Rigley. You need to stay out of it." To his credit, he looked as if he regretted having to say that to her.

"I'm not staying out of it," she insisted as she grabbed clean underwear from her bag on the floor. "But you can come with me to the park, if you want to." She went to the bathroom and turned on the water. He came in right behind her, naked as the day he was born—only a great deal larger and far sexier.

"At least tell me everything you got from his parents. I don't want to interview them again if I can avoid it. They must be worried enough." He closed the lid of the toilet and sat on it, looking at her expectantly.

She stood in bare feet on the cold tile floor and stared.

"What?" he said with that blank look that men seemed to have perfected. Then he looked down at where he was sitting. "Oh! Were you going to use this?"

She laughed out loud. "The possibility had crossed my mind, but I promise you can come back in and sit there while I take a shower. Just give me a few minutes."

His expression became sly as he stood up and sauntered near her. "Or I could join you in the hot, steamy, wet shower," he suggested wickedly.

"Hold that thought," she said as she nudged him out the door for a minute of privacy. He could be quite adorable when he wanted to be, she acknowledged. That had been a nice surprise. She'd never have expected him to have a playful side. But last night had taught her that he was a man of many talents.

It wouldn't last, of course. His commitment issues were bound to catch up with him. But she'd enjoy it while she could. She finished up, flushed, got a big towel ready and decided he could come back in. When she opened the door, he still stood there, leaning against the doorjamb and looking a little like a lost puppy.

"You can come in, but I think you need to stay out of my shower. You know what will happen if you join me."

He just grinned as he took his seat once more on the closed toilet lid.

She stepped into the shower and pulled the curtain across just enough to keep the water in while leaving a wide enough opening to still see him. He looked so cute sitting there. But then she noticed he had his notebook with him. He'd started writing things in it and a crease of concentration appeared between his brows.

Her heart tripped over itself as she looked at him, so handsome, so temporary.

"So tell me what Rigley's parents had to say." He glanced up from his notebook, smiled and added, "You look great all wet like that. You could be in a shampoo commercial."

She laughed, struck a pose with her microbottle of hotel shampoo, and then began to lather it into her hair. "Rigley's parents haven't seen him. He hasn't called either. But they didn't seem to think that was unusual. They complained a lot about his girlfriend who takes up all of his time. I got a picture of him and his girl. Did I mention that he bought tickets to Disney and a diamond ring? I think he planned to come here with this mysterious girlfriend to propose. I thought we could show the photograph around at Disney and see if anyone remembers seeing him."

"The park hosts and hostesses won't like that," he commented as he wrote.

"Who?"

"You know. The Disney security people. They won't want us poking around asking questions like that. I think I should go straight to them, one professional to another."

"And if they tell us we can't show our picture around, then what?"

"I don't know. I have to think about it. And I have a question. Why are you going to all this trouble looking for a man you think died in your warehouse?" He watched her now with those scrutinizing cop's eyes of his.

"Because if I don't find him, then maybe that will help you believe me so we can start looking for him elsewhere, like in a morgue."

"I've already contacted all the morgues around Fort Belvoir. There were no unidentified bodies and no one matching his description."

She sighed. "Well, if I *do* find him, I'll head straight home and make an emergency appointment with a psychiatrist. One way or the other, at least I'll be *doing* something constructive to end this madness." She soaped her body, gratified that Julian watched intently as her hands slid over her skin. "You know, last night was the first time since all this started that I actually slept without nightmares."

"Glad to be of service," he said solemnly. "Sorry you're having nightmares."

"Yeah, me, too." Wishing she didn't have to think about any of that right now, she ducked under the torrent of water and rinsed. When she emerged, he was standing up with the towel open in his two hands, ready to wrap her up.

She stepped out of the tub and into the towel, then leaned against him. He enfolded her in his arms and made her feel safe for long minutes. After a while, she felt stronger and stepped back. "Your turn in the shower."

"Dry your hair. I won't be long," he promised as he disappeared behind the curtain.

She dried her hair, happy that he'd acquiesced to her plan to search all the parks. And then he was there, standing behind her in the mirror in all his naked glory, smiling wickedly. "I like seeing you in your civvies," he said, referring to her shorts and T-shirt. "I only brought my uniform."

"Oh, no!" she said, turning to him. "You can't wear your army clothes!"

"Why not?"

"Because we'll never get anywhere asking questions about Rigley if everyone realizes it's an official inquiry."

"Well, that's fine because you're not going with me."

For a moment, disappointment washed through her. She'd misunderstood. Again. But then, she smiled. "Okay. You do things your way and I'll do them my way."

A crease of apprehension appeared between his eyebrows. "You can't interfere with an investigation."

"I'm not planning to. You just run along and get dressed in your uniform. I'll see you back here in a couple of hours."

"That's not going to work. I know you're just going to go out asking people about this all on your own," he accused. Then, with a sigh, he said, "I suppose there's no way I can make you stay here."

"Not without breaking the law," she retorted.

His gaze slid away as he concentrated. "I need to keep my eye on you."

She laughed and knew she'd won this minor skirmish. "You can't have it both ways. And I have the picture of Rigley with his girlfriend. If you're sticking with me, you're *not* wearing army clothes," she said as she watched him don clean underwear.

"Well, I don't have anything else." His expression had gone mutinous. Clearly, the man preferred to be in complete control of all situations and somewhere along the way, he'd lost it.

"Leave it to me. I'll be back in a flash." She grabbed her purse and dashed out the door, catching his bewildered and frustrated expression as she left.

AFTER THE DOOR CLICKED SHUT, he pulled a clean white T-shirt over his head and down his body. But then, for the first time in his adult life, he didn't know what to do. He'd spent every minute of every day since he'd left his father's control knowing exactly what he was supposed to do. Even in the dying days of his marriage he had no difficulty knowing how to proceed. From the day his ex-wife told him he was a heartless machine incapable of love, he'd calmly seen an attorney, signed papers, put in for a transfer and taken off his wedding ring. And he'd gone on with his life.

But now, standing in the middle of a hotel room where he'd spent nearly the entire night making passionate love with a woman who seemed made just for him, he had no idea what to do. He felt things stirring in the region of his heart that he'd never felt before. Or at least not since childhood. Painful, wonderful things. And in the darkest corners of his mind, he realized that this might be part of the price he'd have to pay for the night just past.

He sat heavily onto the edge of the bed, putting his elbows on his knees and his head in his hands. Breathing seemed difficult, the room suddenly too small. He had to get out of there, had to regroup.

He stood up again, but didn't move from his spot. Time seemed to drift by while he remained rooted to the floor as if he'd forgotten how to walk. And the next thing he knew, a key slid in and out of the lock, the mechanism clicked and the door swung open.

"That didn't take me long!" she said, breezing into the room with a shopping bag from the hotel store. "I picked out the perfect outfit." She rummaged into the bag, oblivious that he hadn't moved. Turning toward him, she held up the most ridiculous Hawaiian shirt in the brightest colors he'd ever seen.

"I'm not wearing that," he heard himself say. And a little of whatever had frozen him to the spot seemed to melt as he heard her laugh, light and airy and sensual.

"There wasn't much to choose from. It's this or the mouse shirt, babe." She threw the offensive garment at him and he caught it reflexively. "At least try it on."

Her good humor must have been infectious, and he realized that a smile tugged at his mouth. He held up the shirt, saw that it buttoned down the front, but figured he could put it on the same way he'd done with the T-shirt. He tugged it over his head and the silky polyester glided over him easily, falling into place as if it had been made for him.

"Great! It's not too small. I was afraid those shoulders of yours would require something more than extra large. Here. I bought you some shorts, too."

The shorts had an elastic waistband. Generic men's shorts. They didn't match the shirt. "They don't go with the shirt."

"Sure they do," she said as she approached him. Somehow, he made himself stay where he was even though his mind screamed for him to run from her before the cost of her company went beyond what he could possibly pay. She moved close, sliding one arm around his waist and under his shirt so that her warm hand splayed over his spine. "See right here," she said as she pointed with the index finger of her free hand. "Right on that flower and over here on the pineapple. There's these spots all through the pattern that match the color of the shorts exactly. See?"

"No," he said as he looked at where she pointed. But what did it matter when she touched him like this. Nothing mattered as much as the sensation of her palm skimming over his back. She gave up and smoothed the material over his chest instead. Her cheek pressed near his shoulder, she hugged him to her. His arms snaked around her and he held her there, imprinting this moment for later consideration. Part of him wanted to stay like this forever, part of him wanted to throw her to the bed and devour her, part of him wanted to bolt like a spooked pony.

"Come on, then," she said as she eased out of his embrace. "We're burning daylight. We need to get to the parks and start asking people about our missing boy and his girlfriend."

He stood still, bereft without her pressed against him. And that, too, seemed like part of the price. A torment of need would plague him now whenever she was too far away.

Kelsey seemed to be bringing so many sentiments back to him. All of them. All at once. He wouldn't be able to function this way, he knew that. And yet, his heart craved what she promised with every smile and every toss of her hair. He wanted just a little more time with her before he ruthlessly closed down the torrent of emotions and got back to the business of making something of himself.

Just a little more time with her. Today, at least.

He smiled and stepped into the shorts. They went almost to his knees and, together with his gaudy shirt, made him look ridiculous. He grinned and held out his arms so she could inspect her work.

"You look wonderful! Goodbye, Major Fordham. Hello, Jules!"

That made him laugh. "My brother Nathan calls me that."

"Because he knows you better than anyone else. He sees the Jules inside you that you work so hard to hide behind that officer facade of yours. We'll leave the officer in the room today and give Jules a little exercise for once." She tossed him a pair of plastic sandals she'd purchased for his feet.

Why not, he asked himself as he put them on. Maybe it was time for just that. He pocketed his wallet and cell phone, and grabbed his sunglasses. Then he followed Kelsey to where they bought tickets into the parks. When they walked out of the hotel, the sun smiled down on them. Julian lifted his face to the warmth.

Just one day of letting go couldn't hurt, he told himself. He ignored the shadow of doubt that lurked just around the corner of his mind and followed Kelsey into the family entertainment capital of the world.

"SHE WENT LOOKING for Rigley, you idiot!" shouted the officer. His voice came through the Wolf's cell phone like a knife. "She's obviously stumbled on to something that's led her that far. It's your job to make sure she gets no farther."

"What we need to do is hurry up and finish the job before she gets back. Then it won't matter what she figures out," said the Wolf as he sweated over the possibility that this insane officer would order him to kill the bitch.

"Yeah, well, that's not gonna work because there's a hold-up with our clients. Money problems since the Feds started cracking down on their bank accounts. So, get rid of Captain O'Roark."

The Wolf looked down at his dog, at the trusting brown eyes that gazed loyally back up at him, and wondered how it had come to this. "Yes, sir," he said into the phone.

CHAPTER ELEVEN

"HI," KELSEY SAID to the young man behind the counter of the first gift shop they saw inside the Magic Kingdom. She gave him her warmest smile and Julian saw that the boy fell for it instantly. The kid grinned from ear to ear.

"I have this picture of my friends." She held up her snapshot of Rigley and his girl. The boy looked at it with more intensity than if Julian had shown him the same thing under the authority of his badge. "I was supposed to meet them," she lied. "But they weren't where they said they were going to be. Do they look familiar to you at all?"

"I see so many people every day. I can't say for sure. They could be this engaged couple who came in here last week," he said.

Kelsey frowned. "Last week?"

The boy looked at the picture again. "Naw, I don't think this is them. Look, you can try talking to one of the hosts or hostesses. They're in those blue shirts. If your friends are looking for you while you're looking for them, the hosts can help get you all back together."

"Like a lost and found for people," Kelsey said, her smile back in place.

"That's right. It happens all the time and the hosts help with that."

"Okay," she said and walked casually back to where Julian waited within earshot. "So, we avoid the people in blue shirts at all cost. They're the security folks and they'll want to help us. That's the last thing we want."

"What exactly are we trying to accomplish here, Kelsey? I mean, you could ask hundreds of shopkeepers all through these parks and if no one recognized the people in your picture, that wouldn't prove a single thing."

She looked at him and he saw that her sunny mood could turn cloudy if he didn't watch his step. "Look, I have to *do* something, okay? I told you, I can't just sit around back at the fort doing nothing. Besides, do you have a better idea?"

"Yes. We go to the security office and tell them we're looking for these people and why." His cell phone began to ring and he ignored it as he stood in the center of the crowded pathway staring at her.

"They'll tell you they'll make an announcement to the employees about the missing people and then they'll ask you to leave. At least, that's what I'd do if I were them."

"I just don't see how this is going to get us very far," he said and just as his cell stopped ringing, he took it out of his pocket to see who had been calling. "Damn!" He was sorry to have missed this particular return phone call. "I have to return this," he told Kelsey.

"You don't have to come, if you don't want to," she said. "Why don't we just agree to meet somewhere in a couple of hours. I could just—"

He held up his hand to her. "Wait. Just one second while I leave another message. It'll only take a second. Then I'll come with you." He turned his back to her and pressed the button to redial the number. Then he took a few paces away, hoping she wouldn't overhear him. It wasn't that he wanted to keep secrets from her. It was just that this wasn't the time to be telling her about this particular call yet.

As he expected, the voice mail picked up. Julian talked to the machine. "Hey, Dr. Moriarty, this is Julian Fordham. You just called me back and I missed answering in time. I still need to talk to you. Or you could leave a message next time with the information I asked for. Thanks." He clicked Off and turned back to Kelsey.

She looked radiant in the sunlight, surrounded by laughing, happy people. He saw her wave bye-bye to a toddler being pushed in a stroller by his mom. The toddler smiled back at her. Kids loved Kelsey. Hell, everyone loved Kelsey.

"Everyone" would include him, so the statement couldn't be entirely accurate, could it? And yet, when he looked at her now, smiling at the passing kids, enjoying the childlike pleasure of being at Disney World, his heart thumped hard, as if it had something to say about this love business.

"C'mon. Let's go ask around with that picture of yours until your heart's content," he said as he slid his arm around her shoulders and drew her along the path. Anything to make Kelsey happy. She rewarded him with a smile.

They spent the afternoon walking through the parks asking sales clerks and ride hosts whether they'd seen Rigley and his girlfriend. A few times, it looked as if the blue shirts were heading in their direction to inquire as to what they were doing. Kelsey proved adept at ducking them and regrouping in a different location.

"How'd you learn to weave and dodge while still looking like you're not actually running away from anyone?" he asked after a while. "Those aren't skills you'd expect to see in a logistics officer."

She laughed and then grew thoughtful. "I learned to do that sort of thing growing up the way I did. We didn't have much. I guess you could say we were from the wrong side of the tracks. Kids can be cruel sometimes. I learned that I could end up either tough and capable or weak and sniveling."

Julian understood this completely. Although his family had settled down into an affluent and stable lifestyle when his father became a congressman, he still remembered the trauma of moving from one air force installation to another every couple of years. He'd had to prove himself at each new place. He'd become one of the tough and capable ones. He looked at Kelsey and realized for the first time that staying in one place for your entire childhood could be just as difficult as moving constantly. "But you're neither too tough nor weak. You found something in between."

"Thank you. But I'm very capable at squeaking past trouble." She did a dance as if she were weaving and dodging bullets. "You know how it is. Kids can be harsh and sometimes even mean. I learned to stay out of the center of things, and how to run and duck for cover. That was the way I dealt with things. Especially after my father died while I was still in high school and we were just hangers-on in that tiny West Virginia town. I was very eager to sign up at my local recruiter's office when I graduated. You can be sort of anonymous as an enlistee in the army."

"I never stayed at one school long enough to really learn how to do anything other than tough it out with the bullies," he said. "And then my father sent me to a private high school once he got out of the air force."

"It probably wasn't so different for you. Aren't private school kids mean sometimes, too?"

"Sure, but in far more subtle and devious ways. Nothing so honest as a left hook. Rich kids are the cruelest of them all, if you ask me."

"You're not," she observed, lumping him in the rich-kid category, but not as a bully. He had to laugh.

"Pretty close," he admitted. "I'm a cold bastard without a trace of a heart. Cool, calculating, brutally by the book." Somehow this truth sounded bitter and regrettable as he spoke it.

She took hold of his arm and hugged it as she walked beside him. "That's not how you were last night, Julian," she said in that low sexy voice that could turn him into a pile of lusting hormones in a matter of seconds.

He actually found himself looking around for a corner to duck behind so he could kiss her until she whispered his name in that same sensual tone she'd used when they'd been making love. Then he reminded himself of where they were and what they were supposed to be doing. He shook his head and chuckled softly.

"For a minute there, I thought you were going to kiss me," she cooed.

"I was. But then I recalled where we are."

"And people aren't supposed to kiss in Disney World?"

"Not the way I want to kiss you. It's a family resort, after all."

The trill of her laughter made his insides feel fluttery. But then she grabbed his hand and jogged off in a new direction, trailing him behind her. He smiled, then laughed, too, wondering what she was doing, where she was going. Before the blur of passing Disney spectacles could actually register, Kelsey had drawn him into the back row of *A Bug's Life*. She pushed him into a seat, took the next one over and then swivelled so she could kiss him. This was one of those kisses that men dream of, where a beautiful woman takes the lead in a way that says she can't stand another moment without bodily contact. The things she made him feel were crisp and vivid and burning hot, as she held his face between her two hands and pressed her lips to his and plied her tongue within.

He'd gone breathless and rigid with sexual excitement when she suddenly jumped back from him. "What was that?" she asked, clearly startled.

Just then, the entire audience, which Julian would have sworn hadn't been there a minute ago, began to screech and squirm as if they were being attacked by ants. Kelsey let out a yelp and then Julian felt it, too. Something seemed to crawl over his ankles, then over his shoulder and into his hair. Kelsey scrambled to her feet in an instant.

"Let's get out of here," he declared as he bolted from his seat, too, and headed for the red exit sign, nudging her along ahead of him.

Back out in the sunlight, he found Kelsey laughing even as she brushed at herself to make certain nothing crawled on her. He tried to be chivalrous and brushed at her back and shoulders. "There's nothing there, I swear," he assured her as he laughed harder.

She couldn't stop laughing. It was infectious.

"It was part of the show," she managed to say. "Air sprayed in tiny bursts to make us feel like there are bugs on us. *A Bug's Life*. The movie, remember?"

"No. What's a bug's life? A kids' movie? Sounds awful." This caused her to laugh some more.

"Not the most romantic place to be making out," she finally said.

He swung her into his arms and put his forehead against hers. "Don't ever be sorry for being spontaneous and kissing me until I can hardly breathe," he said as he ran his hands up and down her back, feeling her ribs and muscles and wanting to take her to bed as soon as humanly possible. She put her arms around his neck and hugged him like she meant it.

It had been a long time since anyone had hugged Julian.

He almost forgot to let her go. She didn't seem to mind. But when she said she was hungry, he recalled that they hadn't eaten much during the day. Still holding her, he tipped his watch up so he could see the time.

"It's almost nineteen hundred hours! We need to eat dinner." He let her go reluctantly, yielding to the basic need for sustenance over the pull of his other urgent need. She slipped from his grasp, but at the last minute she clung to his hand and walked along holding on to him.

They found themselves on Pleasure Island. Kelsey never stopped asking people about Rigley—without success— but they managed to eat and then went to one of the clubs where she talked him into dancing. After an initial rough start, he decided he liked it. It was good exercise and he liked watching Kelsey move. And the slow dancing, as if they were the only two in the crowded room, made him want to take her back to the hotel again. He whispered the suggestion in her ear and she nodded so emphatically that he had to laugh.

"I'm sorry we didn't find any hint of Rigley," he said as they departed.

"So am I," she said. Then she sighed. "Not finding him only points to the possibility that he's dead."

That certainly made the mood less romantic, he thought. And he had no idea how to get things back on track. Guilt that he'd been having a good time when they were supposed to be looking for Rigley didn't help much. So he sat on the shuttle bus with his arm around her shoulder and let her lean her head against him. And this was nice, too. Just sitting on the nearly empty bus, holding each other after a weary day. Still, there remained a nagging sense of dread mewling in the back of his mind. He'd been called again by Dr. Moriarty, but he hadn't listened to the message yet. He wasn't sure he wanted to. Once he did, everything would change between him and Kelsey. He wanted to put that off for a while longer.

But as they walked into the Shades of Green foyer, she commented on the insistent buzzing of his cell phone set on vibrate, reminding him that he'd missed a call and hadn't done anything about it yet.

"It's just my cell. I got a call and didn't answer, so it keeps reminding me."

She unlocked the door to the room and switched on the light. And once again, they were where he wanted to be, nestled in this space where there was a comfortable bed and nothing to bother them. He didn't want to think about the case or his phone, but the sound came again. Exasperated, he pulled the offending cell out of his pocket, pushed the button to let the thing know he was aware of the incoming call, threw the device in his overnight bag and drew Kelsey into his arms. To hell with the rest of the world.

At last, at last, they were alone. And even though he knew he'd ruin everything in the morning, he refused to think about that now. Tonight was his to be with her, to laugh and make love and sleep spooned together.

WHEN KELSEY AWOKE, she knew she'd slept the sleep of the well-laid and if that sounded crude, chalk it up to her earthy mother who was known to say such things now and then. Julian snored gently on and she tried not to wake him as she crawled from the bed and headed for the bathroom.

After finishing up, she realized it was still early. Maybe she could snuggle back under the covers with Julian. But on her way to make good on that thought, she heard a buzzing noise coming from his bag. She paused over the neatly folded clothes that lay in full view inside the open suitcase. And the sound came again.

Her groggy mind finally connected the dots and she realized someone was trying to call him. He'd left his phone on vibrate. Fishing around inside the lip of the bag, she retrieved the phone that he'd tossed there the night before. She didn't mean to look at it—phones were private and sometimes people were funny about others taking a peek. But this was one of those cells with a window right on the front so you could see who the caller was without even trying. It became clear to her, as she held the device in her hand, that no one was actually calling him right now. The thing was just letting Julian know he'd missed some calls. And the front window said he'd missed five of them. That seemed like a lot of calls. She thought they must be important so she flipped open the phone to see if they seemed like something she should wake him up for.

All five were from a Dr. Moriarty. And that seemed extremely important. Maybe Julian's dad was having a problem. Phone in hand, Kelsey leaned over and shook Julian awake. He lifted his lids slowly, yawned and stretched and smiled.

"Your phone says you missed five phone messages from Dr. Moriarty. Is that your dad's doctor?" she asked.

Julian sat bolt upright, smile gone, body tense and alert. "No, not my father's doctor," he said in a voice rusty with sleep. Gently, he lifted his cell phone from her grasp and got out of bed.

"Well, who is he, then?" She knew she shouldn't pry, but curiosity pushed the question out of her mouth before she could think that maybe she should leave it alone. "Never mind. I shouldn't have asked. Let's just go back to sleep for a while."

He eyed her, ran his fingers through his already messy hair, turned away without responding and put on some boxer shorts. Once the important parts of him were covered, he sat on the extra unused bed and faced her as if he had something to say. A thread of alarm unspooled inside her stomach. He looked far too serious for a man who'd made passionate love with her by night and laughed his way through Disney with her by day.

"Dr. Moriarty is *my* doctor," he said.

"Oh my God, you're sick! You have something awful—"

"Whoa!" he called, cutting her off by gently grasping her shoulders and easing her back to where she'd been sitting on the edge of the mussed bed. She hadn't even realized she'd leaped to her feet.

"I'm not sick." He seemed to think about those words and added, "At least not in the way you mean." He wore a half smile that looked full of regret.

Here it comes, she thought. He's got bad news to tell me. Maybe this thing between us is over already. She'd known it wouldn't last, but she'd hoped for more than one day.

"Dr. Moriarty is my shrink. Remember I told you I was seeing a therapist? Well, I called him yesterday. Actually, we played phone tag all day. I asked him by voice mail to recommend a therapist adept in regression therapy. You said that if we found any hint of Rigley being alive, you'd consider hypnosis and—"

She found herself on her feet again. And her body rigid with surprise. "You called and asked about a psychiatrist for *me?* You told your doctor about me and asked about where you could take your crazy girlfriend so she could have her head examined?"

"No!" He got to his feet, too. "It's not like that! I just wanted a recommendation. I didn't want to waste time in case Rigley suddenly showed up or we got a lead on him. You said a hundred times that you wanted to *do* something, that you wanted closure on your nightmare."

"You had no right to make any call regarding my sanity, Julian," she growled.

"This has nothing to do with your sanity, Kelsey. You're perfectly sane. It's your memories that are in question. Only your memories."

"As far as I'm concerned, that's the same thing!" Feeling helpless and lost, she took the coward's way out and stormed into the bathroom, slamming and then locking the door behind her.

"Look, I can't take care of that monster of a dog anymore. I'm just gonna get rid of it," said Private Earlman into his cell phone.

The Wolf growled like his namesake. "I told you to watch it for a few days, and that's what you're going to do."

The man sounded so angry, Earlman almost backed down. Then he recalled what the horrible little animal was doing to his apartment. "But you don't understand. When I go on duty, it chews on stuff and scratches up the doors and cabinets." He knew he was whining, but he had to get rid of the dog. "It totally shredded the carpet in my bedroom when I locked it in there yesterday. I mean, totally destroyed the whole room full of wall-to-wall carpeting! I don't even know how it managed to do it. My roommates are totally ballistic."

"Are you telling me you can't handle a ten-pound dog?"

Private Earlman thought hard about his answer. Then he quietly said, "It poops all over the place. And it pees in places I don't even know about until one of us accidentally steps in the spot barefoot. It's disgusting. I'm gonna be evicted."

"Do you take her out for walks? Are you feeding her

right and giving her water? Did you give her the chew toys I told you to get?"

"I took it out this morning and all it did was snarl and tear at my pants leg. Stupid little ankle biter. And if I give her water, she just pees more!" He'd had enough of the dog. "Why can't I just drop it into the Potomac?"

"You snot-nosed little prick! Why would you do a thing like that! It's just a defenseless creature. If you were nicer to her, she'd probably be your best friend. If you do anything like that, I'll drop *you* into the river. Got that?"

The private didn't speak. The Wolf had a reputation for being a hard son of a bitch, but he obviously had a thing for dogs. He owned a beast of an animal himself. Apparently his regard for canines stretched even to the tiny white demon he'd dropped on Earlman's doorstep.

"Look, just keep her another day or two," said the Wolf. "Don't get rid of her! I have plans for that dog."

"One more day," Earlman reluctantly agreed. "After that, the stupid dog might accidentally get run over by a truck." Maybe his own truck, he thought.

"Just give the dog some damn water and pat it on the head once in a while. If anything happens to it—anything at all—I'll hold you accountable. I can make your life a living hell, Private. Do you understand me?"

"Yes, Sergeant," came the prompt reply. But he knew that if the dog didn't go soon, they'd both be booted from the apartment he shared with three other guys. If it came down to him getting tossed out onto the street or the dog getting tossed into a river, there was no question as to which would happen first.

KELSEY DIDN'T SPEAK to Julian again until they were sitting in the airport waiting for their flight. "Fine," she finally said as if they'd been in the middle of discussing the problem. "I'll see the therapist your shrink recommended."

He turned to her, his face awash with incredulity. "You will?"

"Well, we didn't find Rigley. So that could mean he's my dead guy. And don't even think of launching into your skeptical speech, because I was about to say that I realize now that trying to find him that way was like looking for a needle in the proverbial haystack."

"Yup."

"But the only way I'm going to this doctor is if you go with me. I'm not letting some dude I never met put me under hypnosis while I'm alone and defenseless."

"I'm not sure—"

She flashed him a look and got the same result her mother had always gotten when she'd put on a certain expression. He capitulated immediately.

"Okay, okay! I'll go with you. But it's probably a conflict of interest or a breach of professionalism or something." He looked sulky for a minute, then added, "I'm glad you changed your mind."

"I'm still unhappy with you, calling your doctor without asking me first. That was just not right."

"I should have talked to you about it. But I wanted to see if Dr. Moriarty could get you an appointment with someone he trusts before I told you about it."

"Yeah? Well, don't do stuff behind my back when it's about me, okay?"

"Okay," he said.

"Okay," she said as confirmation. But she couldn't get past fuming just yet. "Did you get an appointment for me?"

He didn't answer right away. "I'm afraid to tell you now. You'll just get angry all over again."

"Just tell me!" she amended. "And since when do you actually worry about making me angry?"

"Since I decided your wish is my command, remember? Didn't I do everything you wanted me to do last night?" he asked with a grin.

She blushed. Yes, indeed. "That's neither here nor there." She stopped and reflected on those words. "Oh, God, I sound just like my mother. What does that saying even mean, anyway?"

"I have no idea. Am I going to get to meet your mother?"

"Maybe," she said. She knew she hadn't completely erased the reluctance from her voice.

"Maybe? Are you ashamed of me?" he said as he sat up straighter and scrutinized her.

"Of course not. It's not you. It's actually her. She's a fairly basic human being from West Virginia. And you're from a rich family. A congressman's son. I'm not sure you'd take to her. And I can't believe you want to meet my mother. Isn't that something like a relationship when people meet each other's parents? You don't seem ready for the meeting parents stage."

He looked horrified for a moment, as if he hadn't thought about what meeting her mother might mean to their commitment level. His gaze skittered away. "I just wondered about your mother. You said you sounded just like her. It would be fun to see if you really *are* like her," he said.

"Well, don't change the subject and try to get on my good side. I'm still mad at you. And I want to know if you got me an appointment with a—what did you call it?—a regression therapist."

"Dr. Moriarty said you can go in tomorrow at noon. It's

a Dr. Calcera you'll be going to. He's all the way out in Bowie, Maryland, but since I'm going with you, I'll make sure you're there on time. This guy is giving up his lunch hour for you because Moriarty said it was urgent."

"How kind of him," she said, making a sarcastic face.

Julian's cell phone rang. He unclipped his phone and looked at the caller ID. "My brother," he told Kelsey. Then he flipped the thing open and answered the call.

After a few minutes, Kelsey became alarmed by the stricken expression on Julian's face. Finally, she heard him say to Nathan, "I'm still in Florida, but I'm at the airport waiting for the plane home." He consulted his watch. "I should be able to get to the nursing home in about three hours. How bad is he?"

Now Kelsey shared Julian's concern. Something was wrong with his father.

He listened for another minute. "Okay. I'll get there as soon as I can." Julian closed his phone. When he looked up into Kelsey's eyes, his expression seemed blank.

She put her hand on his arm. "Is there anything I can do for you?" She didn't want to push him. But she had to offer her help even though she knew he wasn't likely to accept it.

He didn't answer right away. He just searched her eyes with a flat, inscrutable gaze. At last, he said, "You can come with me, if you want to."

She tried not to let her surprise show. This was so far from what she'd steeled herself to hear that she almost gasped. She held herself still, then realized he was waiting for a response, so she nodded, then added, "Okay," in case he didn't understand the meaning of her gesture.

He gave a masculine grunt of acceptance. "It may be the only time you'll get to actually meet him. So, why not? He won't recognize me either way, so it doesn't matter." He looked away then. "It just doesn't matter," he repeated.

Kelsey ached for him. And she thought that was a good thing, because he seemed incapable of aching for himself.

CHAPTER TWELVE

WHY HAD HE ASKED HER to come with him? Julian wondered as she sat beside him in his car, heading east on the Baltimore-Washington Parkway. Putting Kelsey and his father in the same room would never work. Or at least, it would never work to his advantage. At the worst, she'd take his invitation as the next best thing to a marriage proposal, given what she'd said about his innocent request to meet her mother. At best, she'd tag along without expectations and then meet his father and turn around and run away from him as fast as her feet could carry her. His father had that effect on people.

Funny that the prospect of her bolting seemed nearly as awful as having her read too much into the whole thing. With one hand, he rubbed his forehead, trying to make order of his thoughts. Kelsey sat quietly in the passenger seat. They'd had a long, strained flight home during which neither of them had much to say. Now this silent car ride. He never would have guessed she could be quiet for so long. But here she was, saying practically nothing for hours. Was she still angry with him about Dr. Moriarty?

"You're still mad at me," he said warily.

"What?" she said as she turned away from the passing scenery to look at him. One glance told him he'd surprised her.

"You're not talking. When women don't talk it usually means they're angry."

He saw her blinking at him. Her lips moved, stopped, then moved again, as if she couldn't quite formulate any words. Uh-oh.

But she surprised him by laughing. Then she covered her mouth and an apology suffused her expression. "Sorry. It's just that sometimes you say the most ridiculous things."

"What did I say that was ridiculous?" He could hardly believe she'd said that. No one else would ever dare to call him ridiculous.

"That bit about talking and anger. Look, Julian, I'm not angry with you anymore. I just figured you wanted to be alone with your thoughts. You haven't said much yourself, so I took the hint."

He nodded, seeing the logic in this. "The women I've known always stayed mad for a long time."

"That's pretty sad. As for me, I don't have time to stay in a foul temper for long. Such a waste of daylight. Anger is sort of a transient thing with me."

He mulled this over for a while. "You're scaring me," he said after a while.

She sat up straighter. "How could I possibly scare you?"

"You're starting to seem like the ideal woman. Someone I'd be crazy to let slip away," he admitted, wondering why he would say such a thing out loud. He only dug his grave a little deeper.

"Ideal! Please! You haven't seen me when I've been deprived of caffeine for too long. Or when I have to do the physical training test twice a year. I mean, geez! I can be very cranky. Just ask Shannon."

Now it was his turn to laugh. "Okay, so you're not a Stepford wife. I'd say that's a relief." And all at once, he realized he'd used the word *wife* and panic settled into the pit of his stomach for a nice long stay. Why had he said that? What would her reaction be? Surely she'd have expectations now....

"No, I don't think anyone would ever mistake me for one of those," she said lightly. "I can cook and make a room look nice, but that's about as far as my domestic talents go. Besides, I don't know if I'm ready to be anyone's wife just yet."

Say what? He could hardly believe his ears. Had she just announced that she wasn't ready for marriage? What did that say about the two of them? Was he just some sort of casual thing for her? Didn't these past two nights mean anything to her? Were all his preconceived notions about her wrong?

He found himself gripping the steering wheel too tightly. He relaxed his grasp slightly and took inventory of his physical and emotional state.

The review didn't take long. The conclusion—he was a mess.

As always when he needed to order his thoughts, he longed for his notebook. He wanted to make a list of all the things about Kelsey that boggled his mind.

Captain Kelsey O'Roark, he would write. And then below that he'd start with:

Doesn't want marriage. Followed by:

Why not? And beside that he'd write something like *Why take issue with this since that's how you want things, too?* Then, if he were honest, he'd write *Is that how you want things?*

Confusion danced like a dervish inside his head and he rubbed his temple again.

"Do you want me to drive? You look like you have a headache."

"I'm fine," he said. "Besides, we're almost there." In another half mile, he pulled into the parking lot of the nursing home just outside Baltimore where his father had been living for the past few years.

They got out of the car and the hot, humid air hugged them too tightly. He looked up at the sky, wondering if it would rain and wash some of the awful heat away. Then he realized Kelsey was waiting on the sidewalk for him, probably wondering why he wasn't moving.

"Hold on a second." He flipped open his phone and dialed his brother's cell. "Hi, Nathan. How is he?"

"Better," Nathan said. "When will you be here?"

"I'm in the parking lot now. I just wanted to get a handle on what to expect."

Nathan gave a rueful chuckle. "He's bitching about being in a wheelchair, demanding cigarettes and refusing to eat his broccoli."

Julian would have laughed except that this news meant the Honorable Congressman Fordham was now well enough to be his usual horrible self in front of Kelsey. "I brought someone with me. Kelsey O'Roark. Do you remember her?"

"Yeah, I remember her. Cute and sweet, not your type. You usually go more for the cheating, haughty, demanding sort of women, like your ex."

Julian didn't dignify that remark with a retort. "We'll be up in a few minutes. Try to get him calm before we show up." He snapped the phone shut. Yet he had no reason to be upset with Nathan. What his brother had said was true. His marriage had been a disaster not only because he'd been emotionally unavailable, but also because she'd been demanding and arrogant and, in the end, unfaithful. Why had he chosen such an inappropriate match? She would have thrived on politics and his father had approved of her. How pathetic.

He looked at Kelsey, who waited patiently without a word of reproach. And suddenly he knew he'd brought her here to give her every excuse to dump him. That would be the easy way out. Only right now, he wasn't so sure he wanted the easy way out. In fact, it was beginning to look as though *he'd* be the one hurt.

"Maybe you should stay in the car," he said.

Her expression was fleetingly crestfallen, then she hid the disappointment as best she could. He thought she would acquiesce, and he couldn't tell if he felt relieved or disappointed. But then she surprised him again.

"I'd rather go in with you, if you don't mind. I came all this way with you and I don't think I'd be much of a friend if I stayed in the car now." Her voice was gentle and her eyes luminous and soft.

"Suit yourself," he said, defeated. His inability to deny her anything she wanted seemed to be habit-forming.

Inside, elderly people and nurses greeted the two of them cheerfully, making much of his uniform and whispering behind their hands as they eyed Kelsey. He had to admit she looked great in her jeans and T-shirt, simple attire that made him want to peel her naked to see what alluring underclothes she wore beneath. He chased those inappropriate thoughts from his mind as he said hello to the people they passed. He noticed Kelsey had a kind word for everyone, as if she'd been here before and knew the residents. These folks would probably chatter about his love life for weeks on end after this. For some reason, this lightened his mood a little.

He led Kelsey to his father's suite, knocked on the door and heard something heavy hit a wall. He and Kelsey eyed one another warily, then Julian cautiously cracked the door. His initial assessment was that his father had swatted a bowl of vegetables across the room. Green stuff dripped in gobs from the wall. Not a good sign.

"Is it safe?" he asked Nathan who sat in front of their father looking exceedingly put out.

"Sure. He's got nothing else to throw at the moment."

Julian opened the door and preceded Kelsey, just in case the old man went violent again.

"Uh-oh," he heard her say under her breath as she caught sight of the mess. "Someone doesn't like the food here."

"Hello, Dad," he said. Then, without waiting for an answer, he turned his attention to his brother. "Where's Rachel today?"

"Working. She wanted to come, but when the doctor said he'd rallied, I didn't want her to use up her leave for this." He waved his hand toward the curmudgeon in the wheelchair.

Julian's gaze was drawn to his father again. What he saw made him feel old and sad and worn out. The man had been such a mighty figure most of his life. This precipitous decline seemed eerie and unnatural.

"Who's that?" the old man snapped, raising a wizened hand in Kelsey's direction. And the saddest part was that he would have asked the same question even if he'd met her a hundred times before.

"This is—" he began, but then he realized with horror that he hadn't thought of how he would introduce her. Should he just say her name? Should he call her his girlfriend?

"I'm Kelsey O'Roark," she said as she stepped toward his father and took his thin hand in hers. She went down on her haunches in front of his chair so he could see her easily and held his hand in both of hers. And she smiled. "Looks like you don't like the food here much, sir. Maybe you'd like a home-cooked meal once in a while. I could bring you something the next time I visit."

Before he could get over the shock of having her offer to cook for the man, compounded by her assumption that she'd be visiting again, Julian witnessed a miracle. His cantankerous father actually smiled.

"Ohmigod," whispered Nathan. "Even Rachel can't get him to smile."

Julian knew that Congressman Fordham always behaved more civilly when Rachel was around. But he'd never been so charmed by her as he appeared to be by Kelsey. Maybe it was the offer of a home-cooked meal. He'd never have guessed that that's what it took to make the man happy.

Those rheumy eyes glanced toward Julian, then back to Kelsey. "Who's that?" he asked her. Julian sometimes found it a blessing that his father rarely remembered him. Because when he did remember, the man spent their time together questioning his choices in life and berating his achievements. At least Kelsey would be spared that, for now.

"This is your son, Julian," she said as she reached for Julian's hand and drew him a little closer.

"What's he wearing?" asked the old man. Julian usually made a point of wearing civilian clothes. His army uniform tended to upset his father.

"He's in his uniform, General Fordham. Your son is one of the best investigators the army has. He's an officer and a gentleman. You should be very proud."

Behind him, Nathan groaned. They both knew that her speech, said in innocence, was likely to set the old man off. Their father loathed the fact that his sons had joined the army instead of the air force. He'd sworn they'd never see a penny of his money if they joined, but each had done so anyway. For Julian, it was a way to become completely independent of his father. For Nathan, the army had become a new family he could call his own.

"Proud?" asked the congressman as his gaze shifted from Kelsey's face to his son's.

"I was in the air force. Made a career of it," he said to no one in particular. "Went to Vietnam. Bad place. But after that, I made something of myself." So many words in a row made Julian notice a slight slur in his speech. And the shock of what he'd said made Julian take a step back.

Julian glanced at Nathan and saw that his brother was as surprised as he by the revelation that their father had been to Vietnam. How could they have never heard this in all the times they'd each argued with this man about their own desires to join the military?

"Get out of the army, boy!" shouted the general. "You'll be cannon fodder." This, at least, was familiar to the two sons.

Kelsey seemed to see the old man's confusion, so she deftly changed the subject. "So what would you like me to cook for you when I come the next time?"

While she coaxed a menu out of him, Julian huddled in the corner with Nathan and talked over the doctor's diagnosis.

"I hadn't heard about him serving in Vietnam before," Nathan said after a while.

"Me either. I'll look it up in air force records and let you know what I find."

Nathan nodded. "The doctor thinks he had a small stroke, but now he seems to be back to his usual self except for some difficulty speaking," Nathan said. "I'm sorry if I worried you. He was pretty bad off when I called, but in the intervening hours—"

"No, don't talk like that. I'm glad you called. And I don't expect you to handle all this on your own." But even as Julian said it, he realized he hadn't actually pulled his weight when it came to their elderly parent. "I promise I'll help more."

"I know he makes it hard for you to visit," Nathan said. "He makes it hard for you, too, but you don't let it bother you."

"He didn't mess with my head when I was a kid. You made sure he didn't get the chance. But he had full access to your developing mind the minute Mom died."

Julian didn't want to think about the turn his life had taken when their mother had died. He didn't want to deal with the guilt of how little he'd appreciated the buffer she'd provided between him and his father. He didn't want to remember the confusion and turmoil of his father's constant and impossible demands.

Instead, he turned to look once more at Kelsey, chatting easily with his father. She saw him looking and waved him back over. Against his normal inclinations, he did what she wanted, and approached.

"He told me the food here is terrible. And from the looks of those overcooked vegetables dripping down the wall, I have to agree. Can we do something about that?"

It didn't escape Julian that she'd said "can *we* do something." And as was his nature lately, he felt both elated and terrified at the prospect of a future where he and Kelsey faced life's challenges together. "I can talk to the administrator," he offered.

She smiled. "That would be great." Turning back to the old man, she said, "Julian's going to talk to the people in charge about your meals. You have to tell us if they improve or not."

The old man nodded imperiously, as if improved conditions were his God-given right. It mattered not at all that everyone else in the nursing home ate the food without complaint. But at least the old man hadn't begun to berate him.

Hard to figure out why he felt sorry for the old man

when his father couldn't recall his name or their relationship to one another. His visits were much more peaceful when the old man thought he was just another stranger. His therapist had a couple of theories on why Julian's feelings seemed reversed, but he never paid enough attention to them to remember what they were. There was nothing he could do about his relationship with his father, so it never made sense to try to label or categorize the feelings the situation evoked. Better just to stuff it behind one of the many walls inside him so he could get on with his life. Julian was a master at that.

"I'll go find that administrator now," he muttered when he realized he'd been standing there ruminating for several minutes while Kelsey and Nathan attempted to make coherent conversation with a man whose memories were completely unreliable. For all they knew, Congressman Fordham had never been anywhere near Vietnam, he told himself as he left the suite. He made a mental note to check out his father's military history when he got a free minute.

KELSEY COULD SEE Julian's discomfort in being here with his father. So when he left in search of someone in charge of the food services, she couldn't blame him. Still, she burned with questions about his relationship with his dad. The elderly Fordham seemed harmless and really rather sweet. So why did Julian seem to be almost afraid of him?

"Don't be too hard on Julian," Nathan said without providing context.

Kelsey's expression must have indicated she didn't understand.

"If my brother seems closed off, maybe a little standoffish, it's not really his fault. Deep down, he's a very caring guy."

Ah, now she began to grasp what Nathan alluded to. "Why isn't it his fault?" she asked, feeling only a little guilty for probing her lover's brother for information.

"Because our mom died when Julian was fifteen. She'd had a fight with her husband—" he nodded toward his father "—and she had a few drinks, then went out for a drive in her sports car. Now that I'm an adult, I'm surprised it wasn't declared a suicide. But back then, all we knew was that our mother was suddenly gone in a car accident. Julian was in high school by then. My father considered him a man. And any sign of a tear was a sign of weakness according to our dad. So Julian never grieved. Sometimes, I had the impression he actually blamed himself for our mother's death. And Dad was really rough on him, never happy with his grades, never satisfied with his skills in sports even though Julian was the star quarterback. I can't remember anything but criticisms ever coming out of that man's mouth all our lives. But they were mostly directed toward Julian. So my brother learned to file all those terrible emotions away somewhere."

"What about you?" she asked gently.

"I was younger, just turned thirteen. My father didn't acknowledge my existence very often, thank God. I know we moved a lot when Dad was in the air force, but what I remember is living the life of a successful congressman's son years after our mother's death. Julian says he took us to Korea during those air force days and that we all hated it there, but I don't have many memories of that time. Once my mother died, he got us a string of nannies. They gave us as much maternal comfort as they could manage. But it was Julian who stepped into the role of my parent. He let *me* cry on *his* shoulder many times, especially right after Mom's death." Nathan paused and seemed to search for words. "He never told me it wasn't manly. But I can't re-call ever seeing him cry, not even in private. I asked him about it once, right before I got married. He just shrugged and said it was all a long time ago, so why dredge it all up again. He claimed to be happy even though his own mar-riage had dissolved unpleasantly." He shifted restlessly, then added, "He came to our wedding without a date. I've never felt I had the right skills to help him as much as he helped me."

"Did you ever suggest he talk to a professional?"

Nathan nodded. "On several occasions."

She reached out to him and rested her palm on his fore-arm. "You did good, Nathan."

He looked up at her with surprise in his eyes. "Don't tell me he actually went to a shrink."

She wouldn't say more, but she smiled at him and he smiled back. It wasn't up to her to reveal to this younger brother that Julian had talked to a professional, but it seemed okay to let Nathan deduce it on his own. Besides, he looked so glad. And relieved.

"Well, he must really love you," he said after a while.

"Who?" she asked, not following.

"Julian. He must really have a thing for you if he made himself go to a therapist. He never thought he had any rea-son to work on his issues before. But since you popped into his life, he must recognize the value of getting his emo-tional house in order."

Kelsey laughed at this analysis. "I wouldn't jump to so many conclusions, Nathan."

"I see the way he looks at you. I've never known my stoic brother to wear his heart on his sleeve, but since the two of you entered this room, he's acting like a different man. He's all about doing what you ask and thinking of other people."

She pulled back and cocked her head to one side. "Julian's *always* about helping other people. That's all he *does* is help others. He's the most selfless man I know."

Nathan smiled. "Hey, I agree, but most people don't see it because he's so cool and calculating about it. His ex-wife called him the ice man. It seemed funny at first, but then she started saying it with a good dose of bitterness behind it. And you have to admit, he's not big on expressing his deeper feelings."

She scoffed. "What man is?"

"Touché," he said. "But Julian's got his emotions under such tight control, sometimes I worry about him. Now that I see him with you, I can tell that he's making a transformation, and I can relax. And I can't wait to tell Rachel!"

"No, no! Don't do that. Julian's very—" But she stopped midsentence when she saw Julian standing in the doorway.

He stared at the two of them, apparently taking in Nathan's grin and Kelsey's stricken expression, then said, "Julian's very what?"

Nathan leaped to his feet, laughing. "Very kind, very noble, very capable. A very decent guy. Not counting the occasional beating up of his little brother in his ill-spent youth, of course."

Julian laughed. "Obviously I didn't smack any sense into you." He cuffed his brother lightly on the arm as he passed him and came to stand near Kelsey.

Congressman Fordham seemed lost in another world and he didn't look up at Julian's tall figure. "I talked to the administrator and the head chef. They'll take extra care that his food is cooked more gently from now on—for an added fee, of course."

"Of course," Kelsey and Nathan said together.

"We should go," Julian said. He glanced around the room and gave every appearance of feeling trapped.

Kelsey stood, but turned to the elderly man beside her. She gently grasped the wizened hand to urge his distant gaze to focus on her. Then she bade him goodbye and kissed him on the cheek. Julian looked upon the interactions as if they were strangers.

HE WATCHED AS his father peacefully accepted a peck on the cheek from Kelsey. The exhibition moved him to do something he couldn't ever remember doing since he was a small child. He went over to his father, put his arms around those frail shoulders and hugged him. "Bye, Dad," he said as he quickly kissed him on the wrinkled, translucent skin of his cheek.

"Hoo-ah, boy," replied his father. It was the military version of a war chant or a cheer, depending on the circumstances. Hearing his father say it made Julian's eyes burn and his throat feel tight. This was as close as he'd ever come to any hint of comradery from his father.

Julian drew back and stood looking down at his father. The old man looked back, then away. When his gaze returned, the elder Fordham said, "Who are you?"

His confusion broke Julian's heart, but it broke his heart for another reason, too. Because with those three final words, his father had stolen away from him the single expression of approval he'd ever heard from him. That "hoo-ah" from his father hadn't been for him. It had just been the result of a strange and random synapse of his beleaguered mind.

He had to get out of there. Now, before he fell apart. He turned and bolted, moving past people heedlessly, caring nothing for who might be staring, barely hearing that someone called after him. He had to get out in the air, needed to breathe, craved solitude. Hurry, hurry before someone sees him fall apart.

CHAPTER THIRTEEN

KELSEY WENT AFTER HIM, but she couldn't catch up to him without running full tilt and potentially knocking people over. She saw him push through the outside doors, then pause briefly on the sidewalk to scan the parking lot. As she approached, she thought she saw him sway slightly. As he shielded his eyes from the sun, she noticed that his hand shook a little.

Her heart hurt and she wanted to draw him into her arms and let him pour out his pain on her shoulder. But she felt sure that he wouldn't appreciate that kind of gesture right now. So when she caught up with him, she stood silently beside him, waiting to see if he would talk or go straight to the car.

He went straight to the car. But as he crossed the parking lot, he reached behind him with an outstretched hand. When she took it into hers, he clasped her fingers tightly. Hand in hand, they went to their parking space. She noticed he hung his head and walked as if weighted down. The heat didn't help the situation. It bore down on them. At last, they reached the relief of the car and its blessed air-conditioning.

After he started the engine, he put his right hand on the shifter, but she put her hand over his to stop him. He didn't look at her. He just stared at her hand atop his. The muscle at his jaw flexed and released and flexed again.

After a long moment, he cleared his throat. "Let's just go," he said and his voice sounded raw.

"Let's just sit here a minute," she countered. She didn't want to push him, wouldn't insist that he talk to her, but he was in no condition to drive at this particular moment.

He let himself lean back more fully against the driver's seat and slipped his hand from beneath hers. He stared straight ahead through his windshield. After a few minutes, Nathan came out of the nursing home, noticed them in the car and veered in their direction.

He approached with apparent reluctance, hunkering down a little to see his brother through the driver's side glass. As he drew near, Julian made a tsk sound, rolled his eyes and hit the button on the door to lower the window. Hot air immediately whooshed into the cooler interior.

"What?"

"Dad's okay. I got him settled with his nurse."

"That's good."

Kelsey noticed that Julian didn't make eye contact with his brother. It seemed to her that if he looked into the eyes of another person, Julian would shatter.

"Hey, listen," Nathan began. "Are you okay? Dad's not really himself these days."

"Thank God!" Julian barked with a mirthless laugh. "When he's himself, he's a royal son of a bitch."

Nathan stared at him. "Yeah, you got that right," he said softly. His gaze shifted to Kelsey's and she held it, trying to silently reassure the younger brother.

"Okay, you two take care," Nathan said, nodding at Kelsey. As he stood straight, his face disappeared from her view and she had the feeling he'd just placed his brother's emotional health into her hands.

She wasn't sure she was up to the job and wondered if she

should tender a resignation. But as Julian raised the window again, sealing them once more in the coolness, she knew she couldn't abandon him now. Maybe not ever. Because she knew he had a lot to give if he would just let himself.

"How long do you want to sit here?" he asked, sounding annoyed. She noticed his hand still trembled a little.

She thought carefully about her answer. "How about if I drive?"

"Yeah, fine. Anything to get the show on the road." He got out of the car and walked around the hood, still not looking her way.

Kelsey scooted over the console and behind the wheel. She had to move the seat way up to reach the pedals. She buckled up and when he got in on the passenger's side and put on his seat belt, she said, "My place or yours?" Her heart hammered as she waited to see if he would choose to go to his apartment alone.

He sat without speaking for a long time and she listened to the whir of the air conditioner and the throb of her pulse in her ears.

"Your place, if that's okay with you," he finally said.

She realized she'd been holding her breath and had to let it out surreptitiously before she could speak. "Yes, that would be great." She got them on their way.

"We should feed your cat," he added, as if he needed an excuse for opting to avoid his apartment.

"Shannon probably did that, but she'd never empty the litter box. She's a dog person at heart."

"I thought she was staying with that K9 guy from the MP unit."

"Yeah, that's what she said when she called yesterday, but she swore that she left some food out. Still, I should go check. And Jasper will be glad to see me."

Kelsey couldn't believe they were making small talk after the turmoil he'd been in only moments before. But when he put his left arm across the back of her seat and stroked a gentle finger along the plane of her cheek, she felt that they'd made some subtle progress.

Still, he didn't say much on the way home. And once they neared Fort Belvoir, things went rapidly downhill.

"SIR, WHAT DO YOU WANT me to do about Earlman?" said the Wolf into his cell.

"What are you talking about?" barked the officer.

The Wolf knew right then that there were going to be problems. He stared off at the landscape and knew he was about to have a very bad day, starting now. "He said he called you. He said he told you he's bailing out."

"What!" shouted the officer, who, the Wolf noted, didn't have a code name other than sir. "What the hell do you mean? Earlman can't quit when we're so close. We're already down a man." The officer sounded like he could have a stroke at any moment.

"Yes, sir. I know, sir. That's why I called you for your orders, sir." He hoped that placating the man would help. But he doubted it. And suddenly, the Wolf wondered if Earlman hadn't had the right idea by bailing out. The kid might have realized, as the Wolf was beginning to, that this officer was not as clever as he'd seemed at first, back when he'd persuaded them to join in on his scheme. It had all seemed so easy then. Now, there were endless problems.

"Find that kid. Make sure he's never, ever able to talk to anyone about anything. Do you understand?" said the officer.

"Yes, sir," replied the Wolf. He understood. First he'd been ordered to get rid of the female officer, now Earlman. But he hadn't yet decided if he'd do what the officer had implied. The Wolf had signed up for a little grand larceny. He hadn't signed up for murder.

KELSEY HAD DRIVEN them nearly to Fort Belvoir from the nursing home when she glanced into her rearview mirror and saw the black truck tailgating her. "Don't look now, but I think that truck that followed me around the fort is on my tail again now."

He didn't turn around to look but leaned over a little to get a glimpse in the mirror on the passenger door. "Not likely that the same guy would follow you out here. You're not even driving your own car. This could just be an anonymous black truck."

"Maybe," she said. But the truck looked familiar. It had a lot of extra chrome on it and the shocks had been lifted so the vehicle sat high on its wheels. She sped up a little to catch sight of the license plate. Sure enough, the first letter was an M. More than that, she couldn't see because the truck sped up, too, coming right onto her bumper. Fast.

"Brace yourself," she said as she cringed in expectation of a jolt from this guy who seemed to like to play bumper cars.

But the driver surprised her and pulled out into the lane beside them. With the roar of a barely muffled engine, the truck came along beside her, then pulled ahead. In the next instant, it veered into her lane and braked hard. Kelsey smashed down her brake pedal in the unfamiliar car and found herself swerving toward the shoulder of the road, heading into a spin.

"Shit!" she heard Julian cry as his right hand shot out to the dashboard to hold himself in place and his left hand went out to her as if he could keep her safe in her seat that way.

At the last possible second, with the brakes squealing

and smoke billowing behind them from tire burn, she got the vehicle under control.

"Ohmigod!" she managed to say as she came to a stop at the side of the road. Miraculously, they still faced forward in the direction they had been traveling.

But their hearts hadn't even begun to beat normally again by the time they saw that the huge black truck was bearing down on them in reverse. It came on fast, white exhaust preceding it as it sped toward them on a collision course. She covered her head with her arms and turned as far sideways as her seat belt would allow in a hopeless attempt to shield herself from the imminent crash. She felt Julian's arms go around her as he tried to protect her with his body just before impact.

Instead of the crunch of metal they expected to hear, the sound of squealing brakes once again ripped through the air. Then, the gentle purr of two idling engines got past her dread and into her ears. Julian moved first, lifting his head to look forward. Kelsey followed his example, barely believing that nothing had happened. The ominous bulk of the truck swamped their field of vision outside Julian's car.

"Stay here," Julian said as he unbuckled his seat belt.

She made a grab for him. "No way! You're not going to go confront this lunatic all by yourself. You don't even have a weapon!"

"I'm not going to sit here and do nothing, Kelsey," he said calmly. "He could be loading a shotgun right now."

That got her to let go of him and he slipped from her grasp and exited the car. Without him beside her, the vehicle seemed like a ticking bomb and she quickly unbuckled and bolted out of it, too. A passing car swerved just in time to avoid killing her. She took cover by going to the back of the car, intent on providing Julian with as much backup as she could without a weapon. She didn't want Julian to have to worry about her if this nutcase decided to open fire. They were both better off on their feet within a few yards of the trees lining the highway if any shooting started.

Julian edged toward the passenger side of the truck, ducking low so as to stay in the guy's blind spots. He'd moved about halfway along the bed of the vehicle when the passenger door suddenly flew open. From within, Kelsey saw something small and white fly out and land with a thud on the grass. Two masculine arms pulled back into the truck cab after shoving the thing to the ground.

"Take your stupid dog, bitch! Took me forever to find you this time," cried a disembodied voice from inside the cab. "I just want to get the hell out of here for good! And I don't want your mangy dog on my conscience! And if you know what's good for you, you'll get out of town for a few weeks, too!" The arms pulled the passenger door shut again. In the next instant, the souped-up engines howled and the black behemoth skidded out into traffic again, barely missing an oncoming SUV that made an emergency lane change with horn blaring.

While Julian stared after the truck, Kelsey saw the white bundle move. Then she heard a tiny yip. Stumbling and nearly blinded by tears from the exhaust and dust kicked up by the departing truck, she made her way to where Bella lay, stunned but alive.

"Hey, baby Bella," she said in imitation of the way Shannon talked to the animal. "How are you, little girl? Are you gonna be okay? Can I take a look at you, sweetie?" Cautiously, she reached out her closed fist for the dog to sniff.

Bella licked Kelsey's knuckles and whimpered, but she didn't jump up onto her four feet. Julian hunkered down beside them and without bothering to introduce himself to the animal, he gently ran his fingers over the tiny canine body. When his fingers touched her right front leg, Bella barked and gnashed her teeth. But she didn't bite.

"I think her leg is broken. And she looks sick to me," Julian said.

Kelsey looked at the matted, dirty hair, the weeping eyes, the lolling tongue and came to the same conclusion. Bella was in bad shape. "Can we get her into the car to take her to an animal hospital somewhere?"

"Call 411 and get the nearest animal medical facility on the phone. I'll get the dog into the car," he said.

And less than a half hour later, Kelsey found herself behind the wheel of Julian's car again. She couldn't believe she'd gotten her shaking under control so she could drive again so soon, but Bella's condition needed to take priority over everything else. She drove cautiously, as if the black truck could reappear and continue the nightmare. But eventually, they made their way to the clinic that her cell phone provider had found for her.

While they waited impatiently for the vet to look at Bella, each of them made phone calls. Julian called the local police and Kelsey tried to reach her sister. The police appeared right after they got the word that the X ray showed that the dog's leg was, indeed, broken. She was also dehydrated. But Bella would be fine and ready to go home soon.

It didn't take long to file a police report, but neither she nor Julian imagined that it would do any good. The truck driver was long gone by now and if he had any sense, he'd have gotten rid of his vehicle or at least snagged some new license plates somewhere. Even though Julian had managed to get the whole tag number, it wasn't likely to be of much help. Still, they had to try.

At last, a veterinarian called them back to an examining room.

"You two look almost as bad as Bella here," said the doctor as she came into the room after them, without the dog.

"We've had an interesting day," Julian said with a disarming smile. Clearly he didn't want to give details of their harrowing experience to this young animal doctor. "How's the dog?"

"She'll be fine. We've put a cast on her leg. It was only a fracture, but we'll have to keep it in the cast for a couple of weeks. She was very dehydrated, too. What we do for that is we inject water under her skin. She'll absorb it quickly into her system that way. Did my assistant find out who the owner is from the dog tags?"

"She belongs to my sister," Kelsey admitted. "But she's been lost for days." No sense in saying the poor creature had been an apparent kidnapping victim. Or something. Kelsey hadn't had time to puzzle out all that had happened despite all the questions from the police about why the driver of the truck had practically thrown the dog at them.

"Oh! I thought you'd just found her on the side of the road like a stray. Well, that's good. You can take her home to your sister and see that she gets proper care. I'm going to give you some instructions and the X rays so you can bring them to Bella's usual vet," the doctor said.

Kelsey listened as best she could considering the buzzing sound that had begun in her head shortly after she had realized the danger was past. When she reached for the sheet of instructions, she saw that her hand shook. Julian grabbed on to her outstretched fingers before the doctor could notice. Then, with the steadiness of a surgeon, he took the paper himself. In another minute, a technician brought Bella into the examining room.

"I gave her a quick bath before we put the cast on her," said the young woman. "She was really a mess and you can't wash her with the cast on her leg." Then she cooed at Bella as if the dog were a baby. Bella licked the girl's nose.

"She looks fat," Julian observed.

"That's the water we injected," said the doctor. "Make sure you give her plenty of pee breaks for the next day or so. She may have to go more often than usual."

"Got it," said Julian with a firm look directed at the dog. "No peeing in the car, okay?"

Bella looked at him and yipped happily. But she made no promises.

Julian wanted to drive, but Bella had taken a liking to him and didn't seem to want to change hands. She whimpered piteously when they tried.

"I can still drive," Kelsey said. "I'm fine now. Really."

And she was glad she'd ended up driving again. Because, when they finally approached the fort, heading along Route 1, Bella let go a stream right onto Julian's lap. In seconds, his pants and shirt were soaked and clinging to his skin.

"Shit!" he cried as he lifted the dog and aimed the last of her stream toward the floor.

"No, just pee," she said, remembering when Shannon had said the same to her the day after this long nightmare had begun. Kelsey was sorry that Julian's car would likely never be the same again. "Do you want me to pull over?" Kelsey asked, fighting laughter that threatened to be somewhat hysterical.

"Why bother? I'm already soaked and so is my car. Just get us home."

Kelsey didn't ask for a clarification on where "home" might be. She headed straight for her own apartment.

JULIAN PROCESSED the events involving the truck in the time it took to get to Kelsey's place. It was the perfect excuse to avoid thinking at all about his reaction in the nursing home.

Could the guy in the truck have been related to whatever had happened to Kelsey in her warehouse? Or was he some random person who'd found the dog and wanted to be rid of it? But if that were the case, how had he known to look for and follow this particular car? Why hadn't he just called the number on the innumerable signs Shannon had posted or even just dropped the dog off at animal control? Why terrorize them before dumping the dog?

The facts pointed to the black truck being the same one that had followed Kelsey before. And apparently it had followed this car, as well. And that meant that Kelsey had to be involved in something very dangerous. He'd have to stay by her side every second to be certain nothing happened to her.

"So do you believe me now?" she asked as she unlocked her apartment. "Obviously someone's been following me around since the warehouse incident. Doesn't that show I'm telling the truth?"

He tried to hedge his answer. "I've known all along that you're mixed up in something. That's why we need to go see that hypnotist tomorrow. We've got to use all our resources to get to the bottom of this."

Holding the dog gently in his arms, he walked into Kelsey's apartment with her and stood back, observing her gushing reunion with her cat. Or rather, Kelsey gushed and the cat endured, somehow managing to purr and rub while still appearing put out by all the attention. Kelsey stroked the animal and cooed at him. Lucky cat.

There was no sign of Shannon. He followed Kelsey to

the guest bedroom where he found that a tornado had recently passed. Clothes and stuff were everywhere in no order whatsoever. But in one corner was a pile of dog toys and a little bed. Kelsey swept stuff away with her foot to clear an unencumbered path from the dog bed to the door.

"I guess you can put her there for now. I'm hoping when she feels a little better, she'll learn how to walk around on the cast. For now, I'll bring food and water to her in here until Shannon gets home."

Julian watched as Kelsey pulled out some white and blue sheets from a package that looked like disposable diapers. She laid the sheets on the floor near Bella. "Puppy pads for if she has to pee and can't get very far. I bought them the other day after having an in-depth conversation with Shannon about solutions to Bella's tendency to remain silent about her need to go out."

"Good idea," he said. "Did you get a hold of your sister when you called her from the vet's?"

Kelsey shook her head. "She must not have her cell phone on. Or maybe it just ran out of power. But while you were talking to your guy at your office about tracking the license plate number for the truck, I called the K9 unit and the animal shelter and left a message for her. She will be so happy to hear about Bella's return."

He settled the dog carefully onto the dog bed and watched as it awkwardly curled itself up on the cushion, one leg sticking straight out. In seconds, it was breathing evenly in sleep.

"Um, I'm happy she's back, too, but I'm also drenched with her bodily fluids. If I fetch my bag from the car I can put on dry clothes, even if they won't be perfectly clean. May I take a shower?"

She smiled at him, making his heart skip a beat. Then

she came right to him and wrapped her arms around his torso, heedless of his damp clothing. "I haven't had the chance to say thank you."

"For what?" he asked, uncertain as to whether he should hold her close or set her away from his pee-soaked clothing. He settled for putting his hands on her shoulders and rubbing his palms along her back.

"For being so heroic in the face of danger. For putting your arms around me when we thought the truck was going to crush us. For getting out and going after the driver when he might be training a shotgun on you. For holding Bella and not having a fit when she peed all over you."

He chuckled. "What else could I do? She couldn't help it."

"I know, but some people would have at least yelled. I would have pegged you as one of those people. But you were calm and accepting. Very sweet."

"Yeah, I'm a real sweetie. Just your average Joe nice guy." He thought of his father again and wondered if he would be called upon to talk about what had happened there and his reaction to it. He hoped not. He hadn't had time to process that experience himself yet. He wasn't sure he ever would. And it struck him how pretty insane it was that he could react so dramatically to his father, but then be cool and collected in the face of a potential maniac on the road. There was no way to explain it. He prayed he wouldn't have to.

At last, she released him, both from her embrace and from his tortured thoughts. "Hey, you just get into the shower. I'll go get your bag for you."

"No!" he said too emphatically. He didn't want to tell her she shouldn't be outside alone in case the truck driver had accomplices. "I'll get it," he said more calmly. "What are a few more minutes in this condition? And you can feed the animals and make sure Bella has plenty of water like the vet said. And Shannon could call back anytime, so—"

She waved her hands in surrender. "Okay, okay, go ahead and fetch it yourself. You can bring mine in while you're at it. I'll feed the critters."

Bella raised her head when they departed, but she was not otherwise disposed to move. Julian noticed that Jasper lurked just outside the room, peeking in at Bella, skulking back and forth, almost as if he were worried about his arch enemy with the broken leg.

"Do you want something to eat, too?" Kelsey asked as she went through the living room.

"No, I'm not hungry." He headed to the exit.

From the kitchen, he heard her say, "I could make you a sandwich, or whip up some scrambled eggs or something."

"No, really, I'm not very hungry."

When he came back into the apartment with the two suitcases, he saw that she'd changed into clean clothes. And she asked again.

"Are you sure? Because I just found some homemade stew in the freezer and it would only take me a second to heat it up. And I could throw together some biscuits to go with it."

"You go ahead," he said as he retreated to her bathroom. Already he'd begun to feel trapped. But he forced himself to push past those old feelings. She wanted to feed him because she was a nurturing soul who'd had a really rough day. Maybe he should encourage her. Even if he didn't eat it, cooking would make her feel better.

"Hey, you know what?" he called to her. "I probably could eat something after my shower. Make whatever you want."

"Okay!" came her cheerful reply from the kitchen.

Julian grinned as he stripped off his wet shirt and undershirt and then wondered about what to do with it. He didn't want to put it down on anything, given the stuff all over it. He trudged back the way he'd come, shirts in hand.

Rounding the corner to the kitchen, he found Kelsey in the refrigerator. Or at least her head and shoulders were in there. Her delectable backside remained in view until she drew herself out with a huge glass dish in her hands. She was startled when she saw him and almost dropped the dish. The two of them reached to steady the thing at the same time, though he had the presence of mind not to use the hand that held the sodden clothing.

"You scared me. I thought you were in the shower." She looked sheepish as she set down the dish.

"We'll both be a little skittish for a while. That was some scary stuff we went through today."

"I guess you're right, but I hate that. Perfect strangers with the power to make me jittery. That's just not right. I've had just about all I can stand of surprises and scares."

"Well, you're safe here with me, Kelsey. I won't let anything happen to you now." He hoped he could make good on his promise. "I need a plastic bag for these clothes."

She fetched him one and turned a speculative and interested gaze to his naked torso. "I might just join you in the shower, G.I. Joe," she said. "The stew is going to take a while to heat."

He laughed and it felt good to do so after the day they'd had. "Feed the animals first because if you join me in the shower, it could end up being a very long shower."

She smiled at him and there were promises in her eyes. But then the phone rang and she dashed to answer it.

CHAPTER FOURTEEN

"HELLO?" Kelsey said into the phone. "Oh, Shannon! You'll never guess! I have Bella back!"

"Ohmigod!" Shannon shrieked. She turned away from the phone and shrieked the good news to someone. Kelsey assumed she must be talking to Ken or one of the people at the animal shelter. "I'll be right home!" her sister cried. "You can tell me the whole story when I get there."

When she arrived with Ken and his dog, Kelsey did not, of course, tell Shannon the whole story. That would have served no purpose. Shannon spent her time on post where things were fairly safe. Besides, Shannon kept company with the capable MP sergeant who wouldn't let anything happen to her. Telling her the whole story would just upset her for no reason.

But the story they told was serious enough. They explained that the guy in the truck had to be a lunatic the way he'd shoved Bella out of the vehicle and broken her leg. Ken Steinhauser got really angry at that.

"How could anyone hurt a dog? They don't do anything but serve people!" His face had become flushed and his big German shepherd looked avidly up at his master's agitation from his position on the floor.

"As long as she's home safe and she can heal, I don't want to think about that awful man," Shannon said. She held her dog gently and Bella dozed contentedly in the safety of familiar arms.

"Did you get tags on the guy? Did you call the police?" Ken asked. "I mean, this jerk was cruel to a defenseless animal." He looked to Julian for answers to these questions.

"Yes, we called the local civilian police. Probably the driver isn't stupid enough to hang on to that truck. But sometimes we get lucky. I got the impression he was heading out of town from the way he said 'I'm out of here for good.'"

"That's what I thought, too," Kelsey confirmed. The guy had given her the impression that he was bailing out on something. "But what I can't figure out is why he had Bella. I'm pretty sure he's the same guy that followed me before. Was he trying to give Bella back then, too?" It all made no sense to her. But she wondered now if the driver could have been somehow involved in what had happened at the warehouse. Or maybe he was involved in Julian's theft ring. Julian had already asked his paralegal to find out the name of the owner, traced through the tag number.

But now wasn't the time to speculate about all that. "Anyone want more cookies?" she asked, glad she'd been able to cook dinner for the four of them. It had calmed her nerves. Feeding more than just herself had been wonderful. And they'd eaten almost everything she'd made.

"You're going to smother the man," Shannon said.

Ken spoke up. "I don't mind. And I'll take another cookie."

"Not you," Shannon said. She handed Ken the cookie plate, but nudged her head toward Julian meaningfully.

Kelsey held her breath as she glanced his way. She knew he didn't know how to accept caring gestures from others. They made him feel trapped and overwhelmed. Yet, she didn't know how to be aloof or reserved. When she loved someone, she loved in a big way—including the cooking and baking. That was simply part of her nature. But Julian had left her last year because he didn't know how to deal with someone like her. She wondered if he agreed with Shannon now.

"Kelsey can smother me with this kind of cooking any time she wants to," Julian said with a smile in her direction. And he seemed sincere. The smile put the seal of honesty onto his words.

Kelsey's insides went all warm and fluttery as she let out her breath on a sigh. And she loved him even more when he got up and helped her clear the table. "You two sit," he said to Ken and Shannon when they made as if to help. "We can handle this. Besides, the kitchen's not big enough for four of us."

That was true. Someday, she'd have a house with a big kitchen and an island for the stove and lots of counter space. But for now, her apartment had a small dining area outside the galley kitchen in which two people would rub up against each other if they were in it at the same time. When Julian was her kitchen mate, she didn't mind at all.

"Hey, I want to talk to you about something," he began in a near whisper when they were both out of sight of the other two.

She looked at him and felt warmth suffuse her. Her body thrummed in anticipation.

"I think I should be going to my own apartment for the night. You need to spend some time with your sister. And she'll need your help taking care of Bella."

Kelsey's thrum fizzled instantly. She struggled to keep disappointment off her face. Hadn't she just been reminded that he might be feeling smothered? He'd had a day filled with raw emotions. After their wonderful time at Disney, and then that awful experience at the nursing home, she knew he'd need to decompress alone.

And yet, she couldn't keep herself from saying, "You could stay," even though she knew he wouldn't. The words sounded pathetically wishful and needy.

He looked at his sandaled feet, clearly uncomfortable. She bit her lip, wishing she could take back those three words. He'd said he wanted to go and she should let him. Clinging wouldn't help the situation.

"I really shouldn't intrude," he said. "And, as you saw at the nursing home, I don't do family very well."

It was the first overt reference he'd made to what had happened earlier in the day. She was surprised he'd said anything at all about it. She'd expected him to pretend it hadn't happened. She longed to talk to him about his reactions there, but she knew she had to tread carefully.

"And I have to get into clean clothes and all." He plucked at the Hawaiian shirt and shorts from Disney World. They had been the only items in his bag cleaner than his pee-soaked uniform. The man couldn't possibly look more out of sorts in the painfully bright and colorful outfit.

Mercy seemed like the best she could offer him at the moment. "I understand. It's okay. Go home, put on your favorite sweats. Kick back. I'll hang with Shannon. Tomorrow you promised to take me to that Dr. Calcera guy who's gonna shrink my head." She had that, at least. He'd promised to see her tomorrow. Too soon, he'd be able to send her on her way without any hope of a phone call from him. But not yet.

"I'm not sure—" he began.

But she waved him to silence. "You're not getting out of it, Julian. You made the appointment and you promised you'd go with me. I know you think it's some kind of conflict of interest, but if you're not with me, I'm not going." She put on her stubborn face.

That got his serious eyes to take on a sparkle of humor. "I will keep my promise," he said. "The office is out in Bowie, Maryland, so we'll need at least an hour. I'll pick you up at ten-thirty."

She nodded as relief secretly tiptoed through her. She'd thought he might argue about going with her to the doctor appointment. "That'll give me a chance to check in at the warehouse," she said. "Technically, I'm still on leave through tomorrow, but I want to find out how things are going. So you can pick me up there."

"Sounds like a plan." But after he said that, he looked down again and seemed to be debating what his best exit strategy would be.

Kelsey decided on a direct approach. "Are you sure you'll be okay alone tonight? You had kind of a rough time with your visit to your dad."

He looked up again at that and he gazed right into her eyes. "I'll be fine," he said almost too quickly. Something in his expression told her he was aware that it would be a long night of struggles with his internal demons. She wished she could help. But if he wouldn't let her, she had to let him work it out on his own.

"Okay," she said. "Just remember you can call me, even if it's in the middle of the night."

He didn't seem to take offense at her offer and she took this as a good sign. Then he surprised her again by gathering her into his arms. "Thanks," he said softly as he kissed her on the forehead. "It's nice to have good friends."

As she hugged him in return, sadness overwhelmed her usually positive outlook. She wanted to be a whole lot more than just friends with Julian. But she didn't think she'd get it. He didn't even want to talk about such possibilities. And she absolutely hated that he had total control over the future of her love life. But she couldn't force Julian to love her. This detestable lack of control reminded her of why she hadn't made any effort to pursue a relationship with this man before.

But now things were different. Now she was completely in love with the guy. Not just partly or a little bit, but entirely smitten with no hope of recovery. The worst of it was, she'd known full well that he had commitment issues this time around.

As she said goodbye to him at the door, she knew that her situation was all her fault. She should have known better than to start something with this man. Even Shannon would have known better, and she had the worst track record of anyone Kelsey knew. But here she was anyway. And as she watched him go, her heart felt heavy with wishes that would never come true.

THE HOURS IN BETWEEN when he left her and the time he could pick her up for the trip to Maryland were interminable for Julian. During that time, thoughts about his father clawed at his brain relentlessly. No matter how hard he tried to think instead of the time he'd spent making love with Kelsey or the day they'd had together at Disney, his mind kept returning to what had happened in his father's room when he'd suddenly lost control over his emotions.

At last, somewhere in the wee hours of the morning, he gave up trying to fend off the tormenting memories and decided to face them head-on. He took those awful moments out of forced hiding and did his best to examine them intellectually.

If he had to describe what had been going on inside him at the nursing home, he would have said that all the anger and disappointment and hurt caused by his father had suddenly congealed into an overpowering emotional and physical reaction. The only way to regain control, he thought, was to analyze each of those hidden feelings.

But it wasn't that easy. As he examined his emotions, they seemed to only increase in intensity. Because once he started remembering the specifics about his experiences with his father, he realized he had every damn right to be angry and resentful. Anyone would be hurt by the coldheartedness of his old man. The worst of all of the congressman's paternal transgressions had been, of course, the many lectures he'd delivered about how real men don't cry.

As a result, Julian hadn't cried since grade school, though there had been plenty to grieve over. He had not wept at his mother's funeral, not when his first girlfriend had dumped him, not when his dog had been put to sleep at the vet's.

God! He hadn't thought of his dog in years. Probably repressed those memories, considering how vulnerable he'd been when the dog had passed away. His old dog Hanford had stopped being able to climb the stairs by himself. Arthritis had taken its toll. And his father dearest had calmly informed seventeen-year-old Julian that it was time for the dog to be put down. Julian had driven the dog to the vet himself, not trusting his father to stay with the animal until the end. It would have been just like the congressman to drop the dog off, slap down some money and go. But Julian knew even at that tender age that leaving the dog alone for his last journey wasn't the right thing to do. So he'd hoisted the dog into the back seat of his car and talked to the old mutt the entire way there in reassuring tones. When he got to the reception desk with his lifelong companion at his side, his throat had hurt so much and felt so tight, he could barely say what he needed done.

But he'd stayed with Hanford until the end. He had held him in his arms the whole time and for a long time afterward, just rocking back and forth until the weight of the animal made his arms tremble and Hanford's spirit had seemed to slip from the room and from the world forever.

How could he have forgotten old Hanford? But now that he remembered, the pain of that day hit him like a lead pipe to his emotional solar plexus and finally, after nearly twenty years, Julian wept for his dog. And then for his mom. And then for the boy who'd never been allowed to cry.

KELSEY WOKE to the sound of her phone ringing. The bedside clock read a little after oh four hundred. She picked up the receiver before the noise woke Shannon, blissfully asleep with Bella in the guest room.

"Hello?" she rasped.

"Kelsey," Julian said. "I'm sorry to wake you. I...I shouldn't have called. I didn't even realize it was so late... early. I should have looked at the clock and waited."

She sat up immediately, clutching the phone to her ear. "That's okay. What's wrong?"

"Nothing. Everything's fine," he said, but she could hear an edge to his voice that told her he'd had a long, hard night. "But I've been doing a lot of thinking tonight. And I want to thank you for going with me to visit my dad. And for staying with me afterward while I pulled myself together."

"I was glad to be there for you. God knows you've been a good friend to me lately."

"Well, I...I just want you to know," he began. But then he seemed to lose his resolve. He hesitated for a long time.

"Do you want me to come over to your place?" she asked gently.

"No. You should sleep. I need to sleep, too. But I knew I wouldn't do that without talking to you." He huffed a rueful laugh. "Sorry. It seemed so important that I speak to you right away that I couldn't wait. But now that I've woken you up, I'm not so sure."

"Honestly, it's okay. I'm glad you called. What was it you wanted to say?" She held her breath, waiting, hoping.

"I just want you to know I'm really trying this time. To be a better man. To be someone you can count on. I want—" He cut himself off.

Old habits die hard, she supposed, as she heard the struggle behind the unsaid words. But one thing she wouldn't do was help him articulate what he felt or what he wanted. That was the last thing he needed. And he'd likely go along with whatever she guessed even if she guessed wrong. A man like Julian might find that easier than getting in touch with what really stood behind the locked doors of his heart. She refused to give him such an easy out.

"I just don't want you to worry," he said. "I won't stop calling you without warning."

She almost laughed at that. It certainly wasn't very comforting to know he'd be sure to give her warning this time when he decided to stop calling her. Somehow, she managed to keep that thought to herself. She made a sound to acknowledge that she'd heard him, then waited for him to say more.

"And I want to be sure you know that I care for you. I…I know you think that if I can't accept your story on faith and just blindly trust you that this somehow means I don't really care for you. But that's not true," he said firmly. "Because I do."

A dispassionate side of Kelsey noted that he had just affirmed that he did not believe her version of the events in her warehouse, that he didn't trust her memories of that night. She didn't know yet if she could accept the possibility that someone could have so many doubts about a person and still claim to have deeper feelings.

"We'll find out tomorrow whether I'm telling the truth," she said evenly. The instant the words were out, she knew she'd said the wrong thing. She should have told him that she cared for him, too.

She couldn't say it now without sounding forced. She didn't want him to wonder if she said it only because he had. Or worse, that she'd felt sorry for him. He would hate that.

"Yeah, we'll find out tomorrow," he said after a few long seconds during which she had no doubt that he catalogued what she had *not* said. "Okay, well, I should let you get back to sleep."

She wanted to cry out "Julian, I love you!" and to hell with the consequences. But she feared he wouldn't accept those words from her now. The moment had passed.

"Do you think you can sleep now, too?" she asked gently, trying to express her love through her concern for him.

"I think so."

"Because I could come over there, if you want." But even before she finished the sentence, she felt him withdrawing.

"No, that's okay," he said, predictably. "And I'm sorry I woke you. I'll see you at ten-thirty. If your deputy has any inventory reports, maybe you could bring them along. We could talk about them on the way."

"Good idea," she said, but all she could think about was how she'd lost a rare opportunity with him. She yearned for a do-over. But those didn't happen in real life.

They said good-night to each other and Kelsey gently

returned the phone to its cradle. She wondered what torments he'd suffered through all alone in his austere apartment before making his unexpected call to her. And she wondered if she would ever have the kind of relationship with him where she could ask.

JULIAN KNEW he looked like he had a hangover when he walked into Kelsey's office the next day. After he'd called her sometime before sunrise, he still hadn't been able to sleep. He'd found himself recalling how she'd told him the other day that she didn't want to get married yet and then bundling that up with the fact that she hadn't made any kind of declaration about her feelings for him last night. For the first time since he'd met her, Julian questioned what he'd been assuming about Kelsey. She'd seemed to be in love with him a year ago and he'd somehow leaped to the conclusion that she must be in love with him again now. But she'd had every opportunity to say so last night. And she hadn't. So he looked like death warmed over today. Somehow, he knew she wouldn't care. And sure enough, her only remark was to say he looked tired and to offer her driving services again.

Against his nature, he accepted her offer for a second time in as many days. She was a good driver—not too slow, assertive without being aggressive. It came as a complete surprise to him that he didn't mind being her passenger.

As they walked to the car, she handed over a stack of documents she'd carried out with her. "Those are the inventory reports so far. It's for about two thirds of the warehouse. But the thing I don't like is that we do a preliminary inventory of one section only to have stuff moved out afterward and showing up in another section. Or sometimes materiel will be put into an already reviewed area for some reason. I don't understand how that would help thieves, but it sure is confusing the hell out of getting an accurate picture of what's inside that building."

He thumbed the key fob to unlock the car, then handed her the keys. As they settled into their seats, he asked, "Didn't you say you thought maybe someone was just trying to stall for time, mix everything up to make it impossible to get an accurate count?" This had been gnawing at him since she'd mentioned it to him in Florida. If the bad guys were making a mess of things just to buy time, that had to mean they were close to finishing whatever they were up to. If he didn't ID them soon, they'd take off with the goods and be lost to justice forever.

But at least once they were gone, Kelsey would be safe. One of the things that had kept him awake the night before was the thought that he hadn't stayed with her to protect her after the near miss they'd had with the truck. He'd forgotten his vow to look out for her because he'd been self-absorbed. Emotions had clouded his judgment.

He wouldn't let that happen again.

"Yes, I think that's a possibility, don't you?" She pulled out onto the main road and headed northeast. "I mean, why would anyone just keep moving stuff around? I think it's so we can't easily get a good grip on what's missing. Before I have this figured out, the perpetrators will have absconded with my materiel!"

He almost laughed at her use of "perpetrator" and "absconded," but realized just in time that she was in no mood for seeing the humor. In fact, now that he looked at her, he could see that tension just about rolled off of her. She was coiled so tight, she might implode at the slightest provocation.

"Hey," he said as he put a hand on her shoulder and rubbed the taut muscles there. "Are you nervous about this visit to the doctor?"

She smirked at him. "Wouldn't you be?"

Well, yeah, but the likelihood of him ever submitting to hypnosis for any reason seemed so far from anything he could imagine that he hadn't really given it a thought. He would never be able to give up control like that. "Yes," he said. "But remember that he's a professional. He came highly recommended."

"By your therapist, a man I've never set eyes on."

Hmm. When she put it like that, he had to admire her willingness to go along with the whole thing. Would he have done it for her if the situation were reversed?

No way.

"We don't have to go through with it, Kelsey. I can call and cancel." He felt he had to offer even though he hoped she'd decline.

"No. Now that we're on our way, I just want to get it over with. But I want your solemn promise that you won't leave me alone with this guy even for the slightest second."

"I promise," he said. "But what happens if I'm not allowed in the same room with the two of you? I mean, I have no idea how this works, just that Dr. Moriarty said it could produce big results."

"If you can't stay by my side, then we leave without doing it. Simple as that."

"Okay," he agreed. He could hardly do otherwise given his realization that he'd never be caught dead doing what she was about to do. Even if he tried, he doubted he'd be the type who could be induced into a hypnotic trance, no matter how good the doctor was. It was probably a trust issue. And he didn't have any. Didn't that pretty much sum up his whole life?

HE THOUGHT ABOUT THAT AGAIN an hour later when he found himself sitting in Dr. Calcera's office, off to one side, watching him ease Kelsey into a peaceful state from which her subconscious could deliver the unclouded truth. The doctor hadn't wanted Julian inside the same room with them, but Kelsey had been adamant. Dr. Calcera had finally relented.

To ease the doctor's concerns, they had agreed to have Kelsey only answer questions about that night in the warehouse. No personal issues would be broached. Dr. Calcera had assured them that Julian couldn't accidentally be put under hypnosis, too. And he'd been so friendly and open with Kelsey that she seemed far more relaxed than she'd been in the car.

"How do you feel?" Dr. Calcera asked Kelsey after he'd done his thing and counted to three.

"Fine," replied Kelsey in a faraway voice.

"I want to take you back to a particular night when something happened in your warehouse," he said. "Can you remember that night?"

"Yes," she said, frowning slightly. Julian leaned forward in his seat, completely focused on Kelsey and able to feel her tension grow as she remembered.

"You were sitting at your desk in the office in the warehouse. Can you tell me what happened next?"

"I heard a noise," she replied.

Slowly but surely, Dr. Calcera drew the story from her in more detail than she had recalled when she'd gone to Julian's office looking for help. Now, she could remember the hair color and rank of the man on the lift, she remembered a distant sound of a door opening and closing and she recalled the scent of blood mixed with the fragrance of cologne. She described the unit patch on the soldier's uniform. Julian knew this to be the same unit as Rigley's. But other than some added specifics, her retelling of what happened that night didn't differ in any material way from what she'd told Julian immediately afterward.

And he'd spent so long not believing her, that now he had a very hard time adjusting his thinking. And deep down, he wondered if perhaps the hypnosis hadn't worked after all and she'd simply retold the story that she'd built up in her mind since the incident.

Dr. Calcera eased Kelsey to the conclusion of her story while Julian tried to sort out his thoughts. Then he heard the doctor ask if there was anything else she'd like to say about the night at the warehouse. His gaze returned to Kelsey when he heard her speak again.

"I shouldn't have gone to Julian for help," she said.

"Why is that?" Dr. Calcera asked gently.

"Because his life was going along perfectly before I went to him with my problems. Now his life is a mess."

CHAPTER FIFTEEN

JULIAN SAT THERE and stared at her while blades sliced through his heart. She thought his life had been perfect without her? Nothing could be further from the truth. He needed to find a way to tell her that without complicating their relationship more than it already was. After her claim that she wasn't ready for marriage, added to those uncomfortable few moments when she hadn't returned any sentiment during their phone call last night, he wasn't sure how to do that.

"How did I do?" Kelsey asked upon coming back to consciousness. "I feel really good. Like I got in a great nap."

"You did fine," said Dr. Calcera. "Hypnosis frequently makes people feel refreshed. Sometimes the subconscious mind will feel freed of the burden of suppressed memories and the patient will cope better afterward."

"You did great," Julian said. But he had trouble making eye contact with her. He suspected his cheeks were flushed. She didn't realize she'd said the part about his perfect life and he didn't know quite how to handle that.

"Okay. So tell me what I said. Did I give you a different story?" Her eyes were bright, her expression hopeful and wary at the same time.

"No," Julian said carefully. "You gave the same story as before with a few more details." That fact shocked him almost as much as her concluding statements had. He'd been so sure she'd tell them something different. Now, he didn't know what to think. If her story were true, then where was the evidence? There was still nothing to back it up. Unless somehow the test for blood traces had gone wrong and Rigley wasn't actually in Florida but dead and hidden somewhere. Both were unlikely.

"So that means I was telling the truth, right?" She looked to Dr. Calcera for support of this conclusion.

"Yes, that's what it means. Under hypnosis, the subconscious isn't able to lie or hide what it knows," said the doctor.

As Julian sat struggling with all the unexpected things he'd learned, Dr. Calcera and Kelsey talked awhile about the session. When she said she was satisfied that her memories corresponded with what she'd said under hypnosis, Julian paid the man and they departed. Lost in his own thoughts, he gave little attention to what Kelsey said to him on the way to the car. Eventually, she fell silent, too. That silence stretched on and on, even as she got them back on the road.

After a long while, Kelsey growled through gritted teeth, alerting him to her irritation. "Enough of this!" she nearly shouted. "Tell me what's bothering you. Did I say something upsetting? Or are you just struggling with how to balance your lack of evidence against the truth of my story?"

"Honestly, I don't know what to make of it. I can't figure out where I went wrong. I was so certain that something else happened to you that night."

"What did you think happened?" she asked.

"I was afraid you were sexually assaulted and had suppressed the awful memories," he said quietly.

"But now you know that didn't happen."

"Right. But I still don't understand where the evidence is. I'll have to start over completely, retesting everything." He ran his fingers through his hair and rubbed his temples. His head throbbed with a tension headache.

Grasping for a clearer picture, he pulled out his small green notebook and flipped back through the pages, reviewing what he'd already written there. "Something's wrong with how I've been looking at all this. I need to get a fresh perspective."

He rarely made such mistakes. The fact that he'd done so in Kelsey's case proved he should have removed himself from the investigation early on. He was simply too close to her, too emotionally involved, too much in love with her to be clearheaded. How horrible that he could be so deeply in love with her, but unable to show it in any normal way.

"What do the reports from my warehouse tell you?" she asked. He'd forgotten they'd brought them along. He reached for the stack of papers resting on the back seat and brought them forward, glad to have something else to focus on. He prayed they would reveal something—anything— that would help him make some progress in whatever the hell was going on.

THEY TALKED about the confusing reports all afternoon and into the dinner hour while Kelsey whipped up another home-cooked meal. She felt as happy as she'd been in weeks while she whisked a sauce and checked the roasting chicken. Having Julian with her and ready to savor her offerings made the day seem brighter than it had any right to be, given the dire nature of the case they wanted to solve. And Julian seemed happier, too, in a cautious sort of way.

Shannon had called to say that she and Bella would be dining at Ken's place, so Kelsey had Julian all to herself without any threat of him feeling overwhelmed by family. And even though they talked about thieves and accidental deaths all through dinner, Kelsey felt content to have this time with the man she'd fallen in love with. As the summer sun set, the evening seemed to be shaping up to be a memorable one. She wanted all the memories she could collect before the inevitable end arrived and Julian withdrew from her permanently.

Then—as if fate just couldn't stand for the two of them to have another glorious night together—the phone rang. Kelsey had her teacup halfway to her mouth, gazing at Julian over the top of it, when the ringing startled her. She looked at the phone on the little table near the kitchen, puzzled. It didn't sound quite right. But then she noticed Julian fumbling for his cell and she realized the call was for him. She smiled and shook her head in disbelief as he said hello. Of the hundreds of possible unique rings and songs that cell phones could have these days, Julian had set his to sound like an ordinary desk phone.

"Tonight?" she heard him say. Her heart sank as she saw his expression and the way he glanced at her with regret in his eyes. He was being called away. Maybe he'd be able to wiggle out of it.

"Yes, I understand. If he's sick, he's sick. I'll cover for him." He glanced at his watch and Kelsey knew he had to go.

The instant he closed his phone, she said, "I'll go with you."

He stared at her for a moment, then smiled. "You don't even know where I'm going. I could be on latrine duty, for all you know."

"Last I checked, all our latrines were the indoor flushing kind. We're not living out of tents in a foreign country at the moment."

"Have you done a tour overseas?" he asked, avoiding the issue at hand.

"Yes. My second tour of duty was in Bosnia working supplies." She grinned at him. "I even know how to dig latrines. What about you?"

"I went over to Iraq the first time, doing intelligence. Got the ligament in my left knee torn to shreds, so I came home to work in Criminal Investigation."

"Better than coming home in a body bag," she said. "Did you have surgery on it? I didn't notice a scar and you don't even limp."

He nodded. "I worked pretty hard at physical therapy after the surgery for nearly a year to make sure I didn't limp." A grin slid over his features. "And I kept you pretty busy all the times we were naked—too busy to notice a little scar on my knee."

"It must have hurt like hell. How did it happen?"

"I was in Military Intelligence back then. An enemy combatant found our hiding place and we ran for it. He chased us and kept sort of randomly firing his weapon. Honestly, we're lucky we made it out alive. I didn't even know I'd been hit until we were back with our unit. Too much adrenaline, probably. The worst of it was getting sent home in the middle of the action and then being told I was going to be riding a desk from then on."

She could sympathize with the agony of wanting to do more for the American cause but being prohibited from doing so. For Julian, his knee kept him out of the war. For Kelsey, it was the fact of her gender. She could go to the zone of conflict, but she'd have to stay well back and out of harm's way—sometimes digging latrines. The possibility of danger or capture was there, but unlikely. Though her superiors told her repeatedly that she performed an extremely valuable service, it never felt like enough.

"Now you know why I'm here and not overseas." He paused. "My first wife liked marriage better when we were apart. And she didn't like the limp that I still had when she left me."

Kelsey looked at him, wondering if he would notice that he'd referred to his ex as his *first* wife—as if there would be a second. She said, "I'm just glad you lived."

"After I got injured, one of the guys said that I was leading a cursed life. Bad things just kept happening to me. Nothing that would kill me and put me out of my misery, but just enough to keep me from being happy. Funny, he hadn't even met my wife. He might have heaped her in with all the other misfortunes." He looked into Kelsey's gaze and gave her a wry smile. "I chose right then to make sure I didn't live my life as one bit of bad luck after another. I'm not a victim. I had to get past my divorce when I got back to the States, but after that I became determined to stay focused on my new career and be the best investigator I could be."

She saw determination in his eyes. "That's why I came to you that night after things went so crazy in my warehouse," she said. "Because you're the best and I knew you'd figure it out if anyone could. I still think you'll figure it out."

He nodded. "First thing tomorrow, I'm going to do that luminol test over again." He stood. "But tonight, I'm afraid I have to go watch your warehouse. The guy who had tonight's shift came down with the flu and got put on quarters."

She got to her feet. "Like I said, I'll go with you."

He shook his head. "That's not a good idea."

"Of course it is. You've been up all day and didn't get much sleep last night, I'll bet. Now you're planning to stay up most of the night again. You'll need someone to help you stay awake."

"I don't want to put you in danger, no matter how remote."

She put her hands on her hips. "You can't be serious. I'm an officer in the army. I've been trained for danger. And it's *my* warehouse that needs watching."

He matched her pose and they stood glaring at each other. Kelsey broke the stalemate. "I'll just go to my warehouse on my own anyway. You can't stop me."

He chuffed his frustration as he recognized that he couldn't leave her behind. "It's probably better if I keep you with me anyway. Can you shoot?"

"I'm pretty good, actually. I can be trusted to watch your back."

He nodded thoughtfully. "We wear Kevlar, too," he said.

"That's okay with me," she said with a triumphant smile. "Kevlar was invented by a woman."

"Really?"

She pulled a face at him as she passed him in the doorway. "Stéphanie Kwolek worked for DuPont when she invented the fiber that protects us from bullets."

"You're just full of fun facts. If this keeps up, it's gonna be a long night."

She laughed, but then she lost the humor when he stopped on the sidewalk looking thoughtful and serious.

"I need you to be on your guard tonight, Kelsey. These people, whoever they are, may be feeling hemmed in by all our watchfulness. They could be getting desperate to do what they think they need to do. That guy in the truck seemed pretty well panicked and if he had anything to do with all this, that's not a good sign. We have to stay alert every minute."

She nodded. But her stomach tightened and she realized for the first time what she could be getting herself into. If the guys stealing from her building decided to show up tonight, things could get dicey. When they climbed into the car, they were quiet and subdued.

At Julian's office, he secured weapons and protective vests for each of them. As Kelsey put hers on and felt the weight settle over her small frame, a wave of foreboding went through her.

"I CAN'T FIND HIM and he's not answering his phone." The Wolf decided not to mention what he'd found out about Earlman dumping the little dog off with the two interfering officers who could ruin everything if they didn't mind their own business. That news wouldn't help the officer's mood any.

"Find him, goddammit! We can't afford any loose ends. Not now! I'm meeting with our buyers this afternoon. There can't be any problems. You know what these guys are like."

"Yes, sir," said the Wolf. He knew exactly what their buyers were like. He'd had to kill enough of them when he'd been deployed to Afghanistan. Crazy radical fundamentalists who had only one motivation—to kill anyone who didn't agree with their ideals. Sometimes, late at night, it bothered the Wolf that he was going to make his fortune by helping such lunatics. But then he'd think of all that lovely money and the little place he planned to buy in Mexico. That struggling country was unlikely to become a terrorist target, so he'd be safe. And rich. Besides, if he didn't do it, someone else would. Might as well be his own pockets that got lined with green.

"Good luck with your meeting," he said. "We'll have the

crates outside the fence by nightfall." At least, that was the plan. The fact that CID had posted an investigator outside the warehouse each night had been a challenge. But they'd managed to deal with that. The person next on the roster to take over the shift wouldn't be a problem. The officer had assured him of that. All the Wolf had to do now was wait for the call to meet the truck at the gate.

JULIAN DIDN'T LIKE seeing Kelsey in Kevlar because it made him think she could be in worse danger at his side than she'd be at home in her apartment. He had to keep reminding himself that an MP had been watching the warehouse every night since Kelsey had first come to him with her harrowing story and not a thing had happened so far. So there was little chance of action tonight. Still, he couldn't relax.

"So, we just sit here and watch?" she asked as he drove his car slowly toward the building.

"That's about it," he said. "Pretty boring." But as they approached, his heart gave a start and Kelsey let out a tiny squeak when a deer bounded right in front of the car. Luckily, they hadn't been moving at more than a snail's pace and the animal bolted off across the road into more woods.

He pulled along the curb in a spot where he could see the front door and all along one side of the warehouse. "Lots of trees all around this place," he observed.

"I've always liked that about working here. Sometimes I take walks in these woods. I like the solitude and natural setting. But tonight, the trees look downright spooky."

He had to agree. The tree line took in none of the glow that streamed from the street lamps or the security lights fixed to the top of the building. The forest seemed to bring down a black curtain just inside its borders. Anyone could be in that darkness doing any number of things with Kelsey's ammunition and spare parts.

If he'd come alone, he would be thinking about the best way to inspect the border of the property. He could walk the perimeter and look for fresh footprints. "Have you been out in the woods lately?" he asked.

"No, not for a while. Too busy," she said wistfully. "Who's in the other car?" She indicated the other vehicle that sat quietly nearby.

"It's got to be one of Drew's people. I need to go relieve him. You stay here." He looked at her, seeing only what the strange angles of the streetlight cared to reveal. Her features were etched by the shadows. She looked beautiful and he wished he could kiss her. "Stay inside the car," he ordered again.

When he opened the door, the effects of the lighting were erased by the brightness of the overhead lamp. But he still wanted to kiss her. He forced himself to get out before he did something completely inappropriate.

Drew's guy was slouched behind the wheel of his vehicle, sleeping. Annoyed, Julian rapped on the window. The kid jumped so high, he hit his head on the ceiling. Rubbing the injured crown, the young man quickly opened the door and got out. "Yes, sir!" he said, as if he'd been told to stand at attention.

"You were sleeping, Sergeant Bales," Julian growled as he noted the guy's name from his uniform tag.

"Sir," was all the poor kid could think to say. He neither confirmed nor denied the accusation.

"I'll be talking to Major Mitchum tomorrow morning, soldier. Get on home now. I'm taking over the watch."

The young man looked somewhat aghast. Julian thought

he was shocked to get off so lightly until Bales spoke. "Where's Sommers, sir?"

"Who?"

"Specialist Sommers is supposed to relieve me tonight, sir."

"He's sick. I'm relieving you instead. You can go now." He'd had enough chitchat with this slacker. He wanted to get back to his car, back to Kelsey, back to making sure she was safe.

"Yes, sir," said the sergeant, still looking confused. He climbed back behind the wheel, started the car and drove away.

Julian chalked up the young man's nervousness to being worried about what Drew would do to him once he heard about his sleeping on watch. But he pulled out his trusty notebook from the pocket of his BDUs. Flipping to a blank page, he made a note: *Sergeant Bales 1) asleep on watch 2) thought Specialist Sommers would relieve him.* Julian wanted to be sure to check on the name of the sick guy he was relieving. If the bad guys expected this Sommers to be on watch while they got the stolen goods moving out of the warehouse, then Sommers might know some of the thieves even if he didn't realize what they were up to.

Still contemplating this, he walked back to the car. He had a bad feeling about tonight. And he wanted Kelsey away from here, out of harm's way. He tucked away the notebook and opened the car door.

"I'm going to call the MP station and have them come get you," he said as he seated himself behind the steering wheel. "I have this sense that something's going to go down tonight."

Her eyebrows lifted. "I'm not going to leave you out here all by yourself. Especially if you think something's going to happen."

"Kelsey, be reasonable. I can't worry about you and still do my job. I'll be distracted and that's dangerous."

She thought about that for a moment. "Okay, but I'll only leave if you get someone else to sit here with you. Some sort of backup."

He scoffed. "There is no one else. Do you think I'd be out here if we had people lined up to babysit your warehouse?"

She crossed her arms in front of her chest. "Then I'm not leaving. At the very least I can sit here by the phone and call for help if anything happens."

"The car isn't bulletproof," he pointed out, hoping she'd be logical. At the same time, his respect for her went up several notches. As much as he wanted to keep her safe, he also recognized that she was an officer in the army with lots of training. She could take care of herself.

She glared at him. "Oh, so that's supposed to make me feel better about you being here by yourself?"

He didn't want to argue with her. And she had a point. If something was going to happen tonight, he needed backup. So they sat in silence for a while, watching the warehouse and scanning the tree line.

Julian had just begun to relax his guard a little when he heard a noise through the open car windows.

"Did you hear that?" Kelsey asked in a whisper.

"Something's moving around at the back of the building," he said.

"Could be more deer or even a raccoon in the trash," she suggested. "We get lots of animals around here." There were no voices, only the rustle and scrape of something. An animal could be making that sound.

"Is there an entry to the warehouse back there?"

"A fire exit on one end and the door that you and I used

when you went out back to look in the Dumpsters and check for clues on that first day when I asked you for help."

He eyed the area from which he could still hear the faint indications of movement. Darkness hid whatever might be going on back there. "No one's supposed to be inside the warehouse tonight, is that right?"

"That's right. Lieutenant Sorrell said he was going home early to get ready for a big date tonight."

"Okay. Stay here while I go check it out."

"Alone?" she exclaimed. "What if it's the thieves? They're not above violence, Julian! Don't you think it would be better to let me circle around to the other side? Or at least let's call for help?"

Though he knew it was unfair to Kelsey, he could feel the noose of her concern tightening around his throat, just about choking him. Yet another reason he didn't know if he could handle a relationship, even with this woman. He sighed. "If it turns out to be raccoons I'm going to look pretty silly calling for backup. I'm just going to take a look and I'll be careful. You need to stay here by the phone in case it turns out I really do need help." He tossed his cell phone on the seat of the car so it wouldn't go off at the wrong moment. Even set on vibrate, the accompanying flashing light if a call came in would make him a target if the thieves were nearby. He grabbed a flashlight from beside the seat. Then he checked his weapon. "I'm planning to be stealthy. You just stay here so I don't have to take chances saving your pretty butt."

He saw her scowl and mutter curses. "If you get yourself hurt, I'll never let you forget it," she threatened as he climbed out of the car.

"Just stay here. That's an order, Captain." He edged around the nose of the car and hunkered down into the cover of some hedges to make his way to the edge of the building. From there, he began to ease his way slowly along the metal outer walls, hugging the shadows and watching his step to avoid unnecessary sounds.

About a third of the way, he heard a noise behind him. He stopped and glanced over his shoulder the way he'd come. Kelsey had emerged from the car and moved to stand near the trunk. He realized then that he could no longer see the front half of the car. She'd moved so she could keep her eye on him. Her gun was in her hand, pointing at the sky for now, but ready in case he needed assistance. He'd have done the same thing if their roles were reversed. As long as she stayed where she was, hunkered down near the taillights, he could go forward without protective instincts holding him back. Still, he found himself glancing over his shoulder to make sure she stayed put.

The sounds continued to come from the back of the building, still yards away. He stopped and looked around him, trying to pierce the darkness without night vision goggles. Why hadn't he thought to bring a set? He glanced back one more time.

Stopping for a moment to refocus, he reminded himself that he shouldn't keep worrying about her. Doing so was insulting to her as an officer. As he gave himself this two-second pep talk, he heard a clang and a muffled expletive echo from the darkness near where Kelsey had indicated the fire exit could be found. Not a raccoon then. His heartbeat went into overdrive as adrenaline pumped suddenly through his veins. Still, he held himself motionless, listening, gauging, assessing. He needed to get back to the car without being seen so he could call for backup.

Something suddenly spat at the ground near his feet and a split second before he registered what it was, the delayed report of a weapon firing hit his ear. In the next instant, a second bullet ricocheted off the metal wall of the warehouse, too close for comfort. Its sound echoed through the air as birds fluttered from their nighttime roosts. Unable to discern the location of the sniper, Julian ran for cover.

FROM HER VANTAGE POINT near the trunk of the car, Kelsey saw Julian stop to listen. Suddenly, he jumped to the side and looked at the ground. The gun report that followed his reaction to the bullet made her blood run cold. Instinct made her rush toward him with her weapon trained toward the back of the building where the shooter had to be hiding. She was halfway to him even before she heard a second bullet ping off the corrugated steel wall. She heartily approved of his decision to break for the forest to the right of the building—the closest cover—until she saw his progress abruptly halt as if he'd run into an invisible wall. Then, to her horror, she saw him collapse to the ground, face-first.

God, he'd been hit! And she hadn't fired a single shot! She couldn't see her target and if she fired now, she'd draw attention to herself. Since she was Julian's only hope, she held her fire and veered toward the cover of the trees. But she half ran, half crawled closer to him, hugging the shadows of the forest in which Julian had been trying to take cover. As she neared, she saw Julian's gun lying near his lifeless hand. And the instant she left the darkness toward his body, she became a new target. She felt the breeze of a bullet pass by her ear even as she dove toward Julian.

Without knowing how she managed it, she found his gun clasped tightly in her free hand. The repeated bark of the enemy's weapon combined with abject fear forced her to keep moving and she rolled and fired from both handguns almost at the same time, aiming in the general direction of where the unseen shooter had to be hiding. A shout of alarm told her she'd hit someone. On the hope that her return fire had bought her some time, she got her feet under her as she pocketed one of the guns, grabbed Julian's wrist and pulled him along behind her as she lunged for the dark forest once more.

CHAPTER SIXTEEN

AS SHE DRAGGED Julian, using all her strength to do so, Kelsey realized she would end up scraping his face if she didn't turn him onto his back. As soon as she moved into shadow, she tucked her second weapon into her belt and heaved him over, hoping she wouldn't cause him any injury. In the faint light, she saw that he'd already suffered a cut along his cheek. But at least he was breathing. She could just make out the rise and fall of his chest. Grasping both of his wrists, she pulled him farther into the trees until the two of them were as safe as possible behind a fallen trunk. Then she grasped her handgun again and crouched down beside him, listening hard, trying to control her own heavy breathing, doing her best to think clearly even while Julian lay unconscious by her side.

"Don't freakin' go in there!" she heard one of the assailants call out. She agreed with the man's exclamation. If more than one of them came into the woods after them, she and Julian were sitting ducks just waiting to be picked off. Their bodies wouldn't be found until an investigation team finally made its way there after Mark Sorrell discovered there had been another theft.

"They could be calling the authorities right now," came the reply. That made her think of her cell phone, but before she could act on the thought, Kelsey heard a twig snap under her pursuer's foot, too close. She held up her weapon and stared intently into the darkness, reaching blindly for her phone at her waist. It wasn't there. It must have fallen off in all the tumbling. Damn!

"That's why we're getting the hell out of here, idiot. Get back here on the double!" called the person farther away. Behind his voice were sounds of other people scrambling to move heavy objects quickly. How she wished she could call for support. But when she glanced to where she'd rolled toward Julian, she saw her phone glowing faintly in the grass thirty feet away, out of her reach. She knew then that the thieves were going to get clean away.

"Yes, sir," came the reluctant reply from the one nearby. He had to be talking to an officer. But who? An image of Andrew Mitchum came immediately to mind. He would certainly have the knowledge to work out the details of their scheme and to get materiel outside the fence line.

As she heard the footfalls of their stalker retreating, she let her breath out slowly, silently. But her heart continued to pound. Moving carefully so no noise would tempt the guy back toward them, Kelsey pivoted to see if she could better assess Julian's condition.

He was still breathing. His pulse seemed strong. But his eyelids remained closed. How long had he been unconscious? Probably less than five minutes. Everything had happened pretty fast. And she'd lost all sense of time in the chaos.

Gently, Kelsey unbuttoned Julian's shirt. Her vision had adjusted to the darkness enough to make out a flattened bullet in the center of his Kevlar vest. It hadn't penetrated, but the impact to his solar plexus had knocked him out cold. What should she do? Her brain seemed frozen and she couldn't decide on her next move. Lifting her head and looking out to where Julian had been shot, she wondered what her chances would be of retrieving her cell. But she could still hear voices and movement near the warehouse. Going into the open now seemed foolhardy. Worse than the danger to herself, she could draw fire on Julian, lying here helplessly. She couldn't even try to scoop up the phone and then make a run for the car to call for help. That would leave Julian alone and defenseless, too. And besides, she thought she heard movement in the direction of the car. Someone must be checking out their vehicle. She could hear the car doors being opened and closed along with a good deal of indecipherable mumbling.

As she crouched in the woods, tormented by indecision, she tried to listen to what the bad guys were doing. Orders to load up and to hurry were barked by someone in charge. Grunts and curses and the sounds of heavy items being dropped, presumably onto a truck, came to her. They were moving fast and in another minute, the sound of an engine turning over came to her ears. Confusing sounds came from where Julian's car stood, just out of her line of sight. And then the truck was put into gear and seemed to be moving.

They were leaving. They were getting away with the government property she was supposed to protect. But they were also giving her a chance to call for help for Julian. In the balance, the growl of the truck's retreating motor was a welcome sound. And her fortunes must have taken a general turn for the better because Julian's eyelids fluttered as he began to come around.

"Julian," she said as quietly as she could. "Open your eyes now."

He struggled to do as she asked. At last, he found and held her gaze. He grimaced as his hand went to his chest where the bullet had splayed into the miracle fabric that had saved his life. "Shit, that hurts!" he said, but he only managed a whisper, thank God.

"Shh! We're not out of danger yet."

He nodded that he understood. Then he lifted himself to a sitting position, wincing against the pain. He glanced at his surroundings, then cocked an ear to listen. Everything had gone quiet. Even the wind in the trees seemed to have died away, leaving them in ominous silence.

"They're gone. And we need to get moving, too," Julian said softly.

"You stay where you are. I'll get my phone and call for help."

"No, wait. I just need your help to stand up." He reached for her and she crouched and tucked herself beneath his arm.

"Are you sure you want to try to walk? You could have internal injuries."

"I'm okay. I've been shot before."

Well, hell. She didn't want to think about him being shot before. Instead, she did what he asked and slowly lifted. It was like doing a standing press of a couple of hundred pounds, only the weight wasn't even. The muscles in her legs strained, but eventually Julian got to his feet. He listed a little to one side, but he seemed to be steady enough. After a minute, he straightened himself, easing some of his weight from her shoulders without letting go of her.

"Not even a cracked rib," he told her as he took a deep breath and let it out. "How lucky is that?"

"Lucky," she agreed. But somehow she couldn't get out of her mind the picture of him stopping so abruptly and then falling to the ground. She shuddered at the memory.

"How'd I get into the woods? I don't remember crawling in here," he said.

"I dragged you here. Sorry about the scrape on your face."

He lifted his hand and ran gentle fingers over the raw area on his cheek. "That's okay. It's a lot better than being shot in the head, which is what would have happened if you hadn't somehow managed to get me out of sight."

She didn't want to think about that possibility. "You're heavy," she pretended to complain as she started moving cautiously toward the edge of the forest with her arm wrapped around his waist.

"I weigh two hundred and ten pounds. How'd you manage to move me?"

"No idea." She peeked around a tree to see if she could find any trace of their assailants.

"Looks like they're gone," he said. His arm over her shoulders felt warm and comforting and made her glad to have him with her. If she had to find herself embroiled in this much trouble at least she knew she could count on Julian.

"Let's go," she said. "We need to call the police. Maybe they'll catch the sons of bitches before they get too far."

As one, they moved first to where her cell phone sat in the grass. She scooped it up, letting go of Julian, and dialed 911 as they walked toward the car. She noticed that Julian kept a keen eye on where the thieves had been and made sure his body stood between her and any stragglers who might want to take a pot shot at them. Very heroic. But stupid. She didn't have the strength left to drag him to safety again. So she hurried to get behind the car. He followed. They let themselves slide to sitting positions against the back tire while she talked to the dispatcher.

"Yes, there was gunfire. Look, could you also send an ambulance—"

"No! I don't need an ambulance. They'll just want to take me to the damn hospital."

She ignored him. "And you need to see if you can intercept a truck heading out of the installation laden with boxes."

The dispatcher protested that there would be hundreds of trucks moving around post.

"Yeah, I know. But this truck will have ammunition and rocket parts in it. And the driver will be wanting to get out of the post as fast as possible. It ought to stand out." She'd had about all she could take. When the dispatcher continued to question her, Kelsey gave up and handed the phone to the expert. "Here. You talk to him."

As Julian took over explaining what was needed on the scene, Kelsey let her head fall back to rest against the fender. Exhaustion took hold of her even though adrenaline continued to pump through her veins. She closed her eyes, trying to keep the dizzy, trembling feeling at bay. The sound of a siren drifted toward her from a long distance away.

JULIAN ENDURED the poking and prodding of the medics who came in the ambulance for at least an hour, but he flatly refused to go to the hospital. He'd been knocked out by the impact to his chest, not to his head, and he'd endured that ignoble fate before. He knew he'd have a huge and painful bruise between his pectorals for about a month, but he'd survive. He'd been lucky this time and didn't even have any cracked ribs. His sternum might have been fractured, but there wasn't a thing any doctor could do for that. Time would heal it and nothing would hurry it along.

Kelsey took the brunt of the questions from the MPs. Police seemed to swarm the place like ants, but with less organization. Julian despaired that the crime scene would be useless by the time these guys were done with it. They said they were collecting evidence and casting footprints, but he thought they were more likely to cast their own footprints, given the lack of discipline. He wondered where Drew was. The major would have had these people in better order than the lieutenant who seemed to be in charge. But Drew was nowhere to be seen.

That made Julian wonder again about his friend. Did his absence have anything to do with what had happened tonight? Surely Drew would not allow someone to shoot him, even if the MP chief had gotten mixed up in stealing.

Distraction from that unpleasant line of inquiry arrived in the form of Kelsey, looking hot and bedraggled, but nonetheless beautiful, in her BDUs with the Kevlar underneath. She'd probably been too busy to take it off. The police had kept her repeating her story. One part that undoubtedly made no sense to anyone was why she'd been here with him, watching the warehouse. She hadn't given them the long version starting back when she'd seen something she shouldn't have all those nights ago. Instead, she'd simply told them she'd come with him as a friend to help him stay awake. Instinctively, she'd avoided giving too much information to people she didn't know. She didn't even attempt to explain how she'd gotten him into the safety of the woods. She just shrugged her shoulders, as perplexed as any of them, whenever someone asked.

"The MPs said we can go," she announced when she arrived at his side. "And they've assigned someone else to stand watch here. They've decided you've done enough for one day."

"The medics said you can nurse me back to health at home."

A medic gave a disgusted snort at that. "We told you that you need to go to the hospital for X rays, but you refused."

"I can tell when my ribs are broken and they're not," he

protested. Before Kelsey could negate his decision, he stood up from the bumper of the ambulance and took her by the elbow. Turning her toward the car and walking her there, he felt every one of his recently acquired bumps and bruises. He still marveled at what Kelsey had done, especially after he'd heard about her retrieval of the handgun he'd dropped on his way to unconsciousness. He would have suggested she should retrain for CID except he didn't want her to be in such a dangerous job. If she decided to go into that profession on her own, he'd find a way to get used to the idea. But he damn well wouldn't be the one to put the idea into her head.

"You better drive," he admitted as he tossed her the keys and headed for the passenger side.

"Let me take you to the hospital," she tried.

He was already shaking his head before she'd even finished the sentence. "I'd much rather recuperate in your apartment."

She smiled wearily and started the car. He could feel the tension still holding her in its grip. He shared her state of mind. No matter how hard he tried to remember that the police had matters well in hand, he couldn't shake the sense of imminent danger. Even as they rode along, he kept glancing around at the passing scenery as if he would be able to spot an assailant and somehow avert disaster.

"So at least this proves that the people stealing from my warehouse are willing to go to great lengths to do what they're doing," she said.

"Yes, it certainly does. Murder isn't beyond them, given the shot directly to my heart, so I will admit that they might also have gone to great lengths to cover up the death of one of their own in your warehouse that night."

She sighed wearily. "There's only a very small amount

of comfort in having you admit that. Honestly, I just want this whole thing to be over."

When they reached her apartment building, it was midnight and very dark. He worried about the walk from the car to the entrance and scanned every shrub for possible assailants. But they managed the distance without mishap.

"If you look over your shoulder one more time, I'm likely to start shrieking. You're making me nervous," she said.

"It's a post-gunfight sort of reaction. Feels like monsters are going to jump out from around every corner. It'll ease up in a while."

She unlocked the apartment door and he couldn't help but detain her. He walked into the place first, scanned the area, noted the cat making an aborted run to greet Kelsey and figured everything must be normal if Jasper was behaving the same as usual—at least until the feline spotted a man instead of the expected woman.

"All quiet on the home front, Jasper?" asked Kelsey as if she expected an answer.

None came. But the cat skirted Julian and rubbed against Kelsey's legs.

"Have a seat, Julian. If you keel over, I'll never forgive myself. Nor am I likely to find the strength to pick you up. I'll make you tea as soon as I listen to the phone messages."

She went to the phone table while he moved to the couch and sank gratefully into the softness. He watched her push the button and noted how rigidly she stood as she waited for the voices to play. Her nerves were still on edge from the events of the night. He hoped that she would begin to relax now that she was safe in her own home.

But neither of them relaxed when they heard the first recording say, "This is Mrs. Rigley." Julian sat forward, muscles as taut as Kelsey's. He caught her gaze and Kelsey held it as she listened.

"I'm calling you, Captain O'Roark, because you wanted to know if I got any news from my son." A flutter of relief went through him as he surmised that Specialist Rigley must be alive. He stood and moved nearer to Kelsey. She frowned at the answering machine.

The voice continued. "I'm worried, Captain. Very worried. That girl called here and said she was supposed to meet my son last week at her parents' house. He never arrived." Julian's spirits plummeted. Kelsey nodded gravely, lips compressed to a grim line.

"She thought he'd just stood her up for some reason, but when she couldn't reach him, she got worried and finally called here. Her name turns out to be Ginny Januszewski, of all things." The woman gave Ginny's phone number and then closed with a heart-wrenching plea to find her son.

Kelsey paused the machine and ticked through her caller ID until she reached the number from Florida for Rigley's parents. She jotted it down on the pad that sat by the phone. "That doesn't sound so good for Rigley," she said.

"Play the next message," he suggested.

She touched the Play button and the machine whirred on. The next voice was Shannon's. And it was one of the strangest messages Julian had ever heard.

"Hey, she's not home," came Shannon's voice. Julian had the impression that she spoke to someone else in the room with her and not actually to the answering machine. "I can talk to her when I see her." There was a pause and Julian detected the sound of cloth moving across the cell phone's mic. "Tell me again, Ken. Why do I need to talk to Kelsey as soon as possible?"

Then they heard Sergeant Ken Steinhauser let out a

loud, beleaguered sigh. "I told you already. Your sister's got herself mixed up in something dangerous. We need to keep her busy for another day or two while me and the guys clear things up, make some arrests and all. We can't have her poking around in stuff. She'll scare off the people we're after. Some folks are involved that you wouldn't expect."

"Kelsey's not in trouble, is she?"

"Not if she stays out of the way."

"What about Julian?"

"You and the captain need to leave the major to me. He's a dangerous man. The truth will come out in a day or so." Julian's eyebrows went up in surprise. Surely, the sergeant didn't think *he* was the officer involved in the thefts on post—or any other crime. He looked to Kelsey for her reaction, but she continued to listen with her complete concentration focused on the machine.

"And you need to keep Bella here with you while I tell Kelsey that I've lost my dog again," Shannon said. "Then I keep Kelsey occupied searching for her—again. Are you sure she'll fall for that?"

"Look, it's for her own good. And yours, too. And Bella's." There was an unspoken threat in his voice. Would he really harm Shannon's beloved little dog on top of his other veiled threats? Shannon must have heard the implied danger, too, because the sergeant sounded more soothing as he spoke further. "Hey, I don't want to scare you. But this is important and I have my orders. Just keep your sister busy for another day or two. You'll be helping an important government operation."

"Okay. Just let me say goodbye to my Bella and then I'll go find Kelsey." In the next instant, the message ended with a mechanical voice intoning the date and time of the call—only about fifteen minutes prior.

Kelsey stood with her back to him, shoulders slightly hunched, hands pressed flat to the surface of the table. Julian wanted to know what was going through her mind. But he had a pretty good idea what he'd be thinking if he were in her shoes.

"I'm not the officer involved in stealing from your warehouse, Kelsey."

She turned and looked him in the eye. "I never thought for a single instant that you were."

"Or any other crimes," he added as if she hadn't already exonerated him.

"I know," she said. She patted him on the shoulder as she passed by on her way to the kitchen. "Besides," she added when he followed her. "There's no shred of evidence that you could be. You're all about evidence, right? It's clear there isn't any." She shook the teakettle to ensure that water sloshed within. Then she turned on the burner.

"He implied that he thinks I'm involved. He might think he's got some sort of evidence to implicate me." As soon as he said it, he frowned, wondering why he would make a case against himself. Then he realized he needed to be certain that Kelsey continued to trust him. Somehow, that seemed imperative, so he poked at her assertion of his innocence in the hope she'd stand firm.

"He's mistaken," she said calmly.

"How can you be sure?"

"I just am," she said. "You want some tea?"

"It's not that simple," he protested.

"Of course it is. Tea, yes or no?"

"No, thank you. And you're just saying you believe I'm not involved to make a point about me not believing your story from the warehouse before."

"Don't be silly, Julian. I'm not *just* saying anything. If

I really thought you were involved in something nefarious, don't you suppose I'd be calling 911 right now?"

She had him stumped. It *did* make sense that if she had any doubts about him at all, she would call the police rather than calmly make tea. "Well, that's good, then," he said.

"Should I be worried about Shannon?" she asked as she chewed on the inside of her lip. "I mean, she said she was coming to talk to me, so I figure she's on her way. How is she going to get here? She doesn't have a car. Was that sergeant going to let her walk home?" She started to pace.

"Call her on her cell," he suggested. "Make sure she's okay."

"Why didn't I think of that?" she asked herself as she headed for the phone. "And you should be sitting down."

But that was the last thing he wanted to do at the moment. Instead of sitting, he began to pace as well, trying to make sense of what Steinhauser had said, trying to fit it in with what he knew of the theft ring and with Kelsey's situation. Instinct told him they were all interrelated.

"She's not answering," Kelsey said. A worried frown creased her brow. He wanted to comfort her.

Just as he reached for her, there came a commotion outside the apartment. When the front door opened, Shannon walked in. Drew Mitchum followed right behind her.

CHAPTER SEVENTEEN

KELSEY'S HAPPINESS at seeing her sister sifted away as she got a look at who came into the apartment with her. Major Andrew Mitchum had some explaining to do. But she would have preferred he didn't do it in her home. Better to make his confession from behind bars or before General Wilkes at a court-martial. Anywhere but here.

She squinted at him, but said nothing. The last thing she wanted to do was help him to realize they suspected his involvement in this mess. That would only make it easier for him to evade the truth. She hid her anger and worry by hugging her sister.

"We got your message," she said. "We've started to piece it together, but it would help to hear it from you. Tell me what's going on." She led Shannon into the living room, away from Mitchum.

"I needed to get it on tape," Shannon said. "So I thought if I called your answering machine…" Shannon trailed off and looked around with uncertainty in her eyes.

"You did just fine. We saved the recording. Why is Major Mitchum here?"

"He found me walking home. He offered me a ride. I knew he was with the police and that he was a friend of Julian's, so I figured I could trust him." She gave the major a tentative smile.

"She has quite a story to tell," Mitchum said. "I thought you'd want to hear it firsthand, so I brought her here before we go to the MP station."

"You're going to arrest her?" Kelsey couldn't keep the anger out of her voice.

Mitchum's eyebrows drew together in a frown. "No. She agreed to come to the station to answer questions, give a deposition to the JAGs."

Julian approached and his expression begged her to ease up. "Drew is here to help," he said. "He's already heard Shannon's story, so why don't we hear it, too?"

Kelsey understood his message—that there could be no harm in having Shannon speak in front of Mitchum since he'd already heard her story anyway. Kelsey turned her full attention to Shannon.

"He's got my dog," Shannon said as she fought back tears. "Shouldn't you be going after my dog?" She gave Mitchum a meaningful look.

The man returned her gaze with kindness in his eyes. "I have a man on the way right now. We'll get your dog back, Ms. O'Roark. Why don't you sit down and explain things to your sister and Julian."

She sank onto the sofa and Kelsey sat next to her. "I think Ken is part of whatever mess you've been involved in, Kelsey," she said. "I don't think he's a very nice man and he also thinks I'm stupid. Come to think of it, you must all think I'm stupid for imagining he was my friend." She glanced first at Julian and then at Kelsey.

"We don't think you're stupid," Kelsey reassured her. "Just start at the beginning, Shan. We need the details to fill in the whole story."

"I don't really have the whole story. But what Ken said didn't make sense. For one thing, he said he's trying to catch some people involved in crimes on post. I figured out from things he said that it had something to do with your warehouse. Like maybe somebody's stealing from there or something."

Kelsey exchanged a glance with Julian. Her sister had certainly figured things out well enough on her own. "Go on."

"At first, I believed him. Why wouldn't he be working on a case, gathering evidence for an officer in charge? But then he said he needed to keep Bella and that didn't really add up for me. I mean, what kind of police work involves keeping a little defenseless dog? He wanted to keep Bella to make me do what he wants. And what he wants is for me to keep you out of the way." She looked at Kelsey and there was fury in her eyes now. "He thought he could control me, that he could keep me from telling you what I know. But I figured out that he must be involved in some pretty bad stuff. Why else would he hold a dog hostage? And he wants you out of the way, Kels. You could be in danger. I'm afraid for you."

Julian moved closer to Kelsey's side, as if the threat might appear right here in her apartment and he would stand between it and her. Mitchum stayed where he was by the door. No one had invited him to sit. She wished he'd go away.

"You have to be careful," Shannon said. "Who knows what kind of people he's mixed up with."

The kind who would shoot military officers to prevent being caught in the middle of a heist, Kelsey thought.

Shannon looked at Julian and added, "Ken implied that you're involved in whatever's going on. But I knew that couldn't be true. And since I couldn't believe the part about having to keep Bella or the part about you, I knew the whole story was probably a lie. I didn't have a choice about leaving Bella. I couldn't let Ken realize I was on to him."

Kelsey saw that Julian was moved by Shannon's belief in his basic honesty. But he also appeared to be slightly puzzled.

Drew cleared his throat. "I have people heading over to Steinhauser's apartment as we speak. We can pick him up for conspiracy and theft—"

"And dog-napping!" Shannon insisted. And almost on cue, a dog began to howl in the neighborhood.

"—and maybe we can get him to talk," Drew continued. "I'm hoping he'll tell us who else is involved in these thefts."

"Why are you so sure Steinhauser is part of the group that's been stealing? He could have been covering up for any number of crimes," Julian said. Kelsey knew he was probing for Mitchum's reaction.

"But only one case involves Kelsey's warehouse. And why else would he need Kelsey out of the way? You haven't seen fit to tell me much about what you're working on, but after hearing what Shannon had to say, I've figured out that something else happened at the warehouse besides the thefts. You're trying to help the captain determine who's responsible," Drew said. "And it makes sense that her space would be one that got tapped for goods to steal. She's got the ammunition and rockets and stuff."

"There's an officer involved, too," Shannon chimed in. "Ken talked to someone he called 'sir' on the phone just before he came up with this nonsense about keeping Kelsey out of the way and safe by making her believe I'd lost my dog again."

Kelsey glanced at Mitchum and realized that Julian had done the same. The man apparently noted the suspicion in their eyes because he held up his hands in surrender. "Not me!" he protested. "How could it be me?"

To Kelsey's surprise, Julian dropped his gaze to the floor. "No one said it was you, Drew."

Shannon's gaze flitted from one to the other and finally came to rest on Kelsey. "Did I screw up telling Drew everything?" she asked in a whisper.

Kelsey rubbed her palm over her sister's shoulder. "You did great, Shannon. You risked a lot when you made that phone call to the voice mail. I'm proud of you. It must have been hard to leave Bella behind."

"I just chose my sister's safety over my dog's. Sometimes you have to make that sort of decision." But Shannon's eyes were shiny with unshed tears. "We'll get Bella back soon," she asserted. "Right?"

Kelsey nodded as she felt her throat go tight and her eyes sting. Her sister had made a tremendous sacrifice for her. In the past, it had always been Kelsey making sacrifices for Shannon, keeping her safe when she had nowhere else to go, feeding her, finding her jobs, worrying about her. But now Shannon had proven that she was willing to risk what she most prized for her older sister's sake. Kelsey was filled with love for her only sibling.

"Look, I can't convince you I'm not the officer involved in this mess except by solving the case. So I'm going to go find out the status of the Steinhauser arrest." He gave Julian a harsh look and there seemed to be disappointment and hurt in his eyes. "It's late. You can bring Ms. O'Roark to the station for depositions in the morning." He turned to go but stopped in his tracks just as he opened the door.

"Sir!" came a male voice from the hallway just outside. "Glad I found you, sir. There's something strange down in the parking lot." The soldier had appeared out of nowhere. Had he come with Mitchum? Kelsey didn't know.

Julian moved closer and Kelsey stood and followed. Anything strange going on would be of interest to them, too.

"Be specific, soldier," Mitchum demanded.

"There's a K9 down there going nuts sniffing at the trunk of a car, sir." And once again, the howl of the dog registered in Kelsey's brain. She'd been hearing it for several minutes now.

"I didn't call for any K9s," Drew said with a confused scowl. "I only asked for you and Specialist Whitacker."

The young MP shrugged. "Well, there's one outside now. Maybe the officer and the dog were just on patrol. It's First Sergeant Panich, sir. He didn't say why he was there because almost as soon as he arrived, his dog started barking at the trunk of the car."

"Whose car is it?" Julian asked. He wore an expression much like Mitchum's, filled with both confusion and worry.

"We don't know yet, sir. We're running the plates now."

"Did you cordon off the area?" Mitchum asked.

"Yes, sir, we backed everyone up and taped a perimeter, just in case."

"In case of what?" Kelsey asked, dreading the answer.

"The K9s alert to a number of things," Julian said calmly. "We just don't want to take any chances."

Through Kelsey's mind ran the things dogs were usually trained to find: drugs, bodies and bombs.

"Well, let's go take a look," said Mitchum. "Maybe we've got an ID on the owner of the car by now."

The men headed for the stairs and Kelsey and Shannon followed. Mitchum turned on them. "You two stay here. We don't want you down there until we figure out what's going on." Julian nodded his agreement.

"Okay," Shannon said as she meekly backed up a step. But the instant they'd turned their backs to them again, Shannon followed at a discreet distance. So did Kelsey. She knew she should stop her sister, but that would mean staying behind herself. And *that* wasn't going to happen. She'd keep herself out of the way, but she had every right to go outside with the other military people. Besides, maybe she'd recognize the car as belonging to one of her neighbors. She strode out into the night with her sister right on her heels.

Kelsey knew she'd made the right choice when she saw all her neighbors out on the sidewalk, gawking at the chaos. Lights of an MP vehicle flashed blue and red, casting an eerie strobe over the scene. The dog continued to bark and howl.

And the car the dog stood behind was Julian's.

HE STOPPED DEAD IN HIS tracks when he realized the situation. "That's my car," Julian admitted as he gaped at the dog.

"Your car?" Drew said as if he didn't believe it. "Why would the K9 point to *your* car?"

"I have no idea. We only just got back from the warehouse. You heard about that incident, didn't you?"

"Yeah, I heard about it. That's where I was heading when I saw Ms. O'Roark. I stopped to ask her if she was okay, saw she was crying and got the story out of her. They told me you'd been shot."

"Yeah." Julian rubbed a palm over his sore chest. "And lived to tell about it, thanks to Kelsey. While I was unconscious, she somehow managed to pull me to safety."

"Well, what do you have in the trunk—raw hamburger—gunpowder—kilos of cocaine?"

"Not even a pistol. I had that on me at the warehouse and your boys took that for evidence because we returned fire," Julian said over the noise of the dog.

"Panich! Bring the dog over here!" Drew called out to the K9 handler. Panich complied, albeit with a bit of struggle. The dog did not want to leave whatever he'd found. But eventually, the animal obeyed and the pair came to stand before Drew. "What do you think, soldier? Explosives, or what?"

"No, sir. I don't think explosives are the problem. Clyde isn't trained for explosives. He's a search and rescue dog."

Drew scratched his head. "And who told you to come out here tonight?"

"We got a call at the station. Someone said you wanted me over here. The dispatcher told me the address and I came. I assumed you'd had someone make the call for you, sir."

"And your dog is a search and rescue dog. So he alerts when he finds a person who's been buried or something?"

"Something like that. He sniffs out people, sir. He can find the living and the dead."

Julian's eyebrows shot up even as his guts tightened. He had a bad feeling about that piece of news. He could just about feel the net coming down around him as he realized he was being framed. And as the pieces of tonight's puzzle started to fall into place, he had the urge to run for freedom. He took a step backward before he caught himself and stood his ground. Running would do him no good at all.

"So it's safe to open up the car to see what we've got?" Drew asked Panich.

"I couldn't say, sir. But I think the bomb squad is just about done looking over the car."

Sure enough, the explosives guys were just finishing their inspection. "Nothing here, sir," the leader reported to Drew when he went over to the vehicle. "It's safe."

Julian stared at the trusty sedan he'd driven for the past four years and felt certain the thing was about to betray him.

"Mind if we look in your car, Jules?" Drew asked quietly.

No one but Nathan and Drew called him Jules. No one else had ever felt close enough to use a nickname for him.

Julian looked at the man who had been his friend and knew there would be no mercy.

"Sure. Let's have a look," he said, sounding far more calm than he felt. And to make matters worse, Kelsey had wormed her way through the perimeter of police tape and now stood just behind his right shoulder. Julian fished the keys from his pocket where he'd stashed them after Kelsey had delivered them to this parking space such a short time ago. He handed them to Drew.

The man went to the trunk, inserted the key and popped the lid open.

The stench made them all reel backward. Julian stepped on Kelsey's toe before he righted himself. She ended up clutching his arm even as she covered her mouth and nose with her free hand. Julian raised his arm across his face so he could breathe through his sleeve as he strained to see what he already suspected would be in the trunk.

All he could make out was a whole lot of plastic sheeting. It appeared to be wrapped around something large and long. Neither the sheeting nor the thing it encased had been in the car the last time he'd been in the trunk. He kept his car the way he kept his apartment. What word had Kelsey used? Spartan. His trunk was normally completely empty, unless he put a weapon inside for target practice or for protection on an investigation. At the moment, Julian couldn't recall the last time he'd used the trunk.

The hot night breeze swept away much of the reeking odor. The three officers leaned in closer. Drew pulled a small knife out of his pocket and slit the plastic. A face appeared. A mask of death and what appeared to be the remains of frost made the young man almost unrecognizable. But Julian knew who this was. "Specialist Rigley," he said without thinking.

"You know who this is?" Drew asked, his voice laced with incredulity.

"It's the man from the warehouse, I think," Kelsey said. Julian wished she hadn't. Now she might be implicated, too.

"Damn," he muttered as the desire to run came over him again. But he knew he couldn't do that. There was no place to go anyway. And he needed to stay and deal with this mess until he cleared his name. He turned and looked at Kelsey. She'd let go of him now and stood with her hands hanging lifelessly at her sides. She stared at the body lying in his car. And then she slowly turned her gaze up to his.

What Julian saw in her eyes chilled him to the bone. Doubt and sorrow pooled in her eyes and made him want to howl in protest. Her stalwart belief in his innocence had vanished. And how could he blame her? For here was cold hard evidence, pointing to his guilt. "Damn!" he said again.

"Explain what this is, Jules," Drew demanded, his expression grim.

"Someone must have put the body in my car. Then they made a call that sent the K9 out here to discover it. The same guys who shot at us earlier this evening, no doubt."

Drew scrutinized his face, then turned again to the body. Slitting the plastic a little farther, he revealed the name tag on the army uniform the dead soldier still wore. Rigley. Julian had so hoped the young man would be found alive and well in Florida. He thought of Rigley's parents, the worry in his mother's voice from the answering machine.

Drew cleared his throat. "You know I have to take you in until we get this all sorted out, right?" The man had to be thinking of how Steinhauser had all but fingered Julian as the officer in charge of the stealing.

Julian took in a breath and let it out slowly, preparing

for the inevitable. "Yes, I know. I'd like you to call Lieu-tenant Bates and let him work with your guys on this." Bates was from CID and would make sure there were no slipups with evidence.

"Sure, I can do that. You have the right to remain silent," Drew began.

As he delivered the remainder of the Miranda rights, Drew brought forth a set of plastic handcuffs from the back of his utility belt—standard procedure for anyone taken into custody in the face of a violent offense. Julian closed his eyes and wished the nightmare would end. He turned in Kelsey's direction as he submitted to the cuffs without voicing the protests that swam around inside his chest like angry sharks.

He tried to give her a smile, but knew he failed. "I should have believed you in the first place," he told her. "Maybe I'd have already caught the bastard who did this if I hadn't doubted you."

She blinked up at him, her expression tight. "We'll get through this, Julian," she promised fervently even as Drew continued to intone his rights.

"I sure as hell hope so," he said. But just hearing that she wouldn't abandon him helped to lift his spirits a little.

All at once, Kelsey seemed to come out of her torpor. She turned on Drew with all the ferocity of a mother pro-tecting her cub. "Major, stop and think for a minute! You know he's being set up. He can help you if he's free."

Her words made him realize with relief that he might have misread her expression when the body had been re-vealed. Maybe she still believed in his innocence, after all. But Drew had to follow the protocol. Julian didn't blame him. He'd be doing the same thing if the evidence had been in Drew's car. Maybe Drew had already been harboring doubts about Julian. Hadn't the MP chief already asked him if he was holding back information? That must have seemed suspicious to Drew. Everything together would seem suspicious to anyone at first. But Julian had to believe this would all be sorted out in the long run.

"Listen to me, Major," Kelsey tried again as she walked along beside Drew as he led Julian to the police car. "Someone had to have put the body into his car. That's the only thing that makes sense. If Julian was actually involved, he wouldn't be so stupid as to leave the dead body in his car all this time!"

"All what time?" Drew asked.

Uh-oh. Now Kelsey would have to tell him the whole story. "All the time since his death in my warehouse the night I worked late." She gave him a thrifty summary of what had happened to her. "I went to Julian for help and he's had a hundred opportunities to distract me from finding out the identity of the person who knocked me out. But he didn't do that."

Julian saw her look away and frown. Was she remembering the times they had spent together and wondering if he *had* tried to divert her attention? Would she suspect his motives for their lovemaking? And how would she explain the fact that he hadn't believed her story and discouraged her from sticking to it?

Julian shook his head wearily. He could only hope her faith in him would hold. What she'd said to Drew was true. If he were the officer involved in the theft ring, he'd have managed things far more efficiently. For one thing, Rigley wouldn't be dead. But even if he had gotten himself killed, his body wouldn't be thawing in the heat of his trunk.

Drew ignored Kelsey and opened the back door of the police car. For the first time in his life, Julian understood what it felt like to be tucked into a cruiser while hand-cuffed. Drew's palm went to the crown of his head, pushing him down so he didn't crack his skull on the door frame and also to keep him subdued until he was secured inside the vehicle. Once Julian was seated—uncomfortably, with his hands behind his back and the bruise on his chest shrieking for attention—Drew reached across him to secure the seat belt. He clicked it into place around the prisoner. Everything by the book, Julian realized.

Except the prisoner was himself.

"I'll get you out, Julian," Kelsey promised from behind Drew. "Don't worry. They can't keep you. I'll wake up some JAGs and get you out." She looked as determined as he'd ever seen her, despite the doubts that had to be swimming through her mind.

"You already saved my ass once tonight. Get some sleep and go see the JAGs in the morning. I can sleep in the stockade as easily as anywhere." He suspected he wouldn't sleep at all, but he smiled at her as Drew closed the door.

She splayed her hand on the window and he wished he could match the gesture. "I'll get you out tonight," she promised through the glass.

As the car began to drive him away from her, his heart ached. She looked so fierce and determined. No matter how things looked, she clearly *wanted* to believe in him. Her faith, even in the face of both physical and circumstantial evidence, humbled him. And as he lost sight of her, he recognized that he should have had that same degree of trust in her, no matter how the evidence—or lack thereof—had stacked up against her story. He hoped he'd get the chance to show her that he would never doubt her again. Because now he understood what it meant to have someone on your side even when the facts were against you.

He needed her to believe in him, because despite his perfect military record, he had little else to recommend him. He had superiors who extolled his virtues on the job and subordinates who respected him. But he had no friends except for Kelsey and his brother. There was no one else who could stand up for him and attest to his integrity—unless he could also count Drew among his friends. But if Drew turned out to be the officer involved in the theft ring, he'd be perfectly placed to solidify the case against Julian.

CHAPTER EIGHTEEN

SHE'D HAD NO SLEEP, she'd been shot at, her foray into the safety of the woods had scraped the hell out of her legs, her sister's dog was being held hostage and her lover had been arrested. She felt like a walking country-and-western song. Kelsey wanted nothing more than a hot bath and sleep. But she went to the JAG office instead. The duty officer seemed reluctant to wake up any of the JAGs at oh three hundred hours, but when she pounded her hand on the desktop, he started dialing.

The JAG couldn't help her. Julian had been arrested in connection with a murder. There was no way he could be sprung from jail by anyone except maybe General Wilkes, and no one was willing to wake him up. So she would have to wait until morning. With her heart heavy and her body sluggish with fatigue, she headed to the MP station where Julian was being held.

The first person she saw upon arrival was a haggard-looking Major Mitchum.

"You need to let Julian go," she pleaded. "He can't help you resolve this if he's behind bars."

"He already *has* helped. We're on the trail of the guy in the truck who had your sister's dog. If we can find him and persuade him to talk, we'll be able to release Julian."

She blinked at the man. "So, you don't really think Julian killed Rigley?"

He shook his head. "And I didn't murder him either," he added. "But I can't let Julian go without something more than a hunch."

"Who do you think it is, then?" she asked. She still wasn't completely convinced of Mitchum's innocence.

"We've got fingerprints from the trunk of his car. We're running them through the computer now. We'll find whoever put that body in there."

"And what about the body? Do we have a positive ID? Time of death?"

"Yup. It's definitely Rigley. And although it's hard to pin down the time of death on a body that's been frozen before melting in a hot trunk, the coroner thinks he died the same night Julian said you went to him for help. I want you to know I'm annoyed you two didn't see fit to let me in on what happened to you there." He scowled at her.

Kelsey shrugged and felt the weariness in her shoulders. "I wouldn't let him tell anyone. I didn't know who to trust." She still didn't. "Except for Julian."

"Well, technically, I should have arrested you, too, for being involved and for the suspicious behavior of not telling me about what happened in the warehouse. But I figured I could get away with putting just one of you behind bars. Julian understands this."

"And you'll let him out as soon as you get someone to talk?"

"Steinhauser is still saying nothing except that he wants a lawyer. Apparently he's not happy with the JAG he was appointed. At least we got your sister's dog back to her."

Kelsey nodded. "Shannon told me when I talked to her on the phone." She looked up into the man's eyes. They seemed honest and sincere. "Thank you."

He gave her a half smile. "If you ever decide for sure

that I'm not the bad guy, maybe you'd convince your sister to go out to dinner with me."

Kelsey couldn't hide her surprise. Shannon didn't usually attract successful men, officers with solid careers. But a great deal had changed about her sister. She'd shown courage and cleverness tonight—yesterday actually. She had a job with the shelter—one that would start paying her as soon as funding came through. And now she had captured the interest of a man who had everything going for him if he didn't turn out to be a thief and a killer. Kelsey would have applauded her sister's accomplishments if she weren't still worried about whether Mitchum was a criminal.

"Can I see Julian?" She pictured having to talk to him by phone while they peered at each other through thick Plexiglas, just like in the movies.

"Sure," Drew said. "Sergeant!" he hollered over his shoulder. "Bring the prisoner to the interrogation room!" Focusing again on Kelsey, he said, "Follow me."

He led her into a small spare room. Two chairs and a table of gunmetal gray sat in the center. There was mirrored glass on one end of the room.

"Will you be watching through the glass?" she asked.

"No. I'll turn the light on inside the other room so you can see you're alone."

She turned to him then. "Why are you being so nice?"

He captured her gaze and held it. "Because I'm not involved in any of these crimes, because I don't believe Julian is either, because I'm a nice guy and because I'd like to date your sister." He said all this without any hint of amusement.

"We'll see," she said even though she was beginning to feel overly stubborn. She just didn't dare trust him yet.

He left her in the room and she paced in a circle around the circumference several times. Then the light in the observation area flicked on. No one sat in the space beyond the glass. She'd gone another full circle when the door swung inward. Julian stepped into view and her heart leaped with relief and happiness at seeing him.

He turned to her and she saw that his hands were cuffed in front of him. He sported the old-fashioned metal version instead of the plastic strip he'd worn for the ride in the cruiser. She scowled. The door began to close without revealing the sergeant who'd brought him. But she caught it and glared at the man.

"Take off his handcuffs," she demanded.

The sergeant looked as if he might protest, but then he seemed to take a good look at the set of her jaw. He shrugged and stepped back into the room, used his key to unlock the handcuffs and then left. She heard him lock the door behind him.

JULIAN STOOD BACK and waited to see what she would do. He hadn't seen her for hours and for all he knew, she'd changed her mind about his innocence. And yet at least she trusted him enough to be in the same room with him, uncuffed.

Her eyes lifted slowly to meet his gaze. And then she came to him, slowly at first but then with increasing speed. He had to smile even though he knew this was going to hurt. Opening his arms to her, he reduced the force of her welcome assault by backing up even as he embraced her. But then the wall foiled what instinct had dictated, preventing him from hunching his shoulders forward to protect his bruised chest. Pain shot out to all corners of his body, but nothing could undermine the pleasure of having her against him with her arms around his neck and her face buried warmly near his throat.

"I hurt you," she said. "Sorry." But he wouldn't let her pull back.

"All I can feel is your heartbeat against mine and I'm grateful for it," he whispered into her ear.

"Did Drew tell you that Lieutenant Bates couldn't be found to help with the investigation like you asked? They think he's gone AWOL."

"Yeah, Drew told me. I can't believe I trusted him to test for blood in your warehouse. It's too bad our records show he couldn't be the officer masterminding the whole operation so we could name him as the prime suspect and I could get out of here. For one thing, he was in Iraq when the thefts began and for several more months after that."

"Apparently his only involvement was when the bad guys got him to fake his luminol test," she said.

Regret just about choked him. "I should have done that test over again, just because you were so unshakable in your story. After our experience with the hypnotist, I was planning to redo it today. But then I ended up in here."

She sighed and snuggled more completely into his embrace. "I'm sorry I couldn't get you out," she said, sounding strained to the breaking point. "The JAGs said only the general or a better suspect could cause your release."

"I know. I tried to tell you I'd be fine here. Drew is doing everything he can." He kissed Kelsey's forehead. With her here, he felt happier than he could ever have thought possible under such dismal circumstances. "And I don't think Drew is our officer-gone-bad any more than Lieutenant Bates could be."

"I know that now," she agreed. "He's trying too hard to get you released."

"He told me Rigley's body was still partly frozen when they got him out of my car. He'd been in a freezer somewhere. They're looking for all the freezers on post large enough to hold a man's body."

"That could be a lot of freezers," she said, shifting slightly as if to make certain she didn't lean too hard where he was sore.

"Yeah, that's what I said. I mean, people have big freezers in their homes sometimes. But Drew is trying all the commercial freezers first."

"Steinhauser isn't talking," she told him.

"But I bet that Earlman guy will sing when they find him. He's the one with the black truck. His name came up on the registration for the truck plates."

She pulled back and searched his face. "What happens if they can't find him?"

"Drew let me read his file. I have a strong feeling the man went home to Tennessee. Drew has some colleagues from the nearest post heading to his father's place. And a team from here is on the way to bring him back to Fort Belvoir."

"He's put a lot of faith in your hunch about where Earlman will be," she said.

"Drew's worked with me for a while. He knows I can usually read people, especially if I can examine their whole history."

She stepped back from him and he had to force himself not to cling to her. She grasped his hand in hers and drew him to the table so they could sit in the chairs. "What else can I do for you?" she asked. "I feel so helpless, so useless. After all you've done for me…"

"Shh," he said as he stroked his thumb over her fingers. "I've had some time to think while I've been locked up and I need to tell you some things. The first is that your being here now, supporting me—well, it means more to me than I can say. If you'd done nothing else for me, this would be enough. But you've done so much more. Have you even slept in the past twenty-four hours?"

She shook her head wearily. Her eyes shimmered.

"Kelsey, I need to apologize to you. I should have believed you all along. I should never have doubted you for a single second. The evidence be damned, I should have had faith in you. Instead, I dragged you to the hypnotist—and you went! You did that for me, to help me see. And now I do." He took a deep breath and let it out slowly.

"It's okay, Julian," she said.

"No. It's not okay. There needs to be a certain amount of faith between people who care for each other."

She stared at him with those luminous eyes.

"I know this sounds all wrong saying this here, saying it now when I'm in this kind of trouble. But I don't know when we'll see each other again and I need to make sure you know how much you mean to me."

She sat silently for a moment, gazing into his eyes. There were tears there, but they didn't fall. She sniffed once, as if to get a hold of herself. Then, "How could I not fall for a guy who gave me that wowser kiss in my apartment all that time ago."

He laughed out loud. He couldn't help it. He knew he still had some issues to resolve between his heart and his head, but somehow the future seemed to have more promise than ever before.

She smiled and then got to her feet. Was she leaving already? "I don't know how much time we have left," she said. "And I could use one of those kisses from you about now."

He stood up so fast that his sleep-deprived head went a little dizzy. All worth it. Because he had Kelsey in his arms again and he was kissing her again—gently, tenderly, then passionately.

"Hey, you two. Do you want me to leave you alone another couple minutes to, ah, conclude your conversation?" Drew grinned at them from beyond the illuminated glass. "I don't mean to interrupt, but I got other people who need to use the interrogation room. We've got Earlman on his way here and he's ready to talk."

EARLMAN DIDN'T KNOW the identity of the officer in charge of the scheme. He only knew there was someone that the Wolf would talk to on the phone sometimes.

"Who's the Wolf?" Drew Mitchum asked while Kelsey looked through the glass into the room where she and Julian had been two hours ago. Her side of the glass was dark now. Earlman couldn't see her.

"The guy with the dog. Steinhauser. We call him that because of that funny tooth of his. Makes him look like a wolf. And he's got that big dog that looks sort of like a wolf," Earlman added. Kelsey stared at the young man and knew he had to be a city boy. Buddy was a German shepherd and looked nothing like a wolf. But she forgave him because he'd returned Bella—albeit with a broken leg—and he was willing to talk even though his JAG attorney sat nearby with a sullen expression.

After that, the young man spilled everything he knew. Too bad he didn't know much.

Fortunately, Drew felt he had enough from the private to release Julian. The JAG defense counsel had proven to be worth his law degree after all and had arranged an agreement whereby Julian could be freed if he promised to keep the MP chief apprised of his whereabouts. Drew didn't seem to have any desire to keep Julian locked up any longer than necessary and ordered his release.

Kelsey's main interest in listening in was to see if Earlman told anything about where her materiel had gone. She hated the idea of her warehouse being the starting point of ammunition and rocket launchers getting into the hands of terrorists. But it was looking more and more like that was what had happened. She could only hope the stuff hadn't yet left the country and that they'd find it in time.

As she let herself out of the observation room, she wondered what would happen to Buddy now that Steinhauser was in the jail cell so recently vacated by Julian. But her mind went blank when she found Julian just finishing up the paperwork for his release.

"Hey," she said as tenderness for this man washed over her. He had a shadow of beard, his eyes were weary and his clothes were wrinkled almost beyond recognition. But she thought he looked wonderful.

"Hey," he said back as his gaze slid over her and a sweet smile tilted the corners of his mouth up.

"Food or sleep?" she asked.

"Food," he answered promptly. "Then sleep."

But just before they made their escape from the MP station, Drew came out of his office and marched over to them. Onto the counter near Kelsey, he slapped down a can. The red, white and blue label said Old Spice Original on it.

"That's my cologne—an aftershave, really. I know it's old-fashioned, but I like it because it reminds me of my dad." He stared at Kelsey intently. When she didn't respond, he added, "Julian told me you thought I was involved in this mess because you smelled my cologne at the scene. But I want you to realize that a lot of guys wear this same stuff."

"It wasn't familiar to me," she said, unsure of herself and her accusations.

Julian put his hand gently on her shoulder. "I don't believe Drew is involved. I don't have any evidence one way or the other, but I know the scent you noticed was on someone else."

"You're saying that because he's your friend and you don't want to doubt him."

"That's right," he agreed readily.

And all at once she understood what he was trying to say. She smiled at him. "That's pretty risky, trusting your friend without any evidence that he's telling the truth," she noted.

"You're right. And I'll feel a whole lot better when we have the real perpetrator in custody. But for now, I'm going to put my faith in Drew."

"Hallelujah!" Drew cried.

Kelsey said nothing more on the subject. "C'mon. Let's get you fed and to bed." She shook hands with Drew in truce, if not full friendship, and then pulled Julian out of the building.

On the way to the diner, his expression turned serious and he leaned his head back against the headrest. "We don't have any idea where the stolen stuff is except for what they found in that truck that tried to get off post last night while I was being arrested."

She'd heard that a truck had been stopped by vigilant security guards. Unfortunately, none of the occupants had known anything about the goods in the back. They'd just been following orders. Whose orders, nobody knew, confused as they were with names that weren't real. "Maybe we'll get some information from Steinhauser."

He nodded and closed his eyes. "Mr. and Mrs. Rigley are having the funeral in a few days. I figured we'd need to buy tickets to fly down there."

"Yes. We should go." She ruminated in silence about when she'd met Rigley's parents and about how worried they'd been. Sorrow filled her at the thought of them getting the terrible news. The least she could do was go to the service. "Will the authorities let you out of the Commonwealth of Virginia?" she asked.

"The charges were dropped. It certainly wasn't the first time I've been arrested. Probably won't be the last."

"You'll have to tell me sometime about all the other occasions."

"I will. But first, I have to eat some real food."

There was food, then sleep—with only a brief snuggle before dreams captured them both.

Hours later, when they woke up almost at the same time and looked at each other, Kelsey wondered if she mirrored his slightly startled expression. She wasn't used to having a man in her bed. But soon the look in his eyes went all smoldering and he kissed her. Making love with him filled her once more with tenderness. But she continued to feel a yearning deep inside.

He'd said he cared for her, she reminded herself. But declaring that wasn't the same as making a commitment. And she wanted a commitment from this man. She wanted it so much it hurt. And she had no idea if she could just go on day to day without some kind of promise between them. Then she realized how selfish and greedy this might seem. And needy. Pathetically needy. It was what she felt, nevertheless.

Pulling Julian close, she hugged him fiercely and swore to herself that she wouldn't let her craving for permanence and security ruin what she had with this wonderful man she loved so much.

THEY ESCORTED Specialist Ryan Rigley's body back to Florida for his funeral. The event was an emotional roller coaster for Julian, but he saw it through. The young man had been well liked and was remembered as friendly, affable, always wanting to please. His father managed to tell, haltingly and with tears, how his son had always wanted to serve his country. Ryan had been deployed to Afghanistan as a boy and had come home a man. He'd wanted to help his parents to a better life, had sent home money, had promised he'd take care of them.

Those dreams were all gone now. Unsaid was the fact that he'd squandered his life by becoming involved with a gang of thieves and dying in a ridiculous accident. But at least Julian understood now what had motivated Rigley. He had done it in the hope of lifting up his parents and securing a future with his fiancée. The girl Rigley had planned to marry stood just in front of him. Ginny wept quietly all through the service. It was a wonder that she had been welcome, given that she'd never been introduced to Mr. and Mrs. Rigley while their son had been alive. But the parents seemed to believe this was not the time to show hard feelings toward the woman their son had hoped to wed.

Beside him stood Kelsey. Moisture clung to her eyelashes and sparkled in the sunlight that streamed through the church windows. The tip of her nose was a bit red. As he gazed at her, thinking how lucky he was to have her beside him, he saw her glance around as if something had caught her attention. She lifted her face to the air and sniffed delicately. Very carefully, she turned to look first one way and then the other. When she glanced over her shoulder to see who might be behind them, her eyes narrowed.

Her expression demanded that he look behind them, too. In the row just behind them, Andrew Mitchum had come to sit. He wore his class A uniform, just as Julian and Kelsey did. And he must have worn his favorite aftershave, too, because Kelsey had smelled him even though Julian hadn't detected a thing. He gave Drew an acknowledging nod and turned forward again.

What he saw then startled him. Ginny Januszewski had turned around, too. She stared at Drew with dismay, her tears suspended. Then her face crumpled again and she wept in earnest. The pallbearers—all men in uniform—picked up Rigley's casket and carried it down the aisle before Julian could figure out what Ginny found so heart-wrenching about Drew. But he didn't have long to wait before the mystery was solved.

Ginny stepped out of her pew into the aisle just behind Specialist Rigley's parents. But she paused at Drew's row and looked up at him with tears streaming down her cheeks.

"You smell like him," she said. "Your cologne is like Ryan's. When you came in, I thought for a second that everyone had been wrong, that he wasn't really dead, that he was right behind me. But when I turned, I saw you."

Drew gave Kelsey a speaking look, then turned his attention back to Ginny. "I'm sorry if I offended you," he said to her. "I didn't know."

"No, please. I just wanted to explain why I stared at you. And to ask you the name of whatever you wear. So that when I miss him, I can…" Her voice broke and she couldn't go on.

Drew grasped the young woman's hand. "It's Old Spice, ma'am. The original, just like my dad used to wear."

She nodded, her eyes huge and shining and sad. Then she hurried out of the church.

Drew fell into step beside Julian. "I worried she'd looked at me like that because I came in late," he said.

Julian focused on ensuring that Kelsey didn't misstep as they descended the church stairs together. "Did you

wear the cologne on purpose?" he asked. He was fairly certain he knew the answer. He wondered if Drew would
admit it.

"Yes," he admitted. "I don't have any more leads. I
wanted to come to the funeral anyway, and I hoped I might
find some clues by coming here. And this may sound cold,
but I loaded up on the aftershave in the hope someone
would say 'Hey, that's what I wear, too' or something. Instead, I find out the stuff was on Ryan Rigley that night,
and not on the accomplice."

"Well, at least you resolved one thing for me," Kelsey
said. "I don't have to wonder if it's you anymore."

"That's good. I'd rather not divert anyone's attention by
seeming to be a suspect. But wearing the stuff only upset
the fiancée. We're getting nowhere fast. And the stolen
materiel could be anywhere by now. I just hope to God it's
not already in the hands of the terrorists Steinhauser described as the buyers."

KELSEY STOOD in the Rigleys' living room with a cup of
coffee in one hand and a cookie in the other. Sadness
weighted her heart as she studied the pictures of Ryan,
from infant in diapers to man in uniform, that decorated
the place. She'd seen them before, when she'd visited his
parents for information about where he might be, but that
was when she'd hoped to find him alive.

"Captain O'Roark," came a man's quiet voice from behind her. She turned and saw Mr. Rigley, looking much
older than when she'd visited before. "I want to show you
something," he said as he glanced over his shoulder to
make sure no one else heard.

"What is it you want to show me?" she asked, wondering if she should attempt to capture Julian's attention so

he could also see whatever this grieving father wished to share.

"If you would just come with me," Mr. Rigley said, almost pleading. She found she could not deny him. She followed him to the kitchen of the small house.

"Follow me," he urged as he opened the screen door and led her through the backyard.

She saw a large garage in their path and wondered if that was their destination. Feeling vaguely uneasy, she wondered if Julian had noticed her departure and whether he would come after her to see where she'd gone. She hoped so, because Mr. Rigley opened the side door to the garage and she saw gaping darkness within. He stepped through the entrance and beckoned her to follow. She hesitated on the threshold until Mr. Rigley switched on the light.

Before her, in stacks that reached the ceiling, stood crate upon wooden crate. The identifying information on the sides of the boxes had been obliterated with black spray paint, but she recognized what she was looking at. When her heart stopped skipping, it beat hard and fast. She resisted a whoop of glee, remembering the grief-stricken man beside her. But inside, relief and happiness consumed her.

"I'm worried about these," confessed Mr. Rigley. "Ryan had them trucked here a little at a time. He told us not to touch them and said they were just being stored here temporarily. Ryan was always a good boy. I had no reason to think he'd be involved in anything bad."

Without saying more, he shuffled into a narrow aisle that had been left between the crates and disappeared. Kelsey waited, then grew worried and followed. But before she could make much progress in the gloom between the stacked boxes, he reappeared, facing her now. Kelsey had to retreat backward. The space was too narrow for her to turn around. Mr. Rigley emerged with her, holding something heavy in his arms.

When he came into the light, she gasped. He held a missile for a handheld rocket launcher—the kind that tended to be very popular with terrorists. When she met the older man's gaze, his sadness and disappointment hit her hard and diluted some of her sense of conquest at finding this cache of stolen goods.

"I want you to take care of this, Captain. And I'm begging you to find a way to keep Ryan's name out of whatever reports you need to write. His mother couldn't bear to find out her dead son was involved in something so wrong." Tears filled his eyes and spilled over to trail slowly down his cheeks.

Kelsey lifted the ordnance from his arms and placed it carefully out of sight. When she returned, Mr. Rigley had regained control of himself. "I'll do what I can, sir," she said to him.

"He told us he'd been able to buy government surplus and that he planned to sell it. He said he'd make a lot of money. He wanted to help us in our retirement. He—" But he couldn't go on. He covered his face and wept again, gulping past quiet sobs and trembling against the emotional pain.

Kelsey went to him and put her arms around his quaking shoulders. After standing like this for several wrenching moments, she saw Julian appear in the doorway with the afternoon daylight as his backdrop. He glanced around the garage at the quantity of materiel, then met her gaze again. With her eyes, she conveyed her concern for the old man she held. He nodded his understanding and departed to do what he could to arrange for the cleanup of the disastrous mess Specialist Ryan Rigley had made of his short life.

CHAPTER NINETEEN

As HE SAT BESIDE Kelsey on their plane ride home from
Florida the next morning, Julian recalled the sense of relief
he'd shared with Drew when he'd told his friend what he'd
seen in the Rigleys' garage. They'd found at least some of
the materiel before it had been delivered to the illicit buyers.
The two of them had agreed that the best course would be
to call a friend of Drew's at Fort Jackson, South Carolina,
and have him arrange to take immediate possession of the
crates for eventual return to Fort Belvoir. They'd stayed with
Mr. and Mrs. Rigley until the garage had been secured. Some
guards remained to protect the Rigleys, too, just in case.

Julian would do his best to keep Rigley's role in the
whole mess as quiet as possible. Kelsey had promised the
grieving parents he would. He couldn't let her down.
Glancing to his left, he smiled as he watched her sleeping
away her exhaustion as the plane carried them home.

Home. These days, he thought of that as being wherever
Kelsey happened to be. He'd have to figure out what he
should do about that before she decided to give up on him.
She didn't believe he could make a commitment to her.
Right up until his arrest for murder, he'd thought the same
thing. But something had shifted inside him during that
long night in his cell where the memory of Kelsey's stead-
fast belief in him had sustained him.

He loved her and he rejoiced that she loved him, too. So he had to find a way past his knee-jerk resistance to her caretaking and nurturing. He'd already made a series of appointments with Dr. Moriarty. With his goal of bringing Kelsey into his life on a long-term basis, he wanted to overcome whatever made him reject kindness from others.

By afternoon, Julian found himself in the interrogation room with Drew as the two of them questioned Steinhauser, who still refused to give up the name of the officer involved.

"Just give us a name," Drew said in a soft, kind voice.

Steinhauser's expression was completely closed. "I don't know what you're talking about. Can he talk to me like this?" he asked his lawyer who sat quietly beside him.

"My client isn't going to answer your questions until we hear the prosecutor's response to the plea bargain."

Very good at playing bad cop, Julian pounded his fist on the table. The sound reminded him of the gunshots that had been aimed at him the night they'd hauled this asshole into the station after he'd kidnapped Bella. "Were you the one who shot at me? Should we press charges for that, too? Attempted murder of an officer of the United States Army in the commission of his duty. Selling arms to terrorists while soldiers die in the war against them every day. That ought to go over real well with a jury of your peers!"

Steinhauser didn't flinch, but his defiant expression slipped. "I don't know his name even if I wanted to tell you."

"What did you call him, then?" asked Drew gently.

"Screw you."

Without warning, Drew flew over the table and grabbed Steinhauser by his throat. Julian lunged for his friend's clutching hands and pulled them away. "Easy there, lighten up," Julian said to him.

"Don't touch my client," said the attorney without much enthusiasm. The young JAG knew he had a losing case against the recording Shannon had made.

Drew pushed away from the table and began pacing back and forth like a man on the edge. Julian took his empty seat. "Ken, we've got your dog in a holding pen."

Steinhauser's eyes filled instantly with regret and sorrow. He glanced to his attorney, who just looked down at the floor.

"He's a good dog, Buddy," Julian said softly. "How old is he now?"

"He's eight years old." Steinhauser's voice broke on the last word.

"You shouldn't answer any questions until—" the lawyer began.

"It was just about my dog! I can answer the damn question about my dog!" Steinhauser cried.

Julian saw a telltale shine in the man's eyes. "Buddy's getting kind of old to find another handler and carry on with his work. What do you think will happen to him while you're in prison?"

"They retire the dogs. He should be retired," but his voice lacked confidence that Buddy would be properly cared for. Julian knew he had him.

"I can promise to personally look after Buddy if you'll just give us the officer's name."

Steinhauser looked at him, searching his face. Julian looked back steadily. He'd already decided to make sure Buddy found a good home. He could return the sergeant's gaze with complete honesty.

"You'll make sure he goes to a place where people will take good care of him?"

"Yes, I promise."

The prisoner let out a breath. It was the sound of defeat. And then he said the name.

"Damn!" Julian barked as he swept up his beret from the table and bolted for the exit. He had to get to Kelsey. He had to warn her.

WHILE JULIAN TALKED to Steinhauser, Kelsey sat at her desk, going over reports and comparing them to the list of goods they had found in the Rigleys' garage. She'd already found matches for more than half the stolen items on her list of missing inventory. But it was tedious work. Her shoulders ached. She sat back and rubbed at her neck, easing out the kinks.

Mark Sorrell appeared in the doorway. "Hello, Captain," he said.

"Hello, Lieutenant. Where are you going?" She saw that he was in civilian clothes—not unusual at this hour of the day—and carried a packed rucksack. She couldn't recall signing a leave chit for him, but maybe in all the chaos, she'd simply forgotten.

"Mexico," he said as he leaned one shoulder against the doorjamb.

"Mexico? You going to Acapulco to hang with all the young college girls on summer break down there?" She smiled at him. Mark wasn't married yet but with his wholesome looks, he wouldn't have any trouble finding someone to settle down with.

"Actually, I'm bringing *you* with me."

She laughed. "Yeah, that would be great. Let's just leave all this behind and take off for Mexico right this minute," she joked.

"That's right," he said in a silky voice. And that's when she saw the weapon in his hand as he lifted it to aim at her heart.

All at once, she went very still and serious. "What are you doing, Mark?"

"You know. You know perfectly well, interfering bitch that you are." His voice remained eerily calm as he spoke.

Yes, she did know. The instant she'd seen the handgun, her brain had fit the pieces together. Or most of them, anyway. "But you helped me with the inventory," she said, not wanting to believe what had to be the truth.

"What better way to keep you from suspecting me. Besides, I could confuse the data so much more easily from where I sat over there at that stinking desk under your watchful eye in this dead-boring job. Why else would anyone stay in such a God-awful position?"

Well, *that* hurt. She *liked* her job. She didn't think it was boring. And she'd liked Mark, too. Had he been seething with schemes and resentment all this time? Had he hated her the entire length of their professional relationship? "Mark, listen to me. You can't—"

"Do *not* tell me what I can't do ever again for as long as you live—which won't be all that long if you don't get off your ass and come over here. You're coming with me to ensure my safe passage. Your boyfriend will be on to me any minute now and I'll need a hostage. Get up!"

She stood slowly, wondering if he believed he'd really get away with this or if he was making some kind of last-ditch desperate effort that could get them both killed. She nearly jumped out of her skin when the phone on her desk began to ring. They both stared at it.

"Let's go," he said, beckoning recklessly with his gun.

She walked toward him. A door opened and closed from somewhere in the warehouse.

"What are you going to do when we get to the airport?" she asked to distract him. "You wave that gun around in there and about twenty security guards will shoot you full of holes and ask questions later. Me, personally, I don't want to be standing next to you when that happens." She came to a stop, still several feet away.

"Shut up," he said, but his youthful face looked worried. "It's because of you that I don't have the charter plane I'd planned to use. You found our stuff before we could make the sale. Bitch!"

"So what's the plan? I'd like to know what my chances of survival might be." Because if she wasn't likely to live very long, she'd just as soon die here in a heroic attempt to subdue this maniac.

"We're getting in my car and going to the airport."

"And the weapon?" she asked, looking at the way he held it, as if he weren't all that familiar with handguns. "What are you going to do with that?"

"Shut up!" he barked.

Behind him, Kelsey saw a shadow appear. The outline of a man. Somehow, she sensed it was Julian. She wished he'd stay back, stay safe, but he kept coming toward them, slowly and soundlessly.

"Mark—" she began, hoping to distract him. But he cut her off with a curse and spun toward the encroaching officer behind him.

She didn't waste a single second before lunging toward him, closing the distance quickly. With all her might, she lifted her knee directly into his spine while she grasped one of his shoulders to reinforce the blow. With her free hand, she reached for the gun. But as he cried out and fell to his knees, he squeezed off a shot. The surprised grunt that followed told her Julian had been hit.

She kicked wildly toward Mark's gun hand, hoping to

prevent another shot. She heard the snap of bone at his wrist. A split second later she heard him shrieking in pain.

"You...you broke my... God, I should have killed you when I had the chance instead of just knocking you out that night! You've ruined everything!" Then he began to writhe as he held his wrist and moaned.

With a trembling hand, she picked up the discarded gun and trained it upon him where he hunkered in the doorway, preventing her from going immediately to Julian. She moved toward the phone instead and dialed 911. From the dispatcher she demanded the police and an ambulance.

"How many hurt?" asked the dispatcher.

"Two," she said. And she hated the certainty that it was Julian lying on the warehouse floor with Mark's bullet in him. "Hurry."

She didn't attempt to get past Mark who remained on his knees where her first kick had sent him. He looked to be in no shape to tussle with her, but she wouldn't underestimate him. If she approached, he'd try to take her down.

"Move out into the warehouse, Mark," she said.

"I can't, I can't," he moaned. "You broke my wrist."

"Move!" she demanded, gesturing with the gun to remind him she still had it trained on him.

"Kelsey!" shouted Shannon from nearby. Kelsey hadn't heard her come into the building. Shannon stared with wide eyes. "What are you doing?" she asked. Kelsey saw her sister move into the light just behind Mark. Little Bella struggled to get free of her arms.

"Don't go near him, Shan. He's dangerous. This is the bastard who knocked me out that terrible night after Rigley died. And just now, he was trying to take me hostage so he could get away."

Bella finally managed to leap out of Shannon's arms.

As soon as she got her feet under her, she ran to Mark—awkwardly with the cast on her leg, but determined. She snarled and bared her tiny little teeth. When she reached the man on the floor, she bit his pants near his ankles and gave all her strength to tearing the cloth apart by shaking her fluffy white head furiously. It would have been funny if the situation hadn't been so dire.

"Get the damn dog off me!" Mark shrieked as he tried to kick Bella away. She was too quick for him, even with the cast making her clumsy. She danced back out of the way but returned instantly for more terrorizing of his ankles.

"Move out of the doorway," Kelsey demanded of him again.

"I don't understand what's going on," Shannon wailed.

Mark looked up at Kelsey. "You gonna shoot me? You'd just shoot me? I'm helpless here because of you!" He gave Bella a vicious kick that sent her flying.

Kelsey's finger tightened on the trigger and her body trembled with the desire to put the bastard out of everyone's misery so she could go help Julian. She wanted to pull the trigger so much. In her tension, her finger squeezed back slightly. Another few millimeters and the criminal in front of her would be out of her way.

"Don't," Shannon said.

"Stop!" ordered another voice, male and familiar and welcome. Julian emerged from the darkness near the shelves of inventory.

At the sound of his voice, Kelsey let out her breath and released the trigger she'd begun to squeeze. Her heart raced. "You're not dead," she said to Julian.

"Not yet," he agreed, but when he moved into the light, she saw that he clutched at his shoulder and blood pooled beneath his hand, soaking his uniform.

"You're shot!" Shannon exclaimed.

"I'll live," he said.

"You're a tough one to kill," Kelsey observed. A ridiculous thing to say at a time like this, but she couldn't help herself. She wanted to keep on hearing his voice, confirmation that he was alive. Alive!

"Yeah, hard to kill. Seems to me this is the second time you've saved my life, Kelsey." He lifted his head toward the sound of sirens. "They're coming for you, Sorrell, you sorry excuse for a human being. You can forget Mexico, pal. The only place you're going is Fort Leavenworth." Then he collapsed to his knees.

If Shannon hadn't caught him, he would have fallen to his face. Kelsey watched in dismay as her sister eased Julian to the floor and hunched over him with both hands compressing his wound. The dog continued to snarl and tear at Mark's pants. The sirens howled nearby. And Kelsey felt as though she'd fallen into a nightmare again.

JULIAN HAD SPENT more time in the hospital than he could stand. The wound hadn't been lethal but there'd been a chipped bone that had required a second surgery. After a week and a half, he was glad to be walking out of the place, even if he was required to keep his arm in a sling.

Kelsey didn't know he was being discharged today. He hadn't told her. He'd done a great deal of thinking while he'd been confined to the hospital bed and it came down to this: either he convinced her he could change and be the committed partner she deserved, or he went back to his hectic but lonely life as a perpetually single man.

The first place he went to was the animal control office. Shannon was there, as he'd hoped. And so was Buddy. Shannon brought him out and the dog wagged his tail so furiously, Julian's heart filled to the brim with affection for the animal.

"Thanks for taking care of him," he said.

"He's even had a bath," she told him with a smile.

He stroked the soft, thick fur at the nape of his neck and nodded. He glanced back at Shannon. "What are you going to do with yourself now?" He wanted to know how she was taking the fact that her boyfriend, Ken the Wolf, was heading for prison.

"I've been offered a paying job here. Normally I'd get out of town after realizing I'd hooked up with another loser, but I guess I'll stick around. Your friend Drew asked me out. Should I accept?"

He laughed. "Don't ask me! I'm the last person to give out advice on dating."

"Oh, I don't know. I think you know what you're doing." She smiled warmly.

His heart skittered slightly as he wondered what she meant. It sounded as if she was trying to tell him that Kelsey was predisposed to be kind to him. Certainly, Kelsey had visited him often in the hospital. She'd fussed over his pillows, brought him food she'd cooked herself, kept him up-to-date on the retrieval of the stolen materiel and on the fates of the men involved. She'd even gone out to visit his father again, to bring him the home-cooked meal she'd promised him. Nathan had gone with her and she'd had the chance to meet his wife, Rachel.

"Drew's a good man," he told Shannon.

She smiled. "Kelsey should be heading home in another hour. Maybe it would be better if you talk to her there rather than at the warehouse."

He looked at his feet. Was he so transparent that she knew what was on his mind?

"You could take Buddy for a nice long walk. He's been out everyday in the play yard, but that's not much exercise for a big dog like him. And you look like you could stretch your legs, too. And maybe think about your approach." Shannon's eyes sparkled with amusement.

He smiled again, feeling awkward and shy. She knew he intended to talk to Kelsey. And she supported his efforts. That had to be a good thing. "Thanks," he said. "I'm sure she'll let you know how I do."

She put her hand gently on his arm and leaned slightly closer. "You'll do fine, Julian. Just tell her how you feel. Make sure you let her know you'll feel that way for a long, long time."

Easy for her to say, he thought as he took Buddy out into the summer heat. Julian hadn't had enough practice with emotions to know much about his ability for anything long term. But he sure as hell intended to try his best.

The dog began to pant as soon as they started walking, but his tail wagged vigorously and when Julian headed toward the parade ground, the dog fell into step eagerly. He took the dog out into the center of the field and dared to see if the animal could play off-leash without running away. Buddy did great, running after sticks and bringing them back, nearly running Julian down as he galloped over.

It turned out to be good honest fun and brought back happier memories of Julian's dog from his youth—memories he hadn't considered since the day he'd had to put old Hanford down. There had been many happy times in fields just like this one. Carefree days of throwing sticks and pretending to hunt bears in the fields around whatever school he attended at whatever air force base his father had been assigned to. Hanford had been his constant in a life of constant change.

And now, here was Buddy. Making him laugh, filling his heart, reminding him of unconditional love. He hadn't realized his intention to keep Buddy until this moment. It came as a surprise that he hadn't made any conscious decision, and yet it felt as if there had never been any doubt. Buddy deserved a loving home after all his years of service. And he needed someone who would understand his loss. Old Buddy would never see his beloved handler, Ken Steinhauser, again. On that thought, he called Buddy to him, got down on his knee and ruffed the dog's fur affectionately.

"I guess you're going home with me, Buddy," he said. The dog looked at him with his tongue hanging from the side of his mouth. He seemed to understand.

"Now if only we could find a home that's a bit more homey, we'd be all set," he told the dog as he checked his watch. Kelsey would be at her apartment by now. If he could commit himself to caring for this big dog on an ongoing basis, surely he could do the same with Kelsey.

Time to see what she thought of him and his dog.

When they arrived in her parking lot, Buddy just about danced with anticipation. He seemed to remember coming here before. The instant the dog was out of the car, he lunged eagerly in the right direction. Just for practice, Julian told the dog to heel. He did so instantly. The two of them walked side by side to Kelsey's building.

Should he have called first? Would she even be here? What if she had company? What if she had *male* company? That wasn't likely, was it? And even if there was no one there, what if she didn't like the idea he'd come to broach with her?

A litany of such questions bounced around inside of his mind. His steps slowed as he climbed the stairs. Buddy kept looking at him as if to question the change of pace. The dog matched his steps, but continued to silently inquire by turning those big brown eyes up to his face. Julian met the dog's gaze and frowned.

"I have no idea what I'm doing," he told the animal. "But I'm going to do it anyway."

With unfamiliar insecurity twisting at his guts, he knocked on Kelsey's door.

She opened it and the instant she saw him, her face lit with happiness. "You're out of the hospital!" she exclaimed. "I was just getting ready to come see you there. You should have told me you were being discharged. I would have come to get you!"

She stepped back as she spoke and he and Buddy walked into her living room. "I wanted to surprise you," he said, thinking it was a lame way to begin. But she accepted the comment with an even broader smile.

"And I see you have a sidekick now," she said, patting Buddy on the head.

"Yeah. I'm thinking I'll keep him." He waited to see what she would think of that.

Her face eased into a different expression—something softer and more sentimental. "That's so nice of you, Julian. It's not the dog's fault that his handler is going to jail. Buddy needs someone who will understand what he's lost."

"That's exactly what I thought. And I'd be the right man for *that* job," he said with a rueful laugh. Loss had become so prevalent in Julian's life that he expected it. In fact, he was about due for another one, he realized. Standing there, staring at Kelsey, he wondered if he'd be able to bear it.

"I need to get right to the point, Kelsey," he said abruptly. His internal organs felt like they were being squeezed by a phantom boa constrictor. He had to hurry before he found he couldn't breathe at all. "I had a lot of time to think things over while I cooled my heels in the jail cell and then in the hospital." He dared to lift his hands and gently place them on her upper arms. "You believed in me even though I hadn't given you that same trust, even though I failed to have faith in you. I'm sorry for that."

Her eyes grew shiny and she blinked rapidly. "But you gave me something that was just as important as blind faith in my crazy story," she said softly. "You helped me even when you doubted what I told you. You stood by me even when nothing supported my version of events. You were there for me, despite your professional assessment."

His insides felt a little less constricted suddenly. "I've got a bad track record for long-term relationships. But I'd like to try again, if you'll have me. I thought we should start slow with Shannon taking my apartment and you and me living here together. If you can still stand me and the dog in a year, I'll want more than that. So I warn you now—if you agree to share your home with me, you'll be taking on a big responsibility." He took a deep breath and let it out.

She looked up into his eyes and searched his soul for something. Then he remembered Shannon's advice and said aloud what was in his heart. "I love you, Kelsey. From the tips of my toes to the top of my thick head, I love you. I want a life with you."

"Julian," she said breathlessly as she threw herself against him in a crushing embrace. "I love you, too. What took you so long to decide?"

He smiled for the first time since he'd arrived at her door. "I knew it all along, I think. But saying it out loud... I needed time to gather my courage. Because this is the real thing with you, Kelsey. I'm not very good at letting anyone inside my world. But in your case, I have no choice. I belong to you. My heart and soul are in your hands."

"I'll take care of them, Julian. I promise you that." And she kissed him breathless again, just like she had the night he'd begun to suspect how much he loved her and how frightening that could be. But he wouldn't run away this time. He'd stay and find out how to be a loving companion to Kelsey. He had faith that she would show him the way.

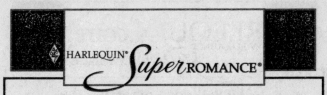

It's worth holding out for a hero....

Three brothers with different mothers. Brought together by their father's last act. The town of Heyday, Virginia, will never be the same—neither will they.

Tyler Balfour is The Stranger. It seems as if his mother was the only woman in Heyday that Anderson McClintock didn't marry—even when she'd been pregnant with Tyler. So he's as surprised as anyone when he discovers that Anderson has left him a third of everything he owned, which was pretty much all of Heyday. Tyler could be enjoying his legacy if not for the fact that more than half of Heyday despises him because they think he's responsible for ruining their town!

Look for **The Stranger,** the last book in a compelling new trilogy from Harlequin Superromance and Rita® Award finalist **Kathleen O'Brien**, in April 2005.

"If you're looking for a fabulous read, reach for a Kathleen O'Brien book. You can't go wrong."
—**Catherine Anderson,**
New York Times bestselling author

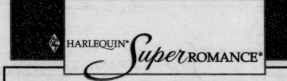